Meera of K

VOL - I

Nitin Antoon

Copyright © Nitin Antoon
All Rights Reserved.

This book has been self-published with all reasonable efforts taken to make the material error-free by the author. No part of this book shall be used, reproduced in any manner whatsoever without written permission from the author, except in the case of brief quotations embodied in critical articles and reviews.

The Author of this book is solely responsible and liable for its content including but not limited to the views, representations, descriptions, statements, information, opinions and references ["Content"]. The Content of this book shall not constitute or be construed or deemed to reflect the opinion or expression of the Publisher or Editor. Neither the Publisher nor Editor endorse or approve the Content of this book or guarantee the reliability, accuracy or completeness of the Content published herein and do not make any representations or warranties of any kind, express or implied, including but not limited to the implied warranties of merchantability, fitness for a particular purpose. The Publisher and Editor shall not be liable whatsoever for any errors, omissions, whether such errors or omissions result from negligence, accident, or any other cause or claims for loss or damages of any kind, including without limitation, indirect or consequential loss or damage arising out of use, inability to use, or about the reliability, accuracy or sufficiency of the information contained in this book.

Made with ❤ on the Notion Press Platform

www.notionpress.com

Contents

1. Bharatam 7
2. The Hunt and Archery 18
3. The News 33
4. My First Tantric Experience 41
5. The Departure of My Beloved Parents 56
6. The Funeral 70
7. My Next Journey 83
8. A Journey to the River of Ganga 96
9. How Do I Find My Guru? 106
10. My Guru Found Me 116
11. The Journey Begins 127
12. First Lesson – Visha Chikitsa 139
13. Meeting Poison Baba 150
14. Jagha Found Me 163
15. The Art of Making a Bonsai Tree 174
16. Carpets in the Air 187
17. Yoga Nidra 201
18. What Do You Choose 213
19. The Festival of Lights 227
20. The Aura of Tranquillity 239
21. Together Till the End 250
22. The Ritual 261
23. Latika Revenge 274

Thank You 287

Bharatam

My story begins in the early ages of the mystical country of Bharatam, which is bound by water on three borders as its fertile soil stretches from tall snowy mountains in the north to the blue ocean in the south. It is home to various landscapes, from impenetrable forests and encompassed swamps spreading across the eastern mountainous terrains to the sand to the west. The monsoons bring rain to nourish the crops, which grew abundantly throughout the land. Many rivers snake through the country and feed into the sea. These rivers are the lifelines of the many villages.

I belong to the picturesque village of Karmana. My parents taught me about love and kindness towards others, especially my fellow villagers. We cherish our culture and traditions. We did not have much but always shared whatever little was amongst us.

Both my parents were teachers at the village school. My mother taught the art of medicine and was intensely passionate about helping people find solutions for any ailment. As a child, I always admired her dedication when I watched her spend countless hours studying the intricacies of the human body. Meanwhile, my father taught the art of music, which became another passion of mine.

I genuinely love both my parents, but secretly, I love my mother more— she made me feel special by getting me the tastiest fruits and cooking the most delectable food, and she was always there when I needed her. My relationship with my father was a strong and humorous bond. We shared a great connection, always on the same page, anticipating each other's thoughts before they were spoken. My father and I always had a good time together and would laugh often.

My parents' love story goes beyond this lifetime. This account of their love story is something that they love to tell, and I always feel blessed to hear it. It is a testament to the power of love and how it can transcend space and time. Because they could not be together in their previous life, they promised to find each other in their next life.

With their Guru's help, they found each other and remembered their promise from their past life. And now, after they had me, their focus shifted to achieving moksha by fulfilling their karma. They were determined to repay their debts to reach their ultimate spiritual goal. Guided by their guru, they continued towards enlightenment, embracing the chance to fulfill their life's purpose. They were grateful for this opportunity and strived to unite in this lifetime and all lifetimes to come.

It is common in the villages of Bharatam for the Guru to also serve as the village priest. This practice is rarely seen in big cities like Hastinapura, where King Maharaj Rajendra Varma, the IX, lives. Our village Guru has a small temple that he preserves, but it is just outside his house and quite far from the other village homes. The temple's intricately stone-carved structure stands tall within the lush green scenery. His daily ritual includes going into the temple every morning and evening to offer prayers to the Lord Maha dev, the Supreme

Lord who creates, guards, and transforms the cosmos. Later in the evenings, just before nightfall, he offers prasad (food) to his disciples and villagers at the temple doorsteps. Once every month, a puja is conducted inside the temple on a moon night to worship our god.

For a profoundly spiritual man, our Guru has a fantastic sense of humor and is always willing to help us understand concepts through experimentation and exploration. He made learning fun and engaging for his students, and his method guaranteed that we retained the learned information long after the lessons.

For me, his teaching methods have provided valuable insights into the importance of what to eat and what to drink. He would often re-iterate that every person's dietary needs are unique, and this realization comes only when faced with the correct information. He has drawn knowledge from various Vedanta schools to gain a multifaceted understanding of the subject. That helped him keep a broad outlook on his students' differing opinions. Even though he often stressed the significance of understanding different perspectives because every human is different, our Guru believed that for genuine service to God, purity of food is essential to sustain the desirable state of mind to reach enlightenment.

Life in Karmana is vibrant and bustling. Our village is well-equipped with all the necessities of life. Located on a trading path, we receive a constant influx of people passing through, making it a busy place for traders. As I grew older, I became more curious about what lay outside our peaceful village. Strangers were a common sight; my friends and I enjoyed chatting. They often set up camp nearby with their animals and caravans. We listened to their stories about the miracles they had witnessed first-hand and where they came from. We were transported to worlds beyond our imagination, and their stories reminded us that anything is possible in this magnificent and mysterious universe. It made us believe that there was a world out there where everything was possible.

The marketplaces in Karmana are a hubbub of commotion. The hustle and bustle of the market are both invigorating and exciting simultaneously. I loved to watch people haggling for prices and observing the way they interacted with each other. The people were warm and welcoming. The streets bustled with traders from all walks of life. From farmers selling their crops and livestock to vendors selling vegetables, fruits, and even spices. Many shops are lined along the streets, stocked with an assortment of merchandise. Many people are skilled in their profession and experienced in a particular craft. Some are herbalists who have learned the workings of Ayurvedic medicine. Many sell jewelry and precious stones.

The entire land surrounding the village is covered in tall trees. The forest's rich greenery and thick vegetation gave a beautiful backdrop for our home.

But my favorite place to visit is the fruit forest, which grows near the village river. The forest is a lush oasis, always packed with various fruits for us to gather. My friends and I are always excited to pick and eat fruits from the different trees. Mangoes, guavas, papayas, and bananas, the list is long. The forest's fresh air and relaxed atmosphere add to the harvest experience. But we could only go out during the daytime when the harmless monkeys were swinging from the vines.

We had to be attentive to their presence and sounds outside. So far, I have not encountered any predators, but it is believed that the forest homes tigers.

The Karmana village boasts an incredible sense of community where familiar faces are around every corner. It's a place where everyone is on a first-name basis, and bonds are easily forged. From annual events to small gatherings, there's always something going on where people can come together and connect. It's no wonder our village is often held up as a great example of how strong communities make for happier, healthier living. Even our school is well-known in the region, attracting many visitors, including other teachers who come to learn from our gurus. There are regular exchanges and knowledge sessions where different philosophies are discussed. My parents enjoyed participating in these events and talking about new ideas. One could always learn something new that added significant value to everyday life.

During one of their visits to our village, a group of spiritual leaders discussed food habits. The topic of eating non-veg arose, and the leaders specified that it could delay meditation as it stays in the stomach longer than other foods.

There was a debate about whether to eat non-veg or only consume veg for optimal nutrition. One of the men who sat under the large Banyan tree argued for a full plant-based diet, but there were concerns from others about meeting all the daily nutrient needs. The challenge lay in finding a sustainable way to provide the body with nutrients. Yet he was able to convince everyone of how it all could work. From this discussion, I discovered that certain types of flowers can be consumed for their nutritional value. Also, there were some types of fungi growing in our area which were edible. This could be a valuable source of food during scarcity.

The following day, curiosity got the better of us. My friends and I decided to approach the stranger to find out what he was talking about. We saw him strolling quietly on the banks of the village river. He looked deep in thought, but we could not resist our curiosity. Our pace quickened as we closed in on him, eager to know what other secrets he was holding onto. He turned towards us with a small smile playing on his lips. It was almost as if he knew that we would corner him that day. He greeted us warmly, before addressing our burning question. He then gestured towards a cluster of colourful blossoms that grew near the river. Their vibrant petals were filled with all the colours of the rainbow and their sweet fragrance was captivating.

"These Mahamakam flowers are very nutritious and will help you reach your desired state of mind," he said.

"But how do we eat them?" asked one of my friends.

He smiled, "Just take a few pieces from the bunch and chew on them slowly."

We were excited and looked at each other, wondering if this was actually possible. It sounded too good to be true. But we were willing to try it, and so we did not think twice. I bit into the flower and chewed slowly as he instructed. The taste was not pleasant but it had a refreshing minty flavour. I felt an instant calm wash over me. It was almost as though my mind was suddenly clear of all my thoughts and worries. I breathed deeply as I felt the fresh air filling up my lungs. My friends followed suit and soon we were all experiencing a similar sensation. We stood there, smiling at each other, feeling content in our moment of peace. The man gave us a handful of flowers and we continued to munch on them until they were all gone. They were really delicious; the taste was unlike anything we had ever eaten in Karmana.

The man bid us goodbye and continued with his walk.

For the rest of the day, my friends and I talked non-stop about what had happened. The experience was exciting and I felt more thrilled than ever.

"We should go and tell everyone," I said to my friends. Everyone agreed.

We hurried towards the village and ran into our parents.

"What happened? Why are you all so happy?" asked my father.

"There is a wonder flower on the river banks, we picked some and ate it!" I exclaimed.

"Oh really? And what kind of flowers were they?" he asked.

"They were a type of flower called the Mahamakam."

"Really? How do you know that?"

"I learned about it from a stranger who visited our village last night. He taught us how to eat them and they made us feel excellent."

"He must have been a great teacher because you look happy and relaxed. Did you learn anything new?"

"Yes, he told us that eating these flowers will help us reach enlightenment," I replied.

"That's wonderful! I'm sure the other spiritual leaders would love to hear about this too. Let's go and tell them right away!" he said.

We walked along the river, and found the group of men gathered around the tall Banyan tree, that sat in the middle of our village. Everyone looked up at us with curiosity and eagerness.

But when I told them what happened, the group of men laughed, "Yes, we do know about the flower. But child, it is an ordinary flower. It has no effect on the minds. The only thing that makes us feel better is the refreshing breeze of the river."

"But the stranger said it did more than that. He also said that these flowers are full of nutrients that are essential for our bodies. We should be able to find all the vitamins and minerals we need from this flower."

"We have been eating this flower since we were young and nothing has changed." said one of the men.

My friends and I felt humiliated. My father saw that and he took a deep breath before responding.

"I believe them, I think there is something special about this flower. I tried it last night and it helped me relax. I could feel my mind slowing down and my worries fading away. And you all should try it too."

The men looked at each other, puzzled by his words. They were still sceptical but they all agreed to try it.

All of us then walked towards the river and picked a few flowers. My father handed some flowers to the men, and instructed them to chew slowly. He repeated the same process with my friends and I. Soon everyone was chewing on the flower with a puzzled expression on their faces. My father looked at me beaming and winked.

There were a group of people who walked by and stood watching us as we ate the magical flowers.

"What's going on? Why are you all smiling?" asked one of the men.

"Let's ask them," said another.

Everyone approached us and asked why we were so happy. I told them how the flowers made me feel relaxed and calmed my mind. I described the experience in great detail and ended with a big smile. The men looked at each other, bewildered.

"What do you mean? How did the flower make you feel?" asked one of them.

"It helped me relax and gave me a clear mind. I felt light and free," I replied.

"You must be lying," said another.

"No, I'm not. It really happened. I am serious. It would be best if you tried it yourself," I insisted.

One of the men stepped forward and took a few pieces from the bunch. He chewed slowly and closed his eyes. After a few minutes he opened his eyes and smiled.

"That's amazing! What did you eat?" asked someone else.

"These flowers are full of nutrients and they help you reach a state of enlightenment," I said.

"But how do we know if it works?" asked another man.

"Just chew slowly and you will feel the effects."

They all looked at each other, unsure about what to do. Finally, one of them agreed to try it. He picked a few flowers and chewed slowly. A few minutes later, he opened his eyes and smiled.

"That was amazing! I feel like I can do anything!" he exclaimed.

The rest of the men followed and were amazed by their own experiences. The spiritual leaders were curious too and asked us to show the stranger who taught us about it. Together, we walked towards the river bank. The man was sitting on the ground under the shades of the forest, deep in meditation.

"You must have done something right because you all feel better for it. But to be honest, the flower itself has no direct effect on the minds," he said.

"But how else do you explain the changes we all experienced?" I asked.

He smiled, "It is a coincidence. You could be just feeling good because you went for a walk in the forest and came across these flowers. Or perhaps it was the fresh air and the sound of the river. You could have been feeling the effects of the change in weather. Or maybe it was your state of mind. The possibilities are endless. So don't get too excited. Just enjoy the experience and keep doing what you love."

My father looked at me with a smile and I smiled back. He understood my curiosity and encouraged me to continue searching for answers. Because my friends and I, definitely wanted to know more and could not wait to return to the river to gather more flowers. As we walked back home, I wondered about the power of the flowers. I couldn't seem to believe that man.

The Hunt and Archery

One afternoon, as I was heading to arching class, a group of young men caught my attention. They were occupied in a conversation about going into the woods to hunt. They were talking about hunting, explicitly targeting an antelope.

Since Antelope are had to catch, it seemed like a thrilling choice. It was a new adventure that I have yet to embark on.

I could not help but wonder if they would be successful or not. In the midst of their conversation, one of them boldly claimed,

"I've taken down an antelope before. It took me three whole days to track its elusive trail."

He confidently asserted, "I know exactly where the animal's path leads. I've encountered numerous animals, so I know precisely what the beast looks like."

An intense fire of passion for hunting coursed through me. So, I gathered my courage and slowly walked up to the men. I expressed my interest in joining their hunting expedition.

The men turned to me with much surprise and curiosity. Even though there was no formal restriction for women from hunting, I, however, did not look like a conventional hunter.

The leader of the hunters was Haroon. With his towering physique, he demanded respect from everyone in the village.

His authoritative presence inspired admiration from those around him. People were naturally drawn to him and eager to follow his lead.

But Haroon's words pierced through my heart like a razor-sharp arrow.

"You? Young and small!" Haroon scoffed, his voice laced with disdain.

"You wouldn't last a moment in the hunt."

His dismissal of my request to join the hunting party echoed in my ears, with each syllable dripping with contempt.

"Antelopes? Ha! I doubt you could even graze their majestic hides, let alone strike them."

His words were a crushing blow that shattered my dreams like delicate clay. But the fire within me burned fiercely still. I smiled at the thought of proving him wrong. He will learn that size and age were weak measures of prowess.

With a steady hand and an unwavering gaze, I turned around. I released an arrow with my bow, and it hit the bullseye on a practice target that was many feet away.

I looked around the group of hunters, as my arrow cleaved through their doubts.

As Haroon's eyes met mine, I felt the intensity of his gaze penetrating my defenses.

"Okay," he uttered, his voice tinged with regret.

"I was perhaps wrong about you."

And in that moment, his words echoed like thunder. It shook the very foundation of my emotions.

"I am sorry, deeply sorry, for my behavior earlier. I hope with every fiber of my being that I did not disrespect you."

His admission hung in the air, fragile like a thread woven in the finest silk. But the weight of his apology bore down upon me. It forced heavily against my chest like an avalanche. Just for a moment, the world around us stood still.

Suddenly, I felt a whirlwind of emotions twirling inside me. I felt hurt but also disbelief, with a twinkle of forgiveness. His vulnerability uncovered a compassionate side that was buried deep inside me.

With a steady breath, I mustered the strength to respond. My words were filled with both caution and the potential for healing. Perhaps, in forgiveness, Haroon and I could forge a stronger bond.

I looked at him directly as I spoke. I sensed that his demeaning words had ignited a spur of defiance in me.

"Don't worry," I declared, my voice dripping with boldness.

"I've heard those words before. Words of doubt still echo in my ears. But mark my words, fellow hunters, I am far from done. I am a force in the making."

In that instance, I realized the true measure of strength was having the courage to admit one's mistake.

"Like an arrow released from the bow," I continued speaking with a steady voice.

"I never miss my target. My aim is true, my focus unbending."

"Very well, you are welcome to join us." Haroon declared, a glimmer of anticipation dancing in his eyes.

The men began to cheer as Haroon continued his speech.

"Together, we are unstoppable!" he roared, his voice echoing like thunder.

He raised his hand to silence the group.

"We will leave before sunrise, to hunt the mighty antelope."

As he spoke, a feeling of urgency filled the atmosphere.

"So, before our journey begins, we will come together and pray. We will ask for divine guidance and protection. We will ask the heavens to grant us a safe and swift journey. We will pray so that our steps will align itself with destiny."

His voice reflected the excitement that matched the beating of our hearts. But I was feeling both fear and excitement at the same time. I was well aware of the lurking danger in the wild.

Later that day, I arrived home in a rush of excitement. I was eager to tell my parents about the upcoming adventure. But I found them both in a state of deep meditation, lost in peaceful thoughts.

I was unsure whether to interrupt their meditation. I paused for a moment, observing the serene expressions on their faces. It was a stark contrast to my own restless thoughts. In their presence, I felt a sense of calm wash over me.

In the end, I decided to retreat to the solace of my room. As I sat on my bed, I could not resist the urge to replay the day's events in my thoughts. The feeling of anticipation grew stronger, making my heart race with excitement.

I was determined to improve my skills in archery and stealth. Until they were as sharp as a hunter's blade. I stepped outside and began training relentlessly. Under the shade of the trees, I practiced my archery and perfected my stealth. Haroon's doubts had taken root in my mind, but I was determined to use them as motivation to succeed. I trained tirelessly, striving to become the best.

As the sun began to set, the surrounding area gradually grew darker. I hurriedly made my way back inside the safety of my home. I knew that this time, I had to share my excitement with my parents. However, they were still deep in mediation. I cleared my throat to get their attention, and they slowly opened their eyes.

"Mother, Father," I exclaimed, "Tomorrow, Haroon and the other hunters are going on a hunting expedition!"

Their eyes widened in surprise, but their expression quickly shifted to one of concern. My parents exchanged a look before turning back to me.

"Hunting is not something to be taken lightly, dear," my mother said. "It can be dangerous, and there are certain rules that must be followed. It's not just about the excitement of the hunt."

"I understand that, Mother," I replied. "But I want to learn about our culture, and hunting is a big part of it. I want to see it first-hand, to witness the skills of the hunters and the beauty of our land."

"Are you sure that's safe, my child?" My mother asked, placing a soft hand on my shoulder. There was a hint of worry in her voice.

"I've heard that there have been attacks by wild animals in the nearby forest," my father added, his eyes full of worry.

"I know, but Haroon and his team are experienced hunters. They know how to handle themselves in dangerous situations." I responded confidently.

My parents exchanged a worried look, but eventually, they nodded in agreement. There was a moment of silence before my father spoke up.

"Very well," he said. "But you must promise not to take a life."

"I promise," I said, feeling a surge of excitement. "I will respect the land and the animals."

My parents nodded, and I could see the pride in their eyes. They knew how important it was for me to connect with our heritage and to learn the traditional ways of our people.

"Very well, but be careful and make sure you stay out of harm's way," my mother said, her voice full of concern.

"I will, Mother. Thank you," I said with a smile.

My father's expression softened, and he placed a hand on my shoulder.

"Remember, Beti, skill and experience can only take you so far. You must also trust your instincts and be prepared to face challenges."

I nodded, determined to take their advice to heart. I knew that I was in for a thrilling adventure but also a challenging one. Nevertheless, I was ready to embrace it head-on with determination and courage.

My stomach growled with hunger, but I was relieved to find that my mother had prepared food for us. I eagerly savored the meal, and soon after, fatigue washed over me, urging me to rest.

As I lay in bed that night, I closed my eyes and uttered a silent prayer, asking for the strength to face the unknown, the courage to overcome any obstacles, and the wisdom to make the right choices.

As I entered the village temple the following morning, I observed the ritual already in progress. Haroon approached me and explained the need to seek forgiveness for hunting the antelope and completing the ceremony promptly. He then led me through the ritual, which included a prayer to Shiva as well as offering flowers to our divine goddess. Together, we stood before the divine statues, fervently pleading for forgiveness.

Afterward, I approached our village priest, who was present, and respectfully requested his blessing.

He addressed me, "Beti, you are way too young to go on this antelope hunt."

In response, I countered, "But Maharaj Haroon told me it was okay, and he was impressed with my skills."

The priest paused for a moment, then relented, saying, "Okay, but listen to your heart. If you cannot release the arrow, please stop. Remember, once you take a life, it will affect your karma."

Understanding the weight of his words, I looked at him and nodded, promising, "I understand. I vow not to take a life if it doesn't feel right."

The priest smiled warmly and encouraged me, saying, "Please go on. Have your adventure."

Returning the smile, I asked him for his blessing, and he graciously granted it, bestowing his divine blessings upon me.

As the first rays of sunlight painted the sky with a golden glow, we stood at the verge of an astonishing journey. With purpose etched upon our faces, we readied ourselves to defy the odds and claim our coveted prize.

Swiftly, I grasped my bow and arrows, joining Haroon's team. We were a group of over five individuals united by a shared purpose. Moments before our departure, our priest approached Haroon, whispering something into his ear. The priest then blessed him, invoking divine protection for the journey ahead.

We had to walk quite a bit to reach the lake where the antelopes habituated. In spite of the potential dangers of alligators and snakes, I was thrilled to venture deep into the forest to see the beautiful lake. As a child, I was not allowed to go this far, but I felt a sense of excitement as we walked for quite a while.

While I strolled alongside the group, thoughts swirled in my mind regarding the conversation between our priest and Haroon. Eager to seek clarity, I approached Haroon, but he met my gaze with a steely resolve and cautioned,

"You are now on a hunt. Maintain a low profile and refrain from unnecessary chatter. Watch your every step and keep an eye out for antelopes. We are nearing our destination."

As we continued our journey, I observed the plan unfolding. We were divided into small groups of two or three, with a designated leader guiding the way while the rest followed closely.

After a prolonged walk, the distinct scent of the lake water filled the air, urging us to proceed with caution. Our pace slowed down, matching the gravity of the situation.

Haroon raised his hand, forming a fist, and glanced at me, his gesture implying a need to halt. Understanding his silent communication, I nodded in affirmation. A smile tugged at his lips as he approached me, his voice hushed,

"You want to take the first shot?"

I returned his smile, confirming my readiness. Just as I was about to respond, he gently placed his fingers on my lips, conveying a more profound message. I comprehended his intention. I retrieved my bow and skilfully strung the arrow, poised for the forthcoming opportunity. Another archer joined our side, preparing her bow as well.

It didn't take long for our keen eyes to spot a herd of antelopes leisurely grazing in an expansive field. With utmost care, we readied ourselves and stealthily advanced toward our unsuspecting prey. Strategy and swiftness were crucial, for any sudden movement could startle the animals and send them fleeing. The adrenaline surged within me as we closed the distance. I aimed my arrow meticulously, tightening my grip on the bow.

Yet, in that moment, a realization struck me. Perhaps the priest's intention was not to discourage me but to protect

The Hunt and Archery

my karma. While I longed to prove myself, I understood the deeper significance. The herd of antelopes approached the lake, their cautious movements hinting at their awareness of our presence.

I spotted a sizeable female antelope and desired to take her down. I was about to make a move when Haroon signaled for us to remain still.

He whispered in my ear, "Don't kill the mother."

"Look at her belly, don't target her. Today, we want to take only one life, not two. She's clearly carrying a calf."

I glanced at the antelope, a sense of unease settling in my stomach. I tried to shift my focus to another target, but the feeling lingered. Then, I overheard the other female archer remark,

"She's not taking the shot."

In an instant, the antelope bolted away, but not before my arrow found its mark. Anger surged within me, and I released the arrow, striking the antelope.

I turned to face the other archers and said,

"Did you see? That was a kill!"

Haroon gazed at me and reassured me,

"I never doubted you. Come, let's claim your prize."

The antelope remained alive; its eyes filled with pain. My anger subsided as I watched her struggle to stand. Her body convulsed as she fought for her life. A wave of guilt washed over me. Haroon asked,

"Do you want to end her suffering?"

With teary eyes, I shook my head. He then instructed me to retrieve the arrow, which I did with utmost care. Haroon removed his knife, and I watched as he carefully slit the antelope's throat. My hands trembled, and I could not bear to watch the gruesome scene. I watched the blood gush from the wound.

As Haroon took the antelope around his neck, he turned to us and declared,

"We must make haste."

As we began our journey, the female hunter who had doubted me walked beside me. She introduced herself,

"My name is Rina."

I greeted her, saying, "Hi, Rina."

Rina nodded, adding, "I am impressed with how you handled yourself. You have the makings of a good hunter."

I smiled, thanking her for the kind words.

I asked, "Can I ask what happened? Why did the priest discourage me from shooting the female antelope?"

Rina replied, "I am not sure why. It seems like he wanted to test your limits. Perhaps he feared your karma would be affected, or maybe he wanted to show his faith in you. But whatever the reason, it was his decision to make. I believe you should do whatever feels right to you."

I smiled and inquired, "So, why did you doubt me? Why did you think I wouldn't take the shot?"

She explained, "When I went on my first hunt, I hesitated. I was scared and reluctant to let go of the arrow. Those feelings can hinder you. I was only trying to help."

I turned my gaze to Haroon, carrying the animal on his neck. As I peered into the antelope's lifeless eyes, a sense of sorrow enveloped me. Rina comforted me, saying,

"Don't worry. The antelope will be reborn, given a new purpose by God. Maybe in her next life, she will be a hunter herself. It's all part of the cycle, karma, and dharma finding balance."

Her words struck a chord within me, and I pondered upon the circle of life and death. We walked back through the thick forest, lost in deep thought. The chirping birds, the rustle of leaves, and the rush of the streams created a melody of their own, weaving together the intricate balance of the universe.

As we reached the village, we were greeted with cheers and celebration. The villagers welcomed us and congratulated us on our successful hunt. But my mind was clouded with mixed emotions. I had experienced the thrill of the hunt but also the weight of taking a life.

Haroon distributed the antelope among the village elders, and we received their blessings in return. I stood there, lost in my thoughts. I silently reflected on the events of the day. The realization suddenly struck me that life is transient. And death is an undeniable part of our existence. Yet, it is our actions and intentions that define our journey.

I wandered and was surprised to find myself at the village temple. I knelt before the divine statues. I prayed for their guidance. I wanted forgiveness for killing the antelope. With tears in my eyes and a heavy heart, I spoke aloud to the gods,

"I am sorry; please forgive me for my actions. I will do my best to learn from my mistakes and will strive to achieve greater heights."

Suddenly, I saw my parents hurrying toward me, their faces displaying worry and concern. My father queried,

"Why didn't you tell us that it was an antelope hunting? Hunting antelope is not a sport or a game. Why did you do it?"

I confessed that I wanted to try my hand at hunting. My mother looked at me intently and asked,

"You must understand that hunting is not just a sport or a form of entertainment. It is a responsibility, one that must be taken seriously. So, did you really kill the antelope?"

With tears welling up in my eyes, I replied,

"Yes, I did."

She inquired further, "How do you feel about it?"

I gazed back at her, overcome with remorse, and answered,

"I feel awful. Deep down, I had a feeling that I shouldn't have done it, but I ignored that inner voice, and now I have taken the life of an innocent creature. I feel so overwhelmed with guilt."

My mother chuckled,

"You must understand yourself before you can understand the world around you. If you don't know yourself, you won't be able to listen to your own instincts, and you'll make hasty decisions that lead to regrets."

Just then, the village priest approached and cast his gaze upon me. He noticed the tears in my eyes and remarked,

"So, you went through with it."

I met his gaze and confessed, my voice trembling slightly,

"I made a promise to you, and now I regret my actions. Allow me to explain what happened."

The priest nodded, with a compassionate expression on his face, urging me to continue.

"There was a moment when I hesitated. I doubted whether I should proceed. I didn't want to go through with it. But then, I changed my mind and decided to take the killing shot."

The priest looked at me with understanding and conveyed his advice,

"No matter what happens, always listen to yourself first before engaging in actions that you might later regret. Whether it's driven by anger or ego, don't let those distractions overshadow your inner peace."

I realized that while it was essential to test my skills, it was equally crucial to respect the balance of nature. The wisdom imparted by our priest had permeated my consciousness, and I vowed to heed his words in all aspects of my life. The antelope hunt had taught me much more than I had anticipated and left a profound impact on the person I was to become.

My father and mother thanked the priest, and then we made our way back home. As we walked back, I couldn't help but reflect on the epiphany I had just had. The weight of my actions had been lifted from my shoulders, and I felt relieved.

"Beti," My father began, and I looked up at him, "we have something important to share with you."

The News

Upon our arrival home, my parents asked me to sit before them. I could sense there was something important that they wanted to discuss with me. Restless and anxious, I positioned myself in front of them as they sat in their usual place on the veranda. The tension in the air was palpable as they gathered their thoughts. Finally, my father cleared his throat. His words pierced through the silence and rang in my ears.

"Beti, your mother, and I have decided that at some point in the near future, we will be leaving our physical bodies. We believe that we're ready to continue our journey, regardless of what others may say."

I looked them in their eye, knowing that they had been talking a lot about this, that this was one of their ways of saying that I needed to be prepared.

I laughed and said, "You can't leave me behind just yet! We still have so much to do together."

My father sighed,

"You're now of age. We trust that you're mature enough to handle your own matters and focus on your responsibilities here on Earth."

My heart raced as his words sank in. The reality of the situation hit me like a ton of bricks. Tears welled up in my eyes, but I knew I had to remain strong for them.

"Mother, Father," I said, gathering myself, "I understand your decision, and I respect it. But please, tell me more about what I can expect once you're gone. How can I prepare myself?"

My mom smiled at me and said, "Beti, our souls are prepared to enter the state of moksha. We don't know when it will happen, but when we recognize the signs, we'll embrace it. It shall free us from another cycle of rebirth."

I was beginning to lose my temper, and so I said, "But you always talk about being selfless to attain moksha, but what you're doing is selfish! You decided to have me, so you should wait until I'm settled before considering leaving. I'll have no one, and I'll be all alone. This won't lead you to heaven; it'll lead you to hell." I stood up in fury.

Dad spoke with a somber tone, "Don't worry; if you hold God and us in your heart, you'll never be alone." With those words, he got up and walked away from the conversation.

Tears welled up in my eyes as I looked at my mom. She pleaded, "But please, Beti, try to understand."

Feeling overwhelmed, I could not bear it any longer. I rushed outside the village and climbed to the top of a tall haystack. There, in the quiet of the night, I let my tears flow uncontrollably until exhaustion took over, and I fell asleep amidst the straw.

The following morning, I stomped my way back home, my footsteps heavy with a mix of sadness and anger. As I entered the house, my parents' faces lit up with relief, and they questioned, "Where have you been?"

"Nowhere. It doesn't matter anyway. You're leaving."

I walked past them, seething with frustration, and collapsed onto the nearest surface, hoping that my display of anger would somehow change their minds. I longed for them to stay by my side for many more years to come. However, as time passed, my worry began to creep in. Neither my mom nor dad came to check on me or inquire about how I was doing. Did I anger them? Did I upset them in some way? The uncertainty gnawed at my heart.

As I stepped out of the house, I spotted my mother and father sitting by a crackling fire, engaged in meditation. Deep down, I wanted them to stop. But I knew that I should talk to the village priest first before taking any impulsive action.

Making my way towards the village temple, I settled down beside the priest, who was absorbed in his own meditation. I patiently waited for him to finish, looking out at the peaceful scenery.

Lost in a daydream, memories flooded my mind. I remembered dancing and singing with my parents around the warm fire and the joy of helping and nurturing stray puppies. Lost in these reflections, I barely noticed the priest regaining his awareness and looking at me.

"You know, according to the Mahabharata, dogs are said to go to heaven. Lord Indra allowed a dog into heaven because its pure conscience is attuned to the cosmic universe," he explained, a smile playing on his lips. "But I sense that's not the reason you came to talk to me, right?"

I replied, "No."

"And I suppose you don't want me to reveal how I knew you were thinking about dogs and gave you a hint about them," he said, his eyes twinkling with a hint of mystery.

I nodded and replied, "I've always been amazed by your ability to understand people's thoughts and emotions."

He smiled warmly and said, "Empathizing with others can be both easy and challenging. It's important to realize that each person's situation is unique, and unless you truly understand yourself completely, it can be difficult to fully comprehend what others are going through."

"Now, tell me what happened and how I can assist you, Beti," he gently urged, his voice filled with genuine concern.

The priest's eyes met mine, filled with a sense of understanding and compassion. He gestured for me to speak, and I hesitated for a moment before pouring out my worries and fears. But his presence and wisdom enveloped me, and I felt comforted by his words. I began to share my concerns and worries, knowing that he would listen attentively and provide guidance from his vast well of knowledge and empathy.

"I will be left alone. I still need them. I think it's a mistake because they might feel ready, but the world isn't prepared for them to leave."

The priest listened attentively, his serene presence offering solace amidst my inner turmoil. When I finished, he took a deep breath and began to speak in a gentle, reassuring tone.

"My dear child, the journey of life is filled with both joy and sorrow. It is natural to feel scared and uncertain when faced with the prospect of separation from loved ones. Your parents have chosen a path they believe will lead to spiritual liberation. While their decision may seem difficult to accept, it is rooted in their own understanding and spiritual growth."

I trusted in his wisdom and guidance, praying that he could convince my parents to reconsider their decision and allow us more time together.

Tears welled up in my eyes, tracing a path down my cheeks. "It's not fair. Why can't they understand? Maharaj, please tell me what I can do to stop them."

He gazed at me with compassion in his eyes and spoke soothingly, "Beti, I've advised them repeatedly that they'll receive a sign from me when it's time for their departure. But they haven't received any such sign. Their impatience will lead them to hell instead of heaven. I will talk to them again tomorrow and try to make them understand."

He paused, allowing his words to sink in before continuing, "Remember, you are never truly alone. The bond of love that connects you to your parents rises above physical existence. Hold them close in your heart and trust that their souls will always be with you, guiding and protecting you."

As his words settled within me, a glimmer of hope began to emerge. I realized that my parents' departure was not a permanent goodbye but rather a transformation into a different form of connection. The priest's wisdom reassured me that I had the strength within me to navigate the challenges that lay ahead.

Feeling a newfound sense of clarity and acceptance, I thanked the priest for his guidance. As I made my way back home, a serene determination filled my being. I knew that although the path ahead might be difficult, I would face it with resilience and love.

As I entered the house, I saw my parents sitting patiently, their eyes fixed on me. Filled with a mixture of apprehension and understanding, I made my way toward them. Tears welled up in my eyes as I reached out and held their hands, feeling the comforting warmth that flowed between us. In that unspoken moment, our bond spoke volumes, transcending the limitations of words.

Whispering softly, I expressed my feelings, "Mother, Father, though I may not fully grasp the path you're embarking on, I want you to know that I will forever treasure the moments we've shared. Your love will forever dwell within me, and no matter where your soul's journey is, our connection will provide me with strength."

My parents stared at me, their eyes brimming with love and pride. Their warm embrace enveloped me, and in that embrace, all worries and uncertainties dissolved.

With a touch of sadness in their eyes, my father spoke tenderly, "Beti, we understand your concerns, but death is an inevitable part of life. We have lived to the fullest, and now we are ready to move on. Please know that we love you more than anything, and we will forever remain as your guardian angels."

Overwhelmed with emotions, I took a deep breath and managed to express, "I will miss you both immensely, but I understand your decision. The memories we've shared will forever hold a special place in my heart."

My mother held my hand firmly, her eyes filled with reassurance, "Remember, Beti, our physical forms may depart, but our love will endure. We will forever be proud of you and watch over you. You are strong, and you will make us proud."

With tears streaming down my cheeks, I held them tightly, knowing that life would never be the same without their physical presence. Yet, I also understood that their love and guidance would forever accompany me.

From that moment forward, I vowed to cherish every precious moment with them and to make the most of our remaining time together. Looking back on that conversation, I realize that their decision to transcend their physical forms was an opportunity for me to grow and take charge of my own life. It was a profound lesson in letting go and accepting the flow of life's journey.

As I nodded, still grappling with the concept of moksha, I recognized the importance of my parents finding inner peace.

My father added, "We will always watch over you and guide you. Our love and support for you will never waver. Remember, you also have our family and friends to turn to for assistance. Don't hesitate to seek their help whenever needed."

After our heartfelt conversation, I sat alone, deep in contemplation. The hues of pink and orange painted the sky as the sun descended, casting a serene ambiance. In the midst of my thoughts, I recognized that my journey without my parents physically present would undoubtedly present challenges. Yet, I found solace in knowing that their presence would forever be with me in spirit.

Death, as tricky as it may be to accept, is an inescapable part of life. Embracing its inevitability and learning to let go are essential aspects of our journey. Though the prospect of losing my parents feels overwhelming, I understand that their decision comes from a place of readiness and fulfillment.

As the sun set and painted the sky with vibrant hues, I sat alone with my thoughts, contemplating the profound conversation we had shared. The beauty of the scene provided a sense of calm amidst the storm of emotions raging within me. I reflected on the love we shared and the memories we had created together, knowing that they would forever hold a cherished place in my heart.

In the days to come, I vowed to make the most of our remaining time together, treasuring each precious moment. I would embrace the lessons they had imparted, drawing strength from their love and guidance. Though their physical presence would be missed, their spirits would continue to watch over me, guiding me along my path.

And so, with a mixture of sadness and gratitude, I embarked on the next chapter of my life, carrying the lessons of love, resilience, and the inevitability of change deep within my soul. The bond we shared, forged in the vessel of unconditional love, would endure all the boundaries of life and death.

My First Tantric Experience

The rays of the early morning sun gently caressed my face, pulling me out of my peaceful slumber. Before my groggy mind could fully grasp the new day, my ears caught the sound of Maadinee's excited voice drifting through the open window.

"Meera, Meera, you have to come now! Our Yoga teacher's guru has arrived in the village!" Curiosity sparked within me, and I couldn't resist the pull of her words.

Throwing off my warm blanket, I hastily got out of bed, my bare feet padding softly across the earthen floor. As I emerged from my room, Maadinee stood before me, her eyes wide with anticipation and her face flushed with excitement.

"He looks like he is only twenty!" Madinee exclaimed, barely able to contain herself. He has long, flowing hair and his presence is so captivating. Her words seemed almost fantastical, and I couldn't help but raise an eyebrow, questioning the truth in her statement.

"You must be crazy, Maadinee," I responded, trying to temper her enthusiasm with a dose of skepticism. But even as the words left my lips, doubt began to creep in. Our village was known for its wise sages and mystics, whose ancient practices held the power to transform lives. Perhaps there was some truth to Maadinee's claims.

Just then, my mother entered the room, her serene countenance emanating an air of wisdom. She listened to our conversation for a moment before interjecting with her gentle voice. "No, Meera beta, it is possible for truth seekers to possess a glimpse of truth and channel it to retain their eternal youth."

A surge of excitement rippled through me. I could not pass up the opportunity to witness it first-hand.

"Alright, Maadinee, I will come with you," I declared with a determination-filled voice.

Maadinee's face lit up with joy as we made our way out of my home. The vibrant energy of the village seemed to swirl all around us. The morning air felt cool and crisp as we embarked on our journey through the woods. Excitement swayed in our eyes, walking hand in hand. The journey to the gathering place was a short one. But every step carried with it a hope that seemed to vibrate through the air. Our destination was the grove where the revered yoga master had chosen to impart his ancient wisdom.

The familiar tranquillity of the woods enveloped us, whispering secrets and tales of times long past. The forest seemed to come alive with every step, urging us to quicken our pace. And so, our leisurely walk gradually transformed into a spirited jog.

Glancing back at Maadinee, her eyes sparkling with enthusiasm, I could not help but smile. We were like two birds in flight, soaring towards the source of enlightenment that awaited us. The faster we moved, the more the anticipation bubbled within us— a shared sense of exhilaration and joy.

My First Tantric Experience

But just as our pace reached its peak, a vibrant burst of colors caught my attention. I skidded to a halt, my gaze fixed upon a cluster of exquisite flowers blooming by the trees. Their delicate petals swayed gracefully in the gentle breeze, their vibrant hues an invitation to pause and appreciate their beauty.

"Please wait, Maadinee!" I called out, my voice carrying a tinge of excitement. "I want to bring some of these flowers as an offering to the Guru." My words hung in the air as Maadinee turned back, her eyes following the direction of my pointing finger.

A mischievous smile played upon her lips as she nodded in agreement. "Oh, what a wonderful idea, Meera! I shall gather some as well." Her voice carried a hint of playful competition.

"But it was my idea," I protested, albeit with a laugh, as I knelt down to pluck the most vibrant blooms from their stems.

Maadinee, not one to be outdone, joined me in the flower-gathering mission. She swiftly plucked her own selection of blossoms, her hands moving with a grace and speed that matched her unyielding spirit. With a gleeful grin, she declared, "I'll gather the most radiant flowers, Meera!"

As I finished my task and prepared to resume our journey, I noticed Maadinee already darting forward, her footsteps echoing through the woods. "Wait for just a moment!" I called after her, my voice filled with playful urgency, but it seemed to be lost amidst the rustling leaves and the symphony of nature.

Undeterred, I clutched my gathered flowers firmly and followed in Maadinee's footsteps. As I ran, I called out to my dear friend, hoping she would hear my pleas to slow down.

"Maadinee, wait for me! We're in this together!" My voice carried a mix of excitement and determination, as if the mere act of calling her name would bridge the growing gap between us.

The forest enveloped me in its embrace, the sounds of my footsteps and breath harmonizing with the rustling of leaves. With every stride, my heart beat in sync with the pulsating rhythm of nature, guiding me forward. The pursuit of the Guru's wisdom had become intertwined with the race to reach Maadinee, merging into a single purpose.

When I finally caught up to her, a glorious smile spread across my face. Maadinee turned towards me, as well. Her eyes were gleaming with exhilaration. Without uttering a word, we both knew that our playful competition had led us to a moment of shared triumph. The flowers we had gathered would become tokens of our devotion and gratitude to the enlightened Guru.

As we approached the gathering, a sea of curious faces filled the space. Their eyes were filled with a mixture of hope and uncertainty. The sound of hushed whispers and murmurs grew louder. We found ourselves standing on a spot, near a towering banyan tree, where we could observe without being overwhelmed.

Time seemed to stretch as we waited, our hearts fluttering with anticipation. And then, as if the universe had sensed our yearning, a figure emerged from the crowd. Tall and youthful, his presence commanded attention. His long flowing hair fell down his back. A serene smile graced his lips.

My First Tantric Experience

In that moment, the air itself seemed to be still. There was a profound energy that enveloped the space. It was as if the guru's aura had transcended the physical realm. My doubts began to fade into a deep sense of reverence and wonder.

Summoning my courage, I approached him with Maadinee by my side. Sitting before us was a young man, his ethereal glow radiating from within. He was clad in nothing more than white sheets. He exuded an aura of spiritual awakening that left me speechless.

"Guru, how old are you?" I ventured to ask, unable to contain my fascination.

A smile danced upon his lips as he met my gaze. "I am 164 years old," he replied, shocking me to the core. My mind reeled at the thought of such an extraordinary lifespan. But then, with a mischievous twinkle in his eyes, he playfully revealed the truth.

"No, just joking. I am only 47. When one takes good care of themselves, nourish their body with the food provided by the divine, and practice yoga diligently, anyone can maintain their youthfulness as long as they desire."

His words resonated within me. It was a gentle reminder of the power we hold to shape our own destinies. I eagerly accepted his invitation to join the yoga session, ready to immerse myself in the transformative practice.

Before joining the group, I approached him, holding the flowers tightly behind my back. As I extended my hand with the vibrant blooms, I shared, "I have something for you." The guru's eyes lit up, and he graciously accepted the gift.

"These are beautiful flowers," he remarked, his voice infused with warmth. "May the flower within your heart grow bigger and more beautiful each day, just like the offering you have given me." His words left me pondering their deeper meaning, a quest for a temple within my own being.

Suddenly, Maadinee arrived, her vibrant energy bursting forth. "So, you're the young-looking guru," she exclaimed, her excitement palpable. The guru's smile widened, and he responded, "No, my dear, that is one of my disciples named Jagha."

Maadinee eagerly presented her own flower to him, her face beaming with joy. "I offer you this flower. Will you bless me?" she asked, her words filled with earnest hope. The guru's gaze softened, and he blessed her with a gentle touch.

Turning his attention to me, his eyes held a mysterious depth. "Open your hand, Meera. I have a gift for you," he said, his voice both comforting and compelling. I obeyed, extending my palm as he placed a small green stone within it.

"This is a special stone called a Naga Mani," he explained, his tone filled with reverence.

"It's breathtaking! The vibrant green hue and the shimmering glow... I've never seen anything like it. But what makes this stone so special, Guru?" I asked him.

"Ah, my dear, the Naga Mani is believed to awaken the dormant spiritual energies within us. It can deepen one's connection to the divine, enhance intuition, and bring about profound transformations. It acts as a catalyst, guiding the seeker towards enlightenment."

"How can I harness the power of this extraordinary stone, Guru?"

"Patience, child. The Naga Mani chooses its own bearer. It recognizes those who are ready to embark on a spiritual journey, seekers like you who are open to the path of self-discovery. It will call out to you when the time is right."

"I am honoured, Guru. The mere thought of being chosen by such a divine artifact fills my heart with anticipation. What should I do in the meantime?"

"It is a gift from the gods themselves. You must keep it close to yourself at all times, for the stone holds secrets and blessings. And as you grow older, I will reveal more to you. Seek me out when you are ready. But for now, let us begin the class. Please find a seat."

Grateful for his wisdom and the precious stone in my hand, I settled into a spot among the gathering. As the session commenced, the guru's teachings washed over me like a gentle stream, nurturing my spirit and expanding my understanding.

As we settled into our positions, the atmosphere brimming with anticipation, the guru began the two-day class. We engaged in warming-up exercises and various yoga poses, each movement gracefully guiding us toward a deeper connection with our bodies and spirits. I encountered some difficulty in attaining the desired stretch, but to my surprise, one of the disciples—a kind-hearted individual a few years older than me, extended his assistance.

With a gentle smile, he approached and offered guidance, helping me navigate the intricacies of the poses.

"You're doing great!" he said. "Just relax into the pose and let your breath guide you."

His reassuring presence infused the air with a sense of camaraderie, and we shared moments of laughter amidst the practice. Gradually, I began to grasp the movements, and he released me to explore them on my own. The group as a whole found a harmonious rhythm, growing more comfortable and fluid in our expressions of the yogic practice.

As the session progressed, we transitioned into sitting in the lotus position, our hands poised in mudras, ready to immerse ourselves in the power of mantra chanting. The guru clapped his hands, signaling the commencement of this sacred practice. With unwavering focus and devotion, we united our voices, chanting the chosen mantras that reverberated through the air.

With each repetition, I felt a stirring within me, as if a dormant energy was being awakened. A subtle warmth coursed through my being, gradually ascending my spine. It felt as though the sun itself was shining upon me despite the waning light of the setting sun. The connection with the divine grew stronger, as if a veil had been lifted, revealing a glimpse of infinite bliss.

In the midst of the chant, I felt something strange. A subtle yet enchanting melody made its way into my consciousness. It was as if celestial beings had joined us, lending their celestial harmonies to our humble gathering. The music wrapped around me, embracing my very essence, and I surrendered to its enchantment.

When the final notes of the mantra echoed through the space, the guru clapped his hands. The sound gently brought

My First Tantric Experience

us back to the present moment. The session had come to an end, and we gradually emerged from our meditative state, our souls illuminated and hearts overflowing with gratitude.

With a sense of deep respect, I bowed before the guru. I accepted the profound transformation that had taken place within me. I thanked him silently for the gift of this experience. And for guiding me on a path of self-discovery and spiritual awakening.

As we dispersed, the residual energy of the practice lingered, infusing every step I took. I carried the radiance of that sacred space within me, knowing that I had tasted a glimpse of divine truth. And with each passing day, I vowed to nurture the inner light that had been awakened, seeking further illumination on my spiritual journey.

Jagha, one of the disciples, approached me with a warm smile, his presence radiating kindness and curiosity. He extended an invitation, suggesting we take a leisurely walk through the enchanting forest. Intrigued by the prospect of spending time with him and indulging in conversation, I eagerly accepted.

The rustling leaves whispered ancient secrets, and the gentle rays of sunlight filtered through the dense canopy, casting ethereal patterns on the forest floor. The ambiance was serene, providing the perfect backdrop for our conversation.

Jagha, his eyes gleaming with kindness, turned towards me and asked, "Meera, how did you find the meditation session? Did it resonate with your soul?"

A smile graced my face as I reflected on the profound experience I had just encountered.

"There's a sense of unity and connection that permeates through our practice. It's truly special." I spoke with a genuine enthusiasm.

I shared that it had been one of the most extraordinary moments of my life. The connection I felt made the inner radiance shine through me. It was unlike anything I had ever experienced before.

"That's the beauty of yoga," Jagha said. "It not only strengthens our bodies but also nourishes our souls. We tap into a deep well of peace and wisdom within ourselves."

"I felt it during the meditation earlier. The chanting, the vibrations... It was as if something awakened inside me."

Jagha's eyes sparkled with a mixture of understanding and excitement. "That's the power of the practice, Meera. It opens doorways to new dimensions of consciousness, allowing us to experience a profound sense of inner peace and harmony."

"I never expected to find such peace within myself. It's like discovering a hidden treasure."

"Indeed, it's a precious gift that yoga offers us. And it's only the beginning. There are countless layers to explore and unfold within our beings."

"Jagha, I'm eager to delve deeper into this path. I want to learn more about the spiritual aspects of yoga and meditation."

"That's wonderful to hear, Meera. Our group is always welcoming new seekers. Whenever you feel ready, we'll be here to support you on your journey."

My First Tantric Experience

He suggested that I join their group and embark on a journey of learning the art of yoga and meditation. My heart yearned to dive deeper into this spiritual path. I wished to explore the boundless potential that lay within me. Yet, a twinge of hesitation tugged at my soul.

"I do want to join your group. And how I wish I could delve into the teachings of yoga," I confessed, "but not at this very moment." I struggled to put my thoughts into words; a sense of loyalty and responsibility to my parents was holding me back.

Jagha nodded understandingly, his gaze filled with compassion. "Family is sacred, Meera. Your devotion and love for them are commendable. Whenever you're ready, we'll be here, waiting with open arms. It's essential to honour your heart's calling and follow your own path."

His words comforted my heart, reassuring me that the door to this transformative path would remain open, patiently awaiting my return. We continued our walk, the conversation flowing effortlessly between us. In his presence, I felt at ease, a sense of comfort and understanding enveloping us.

"I'm grateful for your understanding, Jagha. Your kindness and the energy you bring to the group have been inspiring. I feel a deep connection with all of you."

"The feeling is mutual, Meera. Here, we're like a family. We are bound by our shared love for yoga and spirituality. So, whenever you feel ready to join, we'll be thrilled to have you. I promise you that there always will be a place for you with us."

"I look forward to that day. So, I'm curious about you. Can you share more about your own journey with yoga and meditation? How did you join this group?"

"Ah, my journey has been quite transformative. I was once lost and searching for meaning in my life. It was during a particularly challenging period that I stumbled upon a small yoga ashram. The guru, with his profound wisdom and radiant presence, guided me towards self-discovery and inner peace. From that moment on, I dedicated myself to this path and became a disciple, eager to share the teachings with others."

"That's incredible, Jagha. It's amazing how the right encounters can lead us to our true purpose. I feel a deep connection with this practice, and I know it will continue to guide me."

"Absolutely, Meera. Trust your intuition and embrace the journey with an open heart. The path of yoga is not just about the physical postures but also about cultivating a profound awareness and connection with the divine."

As we chatted, an unanticipated feeling began to stir within me—an unmistakable fluttering of butterflies in my stomach. Jagha's kind spirit, his deep understanding of the spiritual journey, and the way he carried himself with grace and humility captivated my attention. I couldn't deny the growing fondness I felt for him, the inexplicable connection that seemed to strengthen with each passing moment.

Lost in our conversation and the subtle dance of emotions within me, we reached a peaceful clearing in the woods. Jagha revealed their practice of meditating around a carefully

My First Tantric Experience

guarded fire to keep wild animals at bay. His eyes twinkled as he shared this unique ritual, and a smile graced my lips in response. The thought of meditating amidst nature's embrace, surrounded by the warmth and safety of the fire, was intriguing.

Later, we resumed our walk, the evening sun casting a golden glow over the landscape. The enchantment of the forest mirrored the fluttering in my heart, both filling me with a sense of wonder and possibility. I cherished Jagha's company, grateful for the connection we were forging.

As the day drew to a close, we returned to the village, our footsteps filled with a shared understanding and unspoken promises of friendship. I bid him farewell, my heart filled with conflicting emotions—a longing to explore the spiritual path that beckoned, and an unwavering love for my family that rooted me to the present.

The delicate dance between these two desires would continue to unfold, intertwining my personal journey of self-discovery with the bonds I held dear. In the days to come, I knew I would face choices, each offering its own unique path. But for now, I embraced the beauty of the moment, treasuring the connection with Jagha and the promise of a spiritual awakening that awaited me.

Late at night, I found myself lying in bed, surrounded by the peaceful stillness of the hour. My parents were sound asleep, and I could hear their rhythmic breaths rising and falling together. The enchanting experience with the yoga guru and the profound connection I had felt during the meditation session continued to weave into my thoughts.

Unable to find solace in sleep, I decided to adopt the soothing posture of yoga's corpse pose.

As I lay awake in my bed, I immersed myself in the familiar embrace of the yoga corpse pose. Closing my eyes, I focused my attention on my breath. And allowing it to guide me into a state of deep relaxation. My mind became a canvas for the mantra that had taken root within me. Its melodic vibrations vibrated through my entire being. It was then that like a gentle whisper, a familiar mantra flowed effortlessly from my lips.

But as the mantra reverberated in the silence, a subtle shift occurred. The music that had accompanied my previous meditation session resurfaced, but this time it carried a different melody—a colder, more ethereal tone that seemed to transcend the confines of my physical existence. Intrigued and slightly bewildered, I surrendered to the unfolding experience.

All of a sudden, I felt the distinct sensation of weightlessness. It was as if my being was being lifted beyond the boundaries of my earthly body. I remained calm, trusting in the unknown. And then, a voice pierced the silence, gently reassuring me.

"Do not fear, my child. I am Latika, one of the goddesses you have worshipped across numerous lifetimes. I have heard your prayers and felt the love you have offered me. I am here to serve you and protect you from the perils of the world."

My lips trembled with the desire to speak, to express my gratitude and seek guidance. Yet, in this ethereal dimension, words became unnecessary. Latika, the divine presence, smiled understandingly. She assured me that she could hear my thoughts and intentions as clearly as if they were spoken aloud. She encouraged me to keep her close in my heart, like a guiding light in my journey of self-discovery and spiritual growth.

Time seemed suspended as I absorbed the profound encounter. The gentle touch of Latika's presence wrapped around me, filling me with a renewed sense of purpose and inner strength. And then, as swiftly as it had begun, the experience ended. And I found myself back in the familiar embrace of my physical form.

The room surrounding me remained unchanged. I took a moment to gather my thoughts. I could not believe the significance of what had just transpired. Latika's words echoed in my mind. I soon realized that my journey had only just begun. The spiritual path that I had glimpsed was far more extensive than I initially imagined.

A profound sense of gratitude washed over me. There was a gentle curiosity that whispered promises of transformative experiences yet to come. With Latika's guidance etched within my heart, I closed my eyes once more, surrendering to the mysteries that awaited me on this sacred journey of self-discovery.

The Departure of My Beloved Parents

As the gentle sun rays of the early morning caressed the Karmana village, I woke up and felt an instinctual urge to find solace through meditation. With a resolute mindset, I got out of bed and stepped outside, where the atmosphere reverberated with a sacred awakening.

While settling into a comfortable position and preparing to explore the depths of my consciousness, I sensed a companion beside me. It was my dear mother, awakening from her own peaceful slumber. As if summoned by an undetectable force, she gravitated towards me, sensing the divine connection that awaited us. In a graceful manner, she took a seat next to me, her eyes radiating warmth and tenderness. I could sense her unwavering love enveloping me like a gentle, protective covering.

Sensing her gaze upon me, I turned my face and opened my eyes, revealing a tender connection between mother and daughter. "Hello, mother," I greeted her softly. The morning light danced upon her countenance, illuminating her wise and compassionate eyes.

She returned the greeting, her voice resonating with a melodic cadence.

Observing my newfound devotion to meditation, my mother inquired, "I see that you have chosen the path of meditation. It warms my heart to witness your blossoming spirituality. What is it that you seek, my child?" Her genuine curiosity beckoned me to share my innermost desires.

"Certainly, mother," I agreed. "Meditation has become an essential component of my life. Nonetheless, I do not seek to be unrestricted. My aim is to discover my genuine identity, to unleash my inner potential, and to devise ways to promote the betterment of our world."

A warm smile spread across my mother's face, "My dear child," she whispered, "You have aspirations for self-awareness and the admirable pursuit of creating a positive impact. These are truly exceptional objectives."

As the morning sun ascended higher, casting its warm embrace upon the land, my mother's hands delicately unfurled a vibrant mat upon which to lay the Mirchi. With meticulous care, she explained, "We shall let the Mirchi bask in the sun's nourishing rays, preserving its essence for later use. Just as we nurture and store this precious gift, remember to nurture your own spirit and store the wisdom you gather along your journey."

She handed me a pair of bangles, adorned with wooden accents, which she had been wearing on her feet. My mother adorned my wrists with her bangles. Each wooden accent encircling the bangles symbolized grounding, anchoring oneself to the earth's eternal embrace. "These bangles," she imparted, "will hold you steadfast on your path, connecting you to the very essence of our shared existence. As they have nurtured me, may they nurture you, my child. I give them to you so you may stay rooted in your journey."

In a beautiful display of unity, my father, too, joined us, his eyes shimmering with paternal pride. He bestowed upon me his own bangles, a reflection of his unwavering support. Not to be outdone, my father approached us, his eyes reflecting a deep love and unspoken pride. With a gesture filled with profound significance, he offered his bangles, a tangible representation of his unwavering support. The weight of their bangles encircling my wrists infused me with a profound sense of unity, as though the collective strength and guidance of my ancestors flowed through me.

I thanked my parents for their precious gifts. They smiled knowingly, aware of the significance of this moment. As our souls intertwined, they gently inquired if I intended to return to the sacred woods to meditate once more.

"Yes," I responded eagerly, my voice tinged with a mixture of excitement and vulnerability. "I plan to meet with Maadinee, my dear friend, and venture into the forest together. Walking amidst nature's majesty brings solace to my heart, and her presence offers me strength."

My parents nodded in understanding, their eyes gleaming with unwavering trust. "Go, my child," they encouraged me. "Embark on this journey of self-discovery and service."

With their blessings etched upon my soul, I set forth on my path, the woods beckoning me with their enchanting melodies. It was a day filled with possibilities, and I found myself brimming with excitement as I made my way to Maadinee's humble abode. The journey to her house was a familiar one, winding through narrow pathways lined with vibrant flowers and quaint huts, each adorned with colorful tapestries.

As I approached Maadinee's dwelling, I caught a whiff of a mesmerizing scent, a symbol of her family's dedication to spiritual practices. The door opened, and Maadinee welcomed me warmly as I walked inside, as though the walls themselves emitted an aura of tranquillity. We sat on plush cushions with magnificently crafted tapestries that told otherworldly stories of celestial beings.

"My dear Meera! My heart sings with joy at the sight of you," Maadinee exclaimed. "The day is full of promises."

I nodded eagerly, filled with anticipation. "Yes, Maadinee. I feel it in my soul. There is a mystical energy surrounding us as if the universe is ready to reveal its many secrets."

She clasped her hands together, her eyes excited with expectation. "Indeed, my dear friend. We will embark on a journey of self-discovery, delving deeper into the realms of spirituality."

As we drank fragrant herbal tea, Maadinee's mother graced us with her presence.

"Remember, my dear ones," she intoned, her voice heavy with ancestral wisdom. "The path to spiritual awakening lies within yourselves, not in external answers. The journey before you will unlock new doors of self-discovery and illuminate the sacred essence that resides within each of you."

Her words lingered in the air, a gentle reminder of the profound nature of our quest. With newfound resolve, we rose from our cushions, ready to embark on our journey into the heart of the village, where ancient temples, sacred groves, and wise sages awaited our presence.

Maadinee and I set off on the familiar path, winding along the dusty road that led to the heart of our destination. And as fate would have it, we soon caught sight of Jagha.

My heart fluttered, and Maadinee, always perceptive, drew closer to me, her voice filled with a mischievous tone. "Hey, Meera, I think you like him," she playfully whispered.

Caught off guard, I glanced at her, my cheeks flushed with a mix of embarrassment and curiosity. "You think?" I replied, my voice barely concealing a hint of uncertainty.

Maadinee's giggles filled the air, her laughter ringing like joyous bells. "I knew it!" she exclaimed, unable to contain her amusement. The air between us brimmed with a shared secret, a whisper of possibilities that danced on the breeze.

As we walked, our laughter preceded us like a wonderful melody. We walked a brief distance behind Jagha, observing as he effortlessly strolled ahead of us. Suddenly, he turned around, and our eyes locked. I flushed in anxiety. Would he scold us for chasing after him? To my amazement, Jagha directed his gaze towards me and curved his lips into a smile. "Would you charming ladies like me to accompany you to your destination?" he proposed, speaking softly and cordially.

Caught off guard, my heartbeat quickened, and I could not help but exclaim, "Absolutely!"

"Okay, let's go," Maadinee exchanged a knowing smile with me, her eyes silently affirming what our hearts already knew. With Jagha leading the way, we ventured towards the woods, the anticipation of the journey weighing upon us.

The Departure of My Beloved Parents

As we walked in silence, the rustling leaves and chirping birds became our companions. There was an unspoken understanding between us, a shared recognition that words were unnecessary at this moment. We reveled in the tranquillity of the forest, the very presence of Jagha filling the air with a sense of ease and protection.

The sunlight filtered through the dense foliage, casting ethereal patterns on the forest floor. Step by step, we ventured into the heart of the woods, our spirits intertwined in a tapestry of intrigue and discovery.

The three of us arrived at our sacred meditation spot. Nestled amidst a serene grove, the air carried a gentle stillness, as if the very trees whispered ancient wisdom to those who sought solace within their embrace. Our hearts brimmed with anticipation, eager to embark on yet another transformative session under the guidance of our guru.

To our surprise, as we settled into a circle, the guru's countenance seemed tinged with confusion. His voice trembled slightly as he addressed the group, uncertainty lacing his words. "I'm not sure if we can continue today or if we should conclude our session. However, let us give it a try."

A perplexed expression crossed my face. It was unusual for our revered guru to display any hint of doubt. Nevertheless, we followed his lead, finding comfortable positions in Lotus posture. The guru's voice resonated through the stillness, chanting the sacred mantra, "Ohm Santi Santi ohm."

I felt a surge of energy reverberating within me. The collective voices of our group intertwined, creating a tapestry of harmonious sound that seemed to penetrate the depths of my being. At that moment, a profound sense of peace washed over me, as if I had transcended the boundaries of my earthly existence.

A smile graced my lips, unbidden but welcomed. All worries, doubts, and fears melted away, replaced by a profound sense of connection with the universe. The butterflies in my stomach fluttered in joyous harmony as if dancing to the rhythm of the cosmos itself. Time seemed to lose its grip as we continued our communal chant, surrendering to the flow of divine energy.

As the minutes melded into half an hour, the guru's palms came together in a resounding clap, bringing our chanting to a close. His gaze settled on me, his countenance serious yet laced with a mysterious urgency. "My child, you must go home. Your parents are awaiting your presence," he declared, his voice laced with a mix of concern and urgency.

Confusion and curiosity flooded my thoughts as I looked at him, my voice tinged with inquiry. "Why, Guruji? What is happening?"

He responded with a solemn command. "Just go, my child." His gaze shifted momentarily to the bangles adorning my wrist, his words faltering slightly. "May... maybe run."

Maadinee and I exchanged bewildered glances, the urgency in our guru's voice spurring us into action. Without a moment's hesitation, we started running, our voices carrying through the air, calling out to my beloved parents.

"Mother! Father!" my voice echoed through the village, a mixture of excitement and trepidation interwoven in our cries. As we dashed through the winding pathways, our footsteps creating a cadence of urgency.

The Departure of My Beloved Parents

The world around us seemed to blur as we sprinted, the village unfolding in a blur of vibrant colors and familiar faces. As Maadinee and I approached the vicinity of my house, our breath caught in our throats. There, in the midst of the tranquil meditation spot, sat my parents, their figures illuminated by a radiant glow. It was as if they had transcended the realm of mortals, their beings entwined with the very essence of the sun itself.

To my astonishment, a small rainbow circle materialized behind their heads. Maadinee and I stood there, speechless, bearing witness to this wondrous spectacle. It felt as though we were in the presence of a divine miracle, a sacred manifestation that defied all logical explanation.

News of this exceptional incident rapidly disseminated across the town, captivating the inquisitive looks of our compatriots. They congregated at the location, their gazes brimming with fascination and veneration. The atmosphere buzzed with an evident intensity, an amalgamation of astonishment, eagerness, and a tinge of unease.

Our village Pandit, the learned spiritual guide, arrived, his face etched with concern and curiosity. He surveyed the gathering crowd, his gaze falling upon my radiant parents. "Why is everyone here? What is happening?" he inquired, seeking answers to the extraordinary sight that lay before him.

Silence hung heavy in the air as the crowd turned to me, expecting an explanation. My voice trembled as I struggled to articulate the inexplicable. "No, Panditji, I don't know. I have no control over what is unfolding," I uttered, my words laced with both awe and helplessness.

In a swift motion, the Pandit moved towards my parents, his eyes filled with determination to intervene and understand this extraordinary phenomenon. Yet, as he approached them, a sudden shift occurred. Their radiant forms, once bathed in celestial light, crumbled to the ground, collapsing into one another's embrace.

Tears welled up in his eyes as he approached me, his voice filled with a blend of grief and admonishment. "My child, this should not have been done. You should not have accepted their bangles. Those bangles were meant to keep them grounded, to anchor their souls to this earthly realm. But your parents, driven by impatience and a longing for spiritual elevation, prematurely severed their connection to this mortal plane."

His words struck me like an arrow to the heart, piercing through the awe and wonder that had enveloped me moments ago. I struggled to breathe, and it felt as if my heart stopped beating. By inadvertently doing something, I quickened the end of my parent's lives, depriving them of the priceless occasions they needed to finish their responsibilities on earth, notably their duty to take care of me and guide me.

I deeply understood the heaviness of this profound reality, and it crushed me, causing me to collapse to the ground as tears streamed down my face. The observers, who had seen this agonizing chain of incidents, gave me comfort and relief by holding me tenderly and silently asking for me, understanding the immense sorrow that had descended upon me.

As the chaos and confusion engulfed me, my mind raced with a whirlwind of questions and self-doubt. What had transpired before my eyes? Were my parents truly gone?

The Departure of My Beloved Parents

Their departure was signified by the fading glow and golden hue that enveloped their forms. Did they embark on a journey to Indra's paradises, leaving this mortal realm behind? The weight of responsibility bore down on me, and tears streamed uncontrollably down my cheeks.

Overwhelmed by guilt and grief, I questioned my own actions. How could I have unknowingly accepted their bangles, unaware of the consequences it would bring? Should I have known better? The weight of disappointment from both within myself and the community pressed upon me and I yearned to undo the irrevocable.

Amidst my anguish, I felt the comforting presence of Maadinee embracing me, her tears mingling with mine. We were both adrift in a sea of grief and confusion, seeking solace and answers that eluded us. In the midst of our shared pain, Maadinee and Jagha attempted to lift me from the ground. But my body refused to respond, paralyzed by the overwhelming emotional turmoil.

As they struggled to carry me away from the crowd of concerned villagers, I fought against their efforts, desperately craving solitude. My heart yearned to retreat from the prying eyes and the buzzing voices that debated my fate. In a surge of determination, I broke free from their grasp, aching for a moment of respite.

With heavy footsteps, I sought refuge in the tranquil waters of the nearby lake. Underneath the shade of a sturdy tree, I collapsed, my sobs consuming me. I surrendered to the exhaustion that overwhelmed my fragile spirit. Tears stained my face, my body trembling with the weight of sorrow and remorse.

In the peacefulness of that tranquil moment, I slipped into a restless slumber. My dreams were a mosaic of fragmented recollections combined with a feeling of immense hollowness. The soft splashing of the lake's ripples and the murmuring wind acted as a lull, soothing me into a brief reprieve from the havoc that had disrupted my existence. Unbeknownst to me, in that frail moment, the town's religious scholar and the caring citizens encircled themselves, their voices echoing with empathy.

As I slumbered under the shield of the age-old tree, oblivious to the talks that transpired in my absence, a flicker of optimism rose inside of me. I sensed that the route to mending and reformation demanded deep introspection and a reconnection with the sacred domain. I had no notion that this profound deprivation would become the impetus for a transformational expedition, one that would compel me to confront my internal demons, crave forgiveness, and decipher the secrets of our antiquated customs. The venture that lay ahead was doubtful and precarious, but I was resolute in my quest to reclaim my integrity, restore equilibrium, and reunite with the benevolent spirits of my adored parents.

As I opened my eyes, the world around me appeared as if veiled by a thin mist. A rhythmic temple drumming, the melodic chorus of birdsong—but my senses felt dulled, detached from reality. It was in this ethereal ambiance that I noticed movement in the lake in front of me, drawing my gaze. There, in the center of the tranquil lake, a magnificent lotus bud floated gracefully, seemingly suspended in time.

With a sudden burst of energy, the lotus unfurled its delicate petals, revealing the ethereal form of Latika, my personal goddess. She emanated a radiant light that bathed everything in its soft glow. The sight of her brought a rush of relief and hope surging through my veins. Latika had come to me once again, a beacon of divine guidance and solace in my hour of need.

Latika's luscious tresses flowed down her spine akin to a dazzling cascade of water, embellished with fragile, intricately woven floral threads. As she moved, her hair swayed gently, mirroring the rhythms of the divine universe. Clothed in ethereal garments that seemed to shift and change with every step, Latika donned robes of iridescent silk that blended hues of rose pink, opalescent blue, and pearlescent white. Embroidered patterns of lotus blossoms adorned her attire, symbolizing purity, enlightenment, and spiritual rebirth.

Hope ignited within me as I realized that Latika had returned, a beacon of guidance and salvation. Her eyes, mesmerizing and filled with compassion, reflected the wisdom of the ages. They sparkled like twin stars. When Latika looked upon me, it felt as though she could peer into the depths of my very soul, understanding the turmoil and yearning that resided within.

I attempted to speak, to pour out my worries and questions, but my voice failed me. Latika, perceptive as ever, gently silenced me, assuring me that my inability to articulate my thoughts was of no consequence. "I understand," she conveyed, her voice resonating within my soul. "Take solace in the fact that you will learn, and your path will become clear."

The delicate anklet encircling Latika's slender foot emitted a soft jingling sound with each step.

Latika's voice, gentle yet resolute, resonated in my mind. "You will learn in due time," she assured me, her voice carrying the wisdom of the ages. "But for now, know this: your parents are embarking on a sacred journey, a path to be judged by Lord Indra. And you, dear Meera, must confront the burden of guilt that weighs heavily upon your heart."

As the image of Latika and the lake slowly began to fade, I strained to hear a distant cry. It was Maadinee's voice, calling out my name with urgency. Although the details of her words eluded me, her presence brought me back to the present moment.

A tremor coursed through my body, awakening me from a trance. Maadinee, my faithful friend, stood beside me with worry etched on her face. She enveloped me in a warm embrace, and in a soft whisper, she expressed her relief at finding me, her search having consumed hours of worry and uncertainty.

Through a veil of tears, I murmured: "I sought solace in solitude, Maadinee. I needed to find myself amidst the chaos that unfolded."

With unwavering support, Maadinee pulled me up, her touch grounding me in the present moment. "Come," she said, her voice filled with determination. "Everyone has been anxiously awaiting our return. We must return to the village now."

Hand in hand, we slowly made our way back to the village, the concerned faces of our fellow villagers awaiting our return. Their gazes held a mixture of relief and curiosity as they watched us approach. I could sense the unspoken questions lingering in the air, the need for reassurance and understanding. As we entered the village, the collective worry and relief washed over me, mingling with my own emotions in an intricate dance.

The Departure of My Beloved Parents

The villagers encircled us, their eyes filled with a mixture of compassion and curiosity. The village Pandit stepped forward, his voice filled with paternal concern. "My child, we were worried for your well-being. Tell us what transpired, what troubled your spirit so deeply."

Taking a deep breath, I composed myself and looked into the eyes of my people. Their unwavering support and genuine care gave me strength. With a voice that quivered slightly, I began to recount the events that had unfolded—the sudden departure of my parents, the overwhelming guilt that consumed me, and the mysterious encounter with Latika.

The atmosphere became oppressively dense. The inhabitants, bound by a profound spiritual attachment, listened attentively, their hearts receptive to the authenticity of my sentiments.

The Guru, with his eyes glistening with teardrops, uttered words of comfort and sagacity, reminding me that I was not solitarily walking through this journey. He reassured me that the path of liberation and comprehension would unfold effortlessly, but only if I acknowledged the lessons that lie ahead.

In the warm embrace of my community, surrounded by their affection and unfaltering backing, I sensed a glimmer of aspiration reignite inside me. I realized that the journey ahead would encounter several obstacles and revelations, but I was not facing it single-handedly anymore.

The Funeral

Maadinee's parents, compassionate souls, welcomed me into their home with open arms. Her father, the revered Pandit of our village, diligently attended to the funeral arrangements, ensuring that everything was conducted with utmost reverence. It was during this solemn time that Jagha and his wise master guru arrived, offering their support.

Seeking solace, I found a moment alone with the guru in the courtyard.

"I sense that you carry many questions within you, my child."

I nodded in agreement, my eyes welling up with tears. "I cannot help but feel responsible," I confessed. "It seems as though I am to blame for their departure. If only I hadn't taken their bangles, they might still be here with us."

The guru's calm voice enveloped me, his words penetrating deep into my troubled soul. "There is no one to blame, dear one; the departure of your parents was part of a greater plan beyond our mortal comprehension."

Tears streamed down my face, "But it was my greed that led me to take their bangles," I choked out. "If I had not been consumed by such desires, they would still be by my side."

In a gesture of profound comfort, the guru tenderly placed his hand on my head and pressed me gently against his

The Funeral

heart. An inexplicable electric current surged through me, immediately soothing my troubled spirit.

With compassion and unwavering love, he spoke softly, "My child, what you did was not driven by greed but rather by the innocent heart of a child accepting a gift from her beloved parents. Your self-reflection and concern demonstrate the purity of your soul."

A flicker of curiosity danced in my eyes as he continued, "Allow me to share a tale with you, a story of a jeweler who transformed from a greedy man to a saint."

And so, the guru began the story of Sreenivasa, who was born to the kind-hearted trader and jeweler Varadappa Naik and his wife. It was a blessing granted by Lord Venkateshvara upon their eager prayers. Varadappa's wealth flowed not only from his prosperous business but also from his generosity toward the poor and needy. And he handed over his prosperous business to his son, Sreenivasa, who possessed a different nature.

Sreenivasa, driven by a relentless pursuit of profit, turned the family business into a heartless enterprise. He disregarded the needs of the poor. Despite his father's attempts to teach him the values of compassion, Sreenivasa remained unchanged.

One fateful day, Varadappa fell gravely ill, and the physician recommended medicinal ash made from precious gems. However, Sreenivasa dismissed the idea, considering it a wasteful expenditure. He callously remarked that his father was old and would eventually pass away, showing no concern for his life. Sadly, Varadappa breathed his last, leaving behind a son consumed by avarice.

Sreenivasa's wealth continued to grow, earning him the notorious nickname 'Navakoti' or 'the owner of 90 million.' Meanwhile, a poor Brahmana approached him, seeking financial assistance for his son's thread ceremony. Astonished that someone would dare to ask him for money, Sreenivasa repeatedly postponed the Brahmana's request, offering false promises.

Days turned into weeks, and the Brahmana's patience wore thin. Finally, he arrived at Sreenivasa's home, seeking help from his wife, Saraswati. With a heavy heart, he shared how he had begged for six months only to receive a box filled with worthless fake coins. Moved by the Brahmana's plight, Saraswati felt deep shame for her husband's miserliness.

Though forbidden by Sreenivasa to give in charity, Saraswati realized that her diamond nose ring, a gift from her mother, was her own possession. Overcoming her fear, she decided to gift it to the Brahmana, alleviating his burden. Grateful, the Brahmana thanked her, tears of gratitude streaming down his face.

When Sreenivasa discovered the expensive nose ring, he was taken aback. It bore an uncanny resemblance to his wife's jewelry. He requested the Brahmana to return the next day, claiming he needed time to evaluate its price for pawning. Locking the nose ring in his shop, he returned home for dinner.

Unbeknownst to Sreenivasa, Saraswati had planned to end her life out of fear of her husband's wrath. She ground diamonds from her bracelet and mixed them with water, intending to drink the lethal concoction. But as she prepared to

The Funeral

consume the poison, a miracle occurred. The nose ring, fallen from the ceiling, landed directly into the glass. Overwhelmed with joy and gratitude, she bowed before the divine form of Lord Vishnu.

Panic set in when Sreenivasa discovered the nose ring missing from his shop. He returned home and demanded the truth from Saraswati. She revealed how she had gifted it to the poor Brahmana, narrating the entire incident. Stricken with guilt, Sreenivasa realized his profound mistakes. He acknowledged that the Brahmana must have been none other than Lord Vishnu himself, testing his heart.

That very night, sleep eluded Sreenivasa as he recognized the depth of his greed and the pain it had caused. The following day, he approached his wife, Saraswati, with newfound clarity. He admitted his blindness and vowed to donate all his wealth to the poor and needy. Saraswati rejoiced, and together with their children, they embarked on a spiritual journey, singing the praises of God and visiting sacred pilgrim centers.

After a decade of wandering, Sreenivasa now transformed and known as Purandara Dasa encountered Saint Vyasatirtha. The scholar, following the teachings of Saint Madhvacharya, recognized the inner change within Sreenivasa and initiated him into the path of Sannyasa, granting him the name 'Purandara Dasa.'

"My child," the guru concluded, "this story reveals a profound truth. Pursuing material wealth as the ultimate goal can never lead to true happiness. Greed blinds us, numbing our hearts and causing us to neglect our loved ones."

As I absorbed the guru's words, a deep understanding enveloped me, and tears of realization flowed. His voice grew softer as he concluded the story. "My child, do you see the truth within this tale? Genuine happiness blossoms when we make God our ultimate purpose, our guiding light."

I nodded in silent acknowledgment, grateful for the guru's guidance and the timeless wisdom he had shared.

I looked up at the guru, my eyes filled with a mixture of relief and confusion. His words offered me a glimmer of solace. But I could not thoroughly shake off the weight of guilt that lingered within me.

"But Guruji," I whispered, my voice trembling, "if I hadn't taken their bangles... if I hadn't been so attached to them, maybe they would still be alive."

The guru placed a gentle hand on my shoulder, "Child, our lives are governed by a divine plan, and we cannot fully comprehend the intricacies of its design. Your parents' departure was a part of their destined path. The bangles were merely a symbol, a token of their love for you. It is not your fault."

His words gently enveloped me, presenting a ray of comprehension within the turbulence of my feelings. I inhaled deeply, "However, what was the reason for this occurrence in my life? Why was it necessary for me to endure this loss?"

"Life is a tapestry woven with both joy and sorrow, Meera. Sometimes, we are chosen to experience profound loss so that we may grow and awaken to our true purpose. Your journey is unique, and this hardship will shape you into a stronger and wiser soul."

The Funeral

I nodded slowly, finding a sliver of hope within his words. His presence was a soothing balm, guiding me through the depths of my pain. As I rested on his chest, I could sense his affection and knowledge encompassing me, offering the resilience I required to navigate the uncertain course ahead. Tears welled up in my eyes once again, but this time, they were tears of liberation and acceptance. Together, we sat in stillness, permitting the heaviness of our feelings to dissolve into the tranquility of the moment.

The guru's consoling presence reminded me that I was not solitary in my sorrow and that there were guiding forces watching over me. In that sacred realm, I began to discover a glint of acceptance, comprehending that my parents' love would perpetually dwell within me.

After a while had passed, a somber aura entered the abode—the chief of the hunters, Haroon. As his footsteps reverberated through the silence, I lifted my gaze to meet his sorrowful eyes. Haroon was a man of few words, but his presence conveyed a great deal. I cherished his gesture, knowing that he, too, had experienced the loss of loved ones and comprehended the anguish accompanying such a loss.

"Meera," he whispered softly, his voice tinged with empathy. "May the divine grant you the strength during this difficult time."

I smiled gratefully.

As Haroon stood there, his presence emanating both strength and empathy, the pandit returned, his expression filled with the weight of responsibility. He began to explain the traditional funeral rituals, emphasizing the importance of having a living son perform the sacred duties on behalf of the departed.

As the pandit spoke, his words weighed heavily on my heart. The realization that our family lacked a living son to carry out the sacred rituals intensified the ache of loss within me. It was a tradition deeply ingrained in our culture and passed down through generations. The absence of a son to fulfill these sacred duties felt like an unbridgeable abyss.

Tears welled up in my eyes as I turned to the pandit, my voice trembling with emotion. "Panditji," I began, struggling to find the right words, "I understand the significance of these rituals and the importance of a living son performing them. But my parents, despite not having a son, loved me unconditionally and imparted their wisdom and values to me. Can't I, as their daughter, fulfill these sacred duties?"

The pandit's gaze softened, his eyes reflecting both sympathy and understanding. He placed a gentle hand on my shoulder, offering a small measure of solace amidst my inner turmoil.

"Meera, my dear child," the pandit spoke with compassion, "the traditions we follow are steeped in ancient wisdom and hold great importance in our spiritual beliefs. However, they should not overshadow the depth of love and devotion your parents had for you."

A moment of silence enveloped the room, heavy with the weight of an unspoken question. My gaze shifted between Haroon and Jagha, who had accompanied him. Both men stood tall, their faces etched with determination and honor.

I glanced at Haroon, his gaze steady and understanding. Without uttering a word, he seemed to comprehend the weight of my thoughts. He stepped forward,

"Meera," he began, his voice filled with a gentle resolve. "I may not be of your bloodline, but I am willing to shoulder the responsibility of performing the sacred rituals for your departed loved ones."

His offer caught me off guard, and I couldn't help but be moved by his selflessness.

Jagha stepped forward. His gaze fixed on Haroon, tension filling the air.

"I will perform the sacred rituals, Meera," Jagha declared, his voice filled with determination. "I have studied the ancient scriptures and have the knowledge and experience required for this task. And it would be an honor to offer your parents a proper farewell."

Haroon's brows furrowed, his eyes narrowing as he stepped forward to counter Jagha's claim. "Meera, I understand Jagha's desire to help, but I am older than him. I know our traditions, our customs, and have the utmost respect for the spiritual significance of these rituals."

An animosity began to brew between the two men, each vying to prove their worthiness for this revered responsibility. Their voices grew louder, their words escalating into a heated argument.

Confusion and uncertainty gnawed at my heart as the weight of their quarrel pressed upon me. I looked from Jagha to Haroon, torn between the respect I held for both men and the decision that lay before me.

Taking a deep breath, I stepped forward, raising my hands to quiet their voices. "Enough!" I exclaimed, my voice trembling with a mixture of emotions.

Silence fell upon the courtyard, the tension palpable as all eyes turned to me.

The pandit broke the silence, his voice measured and deliberate. "Meera, the time has come to make a decision. Haroon and Jagha have both expressed their willingness to fulfill the sacred duties on behalf of your parents. It is now up to you to choose who shall carry this responsibility."

I looked at them, their expressions filled with earnestness and compassion. My heart ached at the weight of this decision, for it felt as if I had to choose between the two halves of my own being.

At that moment, I realized that this decision was not solely mine to make. It was a decision that needed guidance beyond my own limited understanding. I looked towards the guru, who had been silently observing, his wise eyes filled with a knowing light.

"Please, guru," I implored, my voice trembling with the weight of my indecision, "guide me in this choice. Help me honor my parents' memory in the most fitting way."

As the guru's words filled the air, a profound understanding washed over me. The traditional rituals dictated that the eldest living son perform the funeral rites, symbolizing the liberation of the parents' souls from the cycle of birth and

The Funeral

death, leading them towards moksha. But in this sacred moment, the guru revealed a profound truth.

"Meera, your parents have embarked on a meditative journey, traversing the realms of the divine. Through their spiritual endeavors, their souls have already attained moksha. They have been released from the cycle of re-birth."

"Does this mean I can perform the funeral rites?" I asked, seeking confirmation of the newfound understanding.

The guru nodded, his eyes reflecting the depth of his wisdom. "Indeed, Meera. With your parents' souls having transcended the cycle, the responsibility of the rituals falls upon you. It is through your devotion and love that you can honor their journey and pay homage to the path they have traversed."

The realization that I, their daughter, held the sacred duty to guide their souls further into the realms of peace and enlightenment ignited a sense of purpose within me.

Just then, the pandit moved closer to the guru, and the whispers brought an anticipatory shift to the air. Their hushed conversation seemed to hold secrets and sacred knowledge, leaving me curious yet apprehensive.

Moments later, they approached me with a solemn expression on their faces. The pandit's voice was gentle but carried the weight of responsibility as he spoke, "Meera, it is time to bid farewell to your parents and release their souls back to the world. We will guide you through the ceremony, and it is important for you to follow our instructions. Trust in the wisdom of the ancient rituals and refrain from taking any drastic actions, my child. Can you promise me that?"

I looked into their eyes, sensing their genuine concern and the depth of their understanding. Nodding in response, I assured them, "I will do as you instruct. I trust in the wisdom of our traditions and the guidance you provide."

We proceeded towards the designated area where the funeral ceremony would take place. The flickering flames of the pyres cast an ethereal glow, casting shadows upon the faces gathered around.

The pandit and the guru led the way, their steps deliberate and their words whispered with reverence. I followed closely, my heart heavy with a mix of grief and gratitude for the time I had shared with my parents.

As we reached the pyres, a wave of emotions crashed over me. There, atop the wooden structures, lay the bodies of my mother and father, adorned with vibrant flowers and draped in white ceremonial garments.

My eyes traced the contours of her mother's face, once so alive and filled with warmth. Now, it lay serene and peaceful in death. The lines of wisdom etched upon her brow seemed to whisper secrets of a life well-lived. Turning my gaze to my father, whose strength and resilience had been his guiding light. His hands, once strong and calloused from hard work, now rested tranquility at his sides. I would never again witness his comforting presence or hear the soothing timbre of his voice. I would never see their faces again.

The pandit guided me through the sacred ritual, instructing me on each step with clarity and compassion. I listened intently, absorbing the significance of each action and recitation.

The Funeral

With trembling hands, I took hold of the torch and approached the pyres that enclosed the physical remains of my mother and father. I brushed my fingers against the fabric that shrouded their forms. It felt cool and foreign, a stark reminder that their earthly journey had reached its end. Memories flooded my mind—laughter shared, lessons learned, moments cherished—and a profound sense of gratitude swelled within me.

As I ignited the fire, a bittersweet ache enveloped my being. The flames danced and crackled beneath them, casting an ethereal light that embraced their lifeless forms. My breath got caught in my throat as I beheld the sight before me.

Time seemed to stand still as I sat there, grounded on the ground, gazing into the flickering flames. Questions tugged at my heart, wondering where my parents' souls had ventured, yearning for a glimpse of understanding.

In the silence, the pandit and the guru stood beside me, their presence a comforting anchor. Their quiet strength reminded me that I was not alone in this moment of profound transition.

I closed my eyes, allowing the warmth of the flames and the echoes of the recitations to envelop me. And soon enough, a sense of connection washed over me. It felt as if my parents' spirits were whispering words of reassurance, assuring me that they were in a place of peace and love.

In that stillness, I found solace and acceptance. The path ahead was uncertain, but the love and memories I held in my heart would guide me. The flames continued to crackle and dance, carrying the essence of my parents' journey into the unknown.

With each passing moment, I understood that life is but a fleeting dance, and in the cycle of birth and death, the flame of love and remembrance burns eternal.

My Next Journey

Maadinee and I were making preparations for our journey to the main river, where I would scatter the ashes of my parents. We knew that this pilgrimage was not just a physical journey but also a profound spiritual undertaking. It was a sacred ritual to release the earthly remains of my beloved parents and allow their souls to find eternal peace.

But this was my first time venturing beyond the familiar boundaries of Karmana, and I was unsure of what lay ahead on our path to the sacred river. The anticipation of the unknown swirled within me, mingling with a deep reverence for the spiritual significance of the journey.

The sun had begun its ascent in the sky as I made my way through the slender lanes of Karmana. The morning air filled with the scent of blooming flowers and the gentle rustle of leaves. I had gathered all my belongings from my house and made my way to Maadinee's house.

The villagers had been kind and generous, offering me clothes and fruits for my travels.

When I arrived at Maadinee's house, her mother welcomed me with open arms.

Maadinee's mother, a kind and nurturing soul, had taken it upon herself to ensure we were well-prepared for the journey. Amidst the neatly arranged clothes, she placed a bountiful supply of fresh fruits to sustain us on our sacred expedition. It was a thoughtful gesture, ensuring we had sustenance for both our physical and spiritual needs.

As she packed my belongings, her hands moved with a gentle purpose, folding the clothes with care and arranging them in a manner that allowed for easy carrying. She placed the urn, containing the earthly remains of my parents, lovingly amidst the folds of my clothes, securing it firmly with a crimson cloth and attaching it to a sturdy wooden stick. The sight of the urn and the knowledge that my parents' remains were so close to me stirred a wellspring of emotions within my heart.

I glanced at Maadinee, who stood beside me. We shared a bond that went beyond words.

All of a sudden, an immense burden of sorrow encompassed me as tears streamed down my cheeks. My parents were no longer present. At that point in time, I yearned for the ability to detain them, to hinder their spirits from ascending to a place beyond our earthly existence. The desire to keep them close overcame my thoughts so that I could ensure that they would not have left without me.

As anguish engulfed me, I could not help but question why they had left me so abruptly. Why had they chosen to depart when I still had so much of life ahead? The anguish spilled out of me in a torrent of cries and desperate screams. "Why did they leave me? What was the purpose of their early departure? I hadn't even begun to truly live my life!"

In the midst of my despair, both Maadinee and her mother enfolded me in their comforting embrace. Their warmth provided a fleeting solace amidst the chaos of my emotions. Maadinee's mother, a beacon of wisdom and compassion, leaned in.

"Don't worry, my child," she whispered softly. "Your parents knew what they were doing. They were guided by forces beyond our comprehension. No parent would willingly leave their child behind in such a manner. There are greater forces at play, orchestrated by a higher being, directing their actions. At times, it's the outcome of karma, the manifestation of previous deeds and decisions. We might not have complete comprehension; however, it's certain that this event has transpired. It's imperative that you don't interpret it as a personal attack or entertain the idea of revenge as it'll solely pollute your spirit."

Her words, though difficult to fully grasp in the midst of my grief, resonated deep within me. The notion of revenge had never crossed my mind, yet Maadinee's mother felt compelled to address it. Perhaps she sensed the turmoil and anger simmering beneath the surface of my sorrow. But I knew, deep down, that revenge held no place in my heart. I was determined to honor my parents' departure and to fulfill the duties and responsibilities entrusted to me.

At that moment, Maadinee's mother gently guided my head toward her chest, encouraging me to listen to the rhythmic beat of her heart. As my ear pressed against her warm skin, the steady thud echoed in my ears, bringing a semblance of peace to my tormented mind. It was a reminder that life continued to pulse around me and that love and support were present even in the darkest of times.

As I clung to Maadinee's mother, my tears gradually subsided, replaced by a glimmer of acceptance.

As I grappled with the overwhelming loss of my parents, Jagha appeared in search of me.

"Don't worry, Meera. I will accompany you and Maadinee to the river, ensuring you both safely return to the village. Afterward, I will resume my own journey, guided by the instructions of my guru."

"But how will you know where to go?" I inquired, my voice laced with skepticism. His response, delivered with a touch of mystery, intrigued me further. "Sometimes, he finds me," Jagha explained. "Other times, he appears in my dreams, guiding me to the places I must visit."

An assortment of awe and disbelief swirled within me. The idea that a higher power could communicate with individuals, guiding their path, was not entirely foreign to me. Tales of remarkable yogis and their extraordinary abilities had circulated throughout our village. Yet, at that moment, my mind was consumed by my grief, and thoughts of spiritual advancement seemed distant and inconsequential.

For now, my soul longed for solace rather than enlightenment. The pain of losing my parents weighed heavily upon me, eclipsing any desire for spiritual growth. The world of dreams and ethereal journeys seemed far removed from the raw emotions that consumed my heart.

Although the mighty Ganga herself remained out of our reach, we knew that the river we were bound for held a sacred connection to her sacred waters. It was a tributary, a humble conduit through which the divine energies flowed. The prospect of standing beside its banks, even in its lesser grandeur, filled me with a sense of awe and reverence.

The sun cast its golden rays upon us as if bestowing its blessing on our sacred journey. The village, with its narrow lanes and familiar faces, bid us farewell with words of encouragement and prayers for our safe passage.

Anticipation coursed through my veins. The unknown stretched before us, promising both challenges and revelations. The landscape gradually transformed, revealing a panorama of rolling hills, verdant valleys, and babbling brooks.

A sense of tranquility enveloped our small group. The path before us was shrouded in silence, broken only by the occasional rustle of leaves and the distant calls of birds. Jagha, leading the way, skilfully cleared any obstructions in our path, making our progress through the jungle smoother.

Overhead, notorious monkeys swung from tree branches, observing our movements with curious eyes.

"Don't worry, Meera. They're surely curious creatures. They rarely come close to humans, as some humans hunt them. It's a natural caution they possess." Jagha reassured.

Continuing our trek, Jagha informed us of a rest stop ahead—a small stream with clear, refreshing water where we could refill our flasks. The sound of running water grew louder as we approached, and soon, we came upon the stream. A serene sight greeted us—a deer and its young sipping from the stream, their movements graceful and untethered. Sensing our presence, they darted into the woods, disappearing from view.

We settled by the stream, and Jagha diligently replenished our flasks with pure, cool water. He handed Maadinee her flask first, then extended mine toward me. Our eyes met, and in that fleeting moment, he posed a question that stirred something within me. "Meera, what is the first thing you desire to do? What path would you like to follow?"

Meeting his gaze, I felt a surge of purpose ignite within me. "I want to help people transition smoothly into the next life," I declared. Jagha's smile widened, his eyes filled with understanding. "In that case, Meera, I suggest you study the art of Ayurveda. It encompasses not only physical healing but also spiritual and emotional well-being. It will empower you to provide comfort and guidance to those seeking a peaceful transition."

"Ayurveda," I repeated in confusion and frustration. The mere suggestion of embarking on a healing path so soon after losing my parents felt overwhelming.

Caught off guard by my reaction, Jagha maintained his composure, explaining, "Meera, Ayurveda is the ancient art of healing and restoring health to those in need."

My emotions began to spill over, and I lashed out, unable to comprehend the idea of embracing healing when I was still engulfed in grief. "How can you expect me to consider such things? I haven't even had time to fully mourn the loss of my parents."

Maadinee, sensing the intensity of the moment, interjected, "Meera, please try to understand. Jagha is only trying to offer his guidance and support. Healing takes time, but exploring avenues of wellness may provide solace and a path forward."

Tears welled up in my eyes as a mixture of guilt and uncertainty washed over me. Sitting by the tranquil lake, I contemplated the weight of my emotions. Jagha, ever patient, broke the silence, suggesting that we resume our journey. Reluctantly, I rose to my feet, still grappling with conflicting emotions.

As we continued walking, Jagha matched his pace with mine. In the midst of the journey, I mustered the courage to approach him, my voice filled with vulnerability, "Perhaps I overreacted earlier. I do want to know more."

He turned to me, offering a warm smile, his eyes filled with compassion. "Meera, it's natural to feel overwhelmed and uncertain in situations like these. We have a few more hours until we reach the next village, where we can rest for the night. Take this time to process your emotions."

Walking side by side, our footsteps falling in sync, I contemplated his words. After a while, I found the courage to speak again. "Tell me more about Ayurveda and how it relates to yoga."

Jagha nodded, acknowledging my curiosity. "Ayurveda and yoga are sister sciences intertwined in their approach to holistic well-being. Ayurveda focuses on healing and restoring balance to the mind and body, while yoga complements it by offering practices that alleviate physical and mental imbalances."

I inquired further about finding a teacher in Ayurveda. Jagha explained, "In Ayurveda, just as in yoga, you need a guru, a teacher who can guide you in acquiring the necessary skills and knowledge. But it's not a conventional search. Instead, you must open your heart and allow the teacher to find you. Listen to your inner calling, and the right teacher will reveal themselves in due time."

As the darkness encroached upon us, my mind was filled with contemplation. The mention of finding a teacher through my inner calling reminded me of Latika, the spirit who had introduced herself to me. Perhaps she held the key to unlocking my spiritual journey. Lost in my thoughts, we continued to walk under the fading light, uncertain of what lay ahead.

Just as the night began to envelop us, we encountered a group of hunters on their way back to their village. Jagha seemed familiar with them, and they greeted us warmly, their faces radiating kindness. Although we were strangers, their embrace and hospitality made us feel like long-lost friends. Their cart was adorned with a deer and a few monkeys.

We followed their lead, traversing the final stretch of our journey. Soon, we arrived at their village, and the sight of the bustling community brought a sense of relief. They led us to a well where we could quench our thirst and freshen ourselves with the cool water it provided. The villagers' generosity continued as they guided us to the central gathering area. A lively fire crackled, casting dancing shadows upon the faces of the villagers.

As the aroma of their freshly caught game wafted through the air, I hesitated, leaning in to whisper to Jagha, "I'm not sure if I can eat this." My eyes fixated on the roasted Non-ved, my mind wrestling with conflicting emotions.

Sensing my hesitation, Jagha leaned in closer, his voice gentle yet firm. "Meera, it is essential to honor the generosity and love bestowed upon us by these villagers. Refusing their offering would be disrespectful. They have prepared this meal with care; don't you think we should honor it?"

At that moment, I made a choice to set aside my personal reservations and embrace the spirit of unity and gratitude.

We settled down on the ground near the fire, surrounded by the lively sounds of folk songs and clapping. The aroma of the roasting food wafted through the air, enticing our senses. As the villagers joyously shared their songs and stories, I felt a sense of belonging in this tight-knit community. They had welcomed us with open arms, and it was in this warmth that I began to glimpse the beauty of their way of life.

While I soaked in the atmosphere, Maadinee approached me, her eyes brimming with excitement. She spoke with an urgency in her voice, "Meera, you have to meet the local Doctor. She is not only an Ayurveda expert but has also embarked on an incredible journey with her teacher, learning everything from meditation to the art of selecting healing spices. You must meet her."

My curiosity was piqued, and I eagerly replied, "Yes, please show me where she resides."

Jagha and I followed Maadinee's lead, making our way to the humble hut where the Doctor resided. Upon entering, I found her seated in the graceful posture of the lotus position. Her serene presence immediately put me at ease, and I greeted her with a respectful "Namaste."

The doctor's eyes sparkled with wisdom as she welcomed me to sit beside her. She encouraged me to share a bit about myself and the motivations that led me to Ayurveda. With vulnerability in my voice, I explained, "I recently lost my parents, and I can't help but wonder if there was something I could have done to prevent it. I yearn to learn Ayurveda so that I can heal and protect those I care about."

She listened attentively, her compassionate gaze unwavering. When I finished speaking, she spoke gently yet firmly, emphasizing the delicate balance of life and death. "Dear Beti, we can play a role in ensuring their well-being while they are with us. The art of Ayurveda teaches us to honor life's cycles and promote health and harmony."

Eager to learn, I asked if she would teach me all she knew. Her laughter filled the air, carrying a wisdom beyond my comprehension. As her gentle chuckles subsided, I mustered the courage to ask, "But why can't you teach me? I am eager to learn." The surprise in my voice was evident, unable to fathom why she couldn't share her knowledge with me.

With a serene smile, she explained, "My guru bestowed upon me the knowledge and tasked me with its practice. I, too, must wait for a sign from my own guru before passing on her wisdom. However, I can inform her of your deep desire to learn."

As my thoughts swirled, I noticed her gesture towards Jagha, who stood nearby. Confusion clouded my expression as I asked, "How did you know that he is practicing and has a guru?" I could not comprehend the subtle signs that eluded me.

She met my gaze, "My dear child, you will come to recognize the signs when someone is on the path of spiritual growth. It is an intuition that awakens within you as you mature on your own journey. Rest assured, with time and experience, you too will possess the discernment to recognize the seekers."

Yearning to dive deeper into the mysteries that lay ahead, I couldn't contain my curiosity any longer. I implored her, "But how can I meet your guru? Where can I find her?"

She lowered her voice, "I cannot disclose the precise time or location of her arrival. However, I can share that she is drawn to places like ours, especially during the end of the monsoon season when the specific spices she seeks are abundant. She has her own way of finding her students, guided by a higher power. I can relay your desire to learn to her. But ultimately, she can only find you if you truly desire her presence and open your heart to the search for a guru."

As the aroma of the freshly prepared meal filled the air, a kind-hearted man approached us, sensing our hunger. He extended an invitation to join the villagers in partaking in the food that had been lovingly prepared for the community. As guests of the village, we were given the privilege of being served first.

Seated alongside the chief of the village and his family, we engaged in heartfelt conversations, sharing our stories and the purpose of our visit. The chief, filled with compassion, offered his condolences, and to our surprise, he extended the services of his priest, who would accompany us to the river, guiding us along the way and imparting his wisdom.

Gratefully accepting this gesture, we savored a bit more of the delectable meal before retiring for the night in the cozy guest house provided by the village.

As the night draped the village in its tranquil embrace, I found solace in the embrace of sleep. It was in this realm of dreams that I felt a familiar presence approaching—a gentle, ethereal energy enveloped me, and I knew it was my Devi, Latika, gracing me with her presence.

In my dream, I stood in a serene garden, illuminated by a soft, radiant glow. Latika appeared before me, her form ethereal. Her voice, like a gentle breeze, whispered comforting words that caressed my soul.

"Meera, dear child," Latika's voice echoed with a soothing melody, "your parents have transitioned to a realm beyond the earthly plane, guided by the divine plan of the universe. Their departure was not a result of abandonment or neglect, but rather a culmination of their soul's journey and karmic cycle."

Tears welled in my eyes as I yearned for their physical presence. Latika's touch gently wiped away my tears, assuring me of their eternal love and connection. She continued, "Though they may not be physically present, their love and guidance continue to surround you. Their spirits watch over you, guiding and protecting you every step of the way."

Latika's presence filled me with a renewed sense of purpose and determination, instilling within me the belief that my path would intertwine with that of a guru who would guide me further along my spiritual journey.

"Meera, dear child, open your heart and trust in the divine timing of the universe," Latika whispered gently. "Your guru will find you when the time is right, unveiling the wisdom and knowledge that awaits you. Until then, focus on nurturing your inner light and embarking on the path of self-discovery."

As I embraced the comfort and guidance offered by my Devi, a profound sense of peace washed over me. I knew that in this intricate tapestry of life, everything would unfold as it was meant to.

With a final loving gaze, Latika's form dissolved into the luminous surroundings, leaving me with a renewed sense of resilience. As sleep enveloped me that night, I could not help but feel a sense of anticipation and hope. The encounters and conversations of the day had ignited a flame of purpose within me. I knew that the path to finding my guru and deepening my knowledge of Ayurveda lay ahead, and with the support of the village and the guidance of my Devi, I was determined to embrace this sacred journey with an open heart and a steadfast spirit.

A Journey to the River of Ganga

The next morning, as the sun began to rise, I and Maadinee sought shade beneath the majestic embrace of a towering banyan tree, its sprawling branches providing a sanctuary from the world's burdens. The air danced with the intoxicating fragrance of nearby blossoms, as if nature itself conspired to uplift our spirits.

With tender care, Maadinee untied the knot of the sack her mother had packed, revealing a vibrant medley of fruits nestled within. I chose a ripe mango, its golden skin adorned with blushes of crimson. With a swift motion, I sliced open the fruit, revealing a succulent, vibrant orange flesh that beckoned me closer. A smile formed on my lips, an involuntary reaction to the sheer delight of the moment.

Soon Jagha joined us, his eyes crinkled at the corners with a playful glimmer. He observed us indulging in the succulent fruits, our lips stained with their juices and our faces radiating contentment.

"Would you like some fruits?" Maadinee offered.

"No, I am still quite full from last night's feast." Jagha chuckled, his eyes sparkling with amusement. "I must admit, the feast was quite extravagant. The villagers really know how to honour their guests."

I nodded in agreement, my mouth still filled with the refreshing sweetness of the fruit. The flavours burst on my tongue, momentarily distracting me from the weight of grief that lingered within me. It was a small respite, a fleeting moment of solace in the midst of sorrow.

Finally, the priest emerged from the village, wearing a serene expression, his gentle demeanour and wise countenance inspiring a sense of reverence within us.

"Namaste, Meera," he greeted us with a gentle smile. "I hope you had a peaceful night."

"Namaste, panditji," I replied, my voice tinged with gratitude. "The night brought some measure of solace, and I hope that the rituals that we will perform today, will help me find closure."

The priest nodded. "Rituals have a way of bringing us closer to the divine and helping us find peace amidst the storms of life. Now, if you're ready to leave, we shall make our way to the river."

We gathered our belongings and followed the village priest as he led us towards the river. The priest, adorned in vibrant saffron robes, walked with a grace that seemed to harmonize with the rhythms of nature around us. The path meandered through lush green fields, alive with the vibrant hues of blooming flowers and the melodious symphony of birdsong.

As the priest shared his wisdom, Maadinee and I listened intently, our hearts open to the sacred teachings that flowed from his words. The weight of our grief seemed to momentarily lift, replaced by a sense of reverence for the journey we were about to embark upon.

"Panditji, what is it about the Ganga that makes its waters so potent and transformative?"

He paused, "Dear Meera," he began, his voice infused with a warmth, "the Ganga is not just an ordinary river. It is considered a divine manifestation, carrying the blessings of the gods themselves. It is believed to possess healing properties that can purify both the physical and spiritual realms."

"But how can the waters of our humble river have the same power? Are they connected somehow?" Maadinee interjected.

"The Ganga is not confined to a specific physical location," the priest continued, his voice carrying a mystical air. "Its essence flows through all rivers, interweaving the divine current with the humble streams that crisscross our land. The river we stand before, though distant from the mighty Ganga, is intricately connected. Its waters carry the sacred energy, ultimately merging with the divine flow."

I felt a surge of gratitude for the interconnectedness of all things, for the knowledge that even in our small village, we were intricately connected to the ancient traditions and sacred rivers that had shaped our land for centuries.

I found solace in his words, as if each tale he shared was a thread weaving together the tapestry of my understanding.

"Meera," the priest's voice carried a gentle yet resolute tone, "the Ganga is not just a river; it is a divine manifestation, a sacred conduit that connects the earthly realm with the realm of the divine. Its waters hold immense power."

I listened intently, my curiosity blending with a newfound reverence for the mystical Ganga.

"Countless pilgrims embark on arduous journeys, drawn by the call of the Ganga's purifying embrace. They seek not only physical cleansing but also spiritual liberation, a release from the karmic bonds that bind them. The Ganga, they believe, has the power to absolve sins, bestow blessings, and guide departed souls towards higher realms of existence."

It became clear to me that the act of dispersing my parents' ashes in this river was not merely a symbolic gesture but a sacred passage, an offering that would allow their souls to embark on a transformative journey.

Listening to his words, my heart felt a glimmer of hope and peace. I began to understand that this ritual was not just a farewell to my parents' physical forms but a transcendence of their souls to a realm of eternal serenity. Their journey would be intricately woven into the fabric of the divine river, flowing through the vast expanse of time and space.

As we reached the tranquil riverbank, its gentle currents reflecting the sun's radiant glow, a sense of reverence filled the air. We formed a small circle, with the village priest standing at the centre, guiding us through the ritual. The priest closed his eyes, invoking the presence of the divine, his voice resonating with an otherworldly grace.

He spoke of our parents' journey, their lives intertwined with the cosmic dance of creation and dissolution. He reminded us that death was not an end, but a transformation, as the soul embarked on a new voyage.

"Let us now release the ashes," he said softly. "Allow the river to carry their essence, to merge it with the eternal flow, so that they may find solace and eternal peace."

I reached into the urn, taking a handful of my parents' ashes. My heart trembled with a mix of emotions. The grey ashes were once my living, breathing parents.

Jagha, standing beside me— a source of quiet strength, noticed my trembling hands. His empathetic eyes, met mine, and in that fleeting moment, a silent connection was forged between us.

"Meera," the tenderness in his voice soothed the ache within me, "let me guide you in this final act of love for your parents."

I nodded as my eyes were gushing with tears that threatened to spill over. Gently, Jagha extended his hand towards me, his fingers reaching out to meet mine. As our hands touched, a surge of warmth coursed through me. It was a comforting reassurance that I was not alone in this journey.

Together, we leaned forward, our fingers releasing the ashes into the river's gentle current. It felt as if time stood still, our collective sorrow and love merging with the flowing waters, carrying the essence of my beloved parents towards eternity.

Tears streamed down my cheeks, intermingling with the sacred ashes. Jagha's presence beside me provided an anchor amidst the overwhelming sca of emotions, his touch a guiding light in the midst of darkness.

Jagha turned towards me, his gaze tender and compassionate. Without saying a word, he reached out with his other hand and dipped it into the cool waters of the river. He brought the wet hands to my face, as he gently brushed away the tears that stained my cheeks.

As the ashes dispersed, carried away by the river's tender embrace, a sense of bittersweet acceptance settled within me. I closed my eyes, offering a silent prayer to the universe, seeking solace and peace for my parents' souls.

In that intense moment, I closed my eyes, feeling the weight of my sorrow and longing slowly lift from my heart. I imagined my parents' spirits embracing the soothing the river, their souls carried forth on a mystical journey towards a realm of eternal peace and liberation.

Jagha's hand remained clasped with mine, as we witnessed the final moments of this sacred ritual. His presence, once a stranger, had become an integral part of my journey, a steady companion who understood the depth of my grief and the longing in my heart.

As the last remnants of ash dissolved into the river's embrace, Jagha gently released his grip on my hand. His eyes met mine, shimmering with unspoken emotions, conveying a shared understanding of the profoundness of this moment. Although my heart still ached with the absence of my parents, I found solace in the knowledge that their souls had found a sacred path, guided by the divine currents of the river.

With the ritual complete, we stood in silent contemplation, our thoughts and prayers mingling with the gentle whispers of the flowing water. The village priest bestowed blessings upon us, offering words of comfort and encouragement as we embarked on our individual paths of healing and self-discovery.

Their departure had marked the beginning of a new chapter in my life. It was a chapter where I would seek to honour their memory and to embrace the teachings of Ayurveda. By opening my heart to the possibility of finding a spiritual guide, I would find a guru who would illuminate my path with divine wisdom.

The journey back to the village was contemplative, our footsteps falling in sync with the rhythm of our thoughts. The weight of grief still lingered, but a glimmer of hope ignited within me. I knew that the memories of my parents would forever reside within my heart, guiding me as I ventured into the realm of Ayurveda, seeking healing not only for myself but for those who crossed my path.

The funeral rites had marked a transformative moment in my life. The departed souls of my parents now danced upon the sacred currents, whispering their love and guidance from realms unseen. I would carry their spirits within me, their presence serving as a constant reminder to embrace life's journey with courage, compassion, and a deep connection to the divine.

Upon our return to the village, we were met with compassionate eyes and understanding smiles. The villagers, having witnessed our journey, offered their condolences once more. Their presence was a balm to our wounded hearts, a reminder that we were not alone in our grief. I could feel their collective strength and compassion embracing us, enveloping us in a warm embrace of communal love.

We thanked the chief and with a final exchange of nods, we bid farewell to the chief and the villagers who had embraced us as their own. I carried with me the lessons learned and the warmth of their support, knowing that their kindness had left an indelible mark on my soul.

The journey back, Maadinee and Jagha walked alongside me, their presence a source of strength. A gentle breeze rustled through the trees. The weight of our grief was softened, if only momentarily, by the beauty of nature surrounding us.

Breaking the silence, Jagha's voice cut through the stillness. "Meera, have you ever explored the healing practices of Ayurveda and yoga? They hold profound wisdom that can bring balance and restoration to the body, mind, and soul."

I turned to him with a glimmer of interest in my eyes. "Ayurveda and yoga?" I echoed, intrigued. "Tell me more, Jagha. How can this heal me?"

Jagha's gaze met mine, "Ayurveda is a holistic system," he explained. "It focuses on maintaining balance within the body, using natural remedies and treatments tailored to individual needs. Ayurveda recognizes that our well-being is influenced by various factors, such as our diet, and also the harmony of our mind, body, and spirit."

"And yoga," I prodded, eager to delve further into this realm of healing.

A smile graced Jagha's lips as he began to unravel the wonders of yoga. "Yoga is a divine and bodily practise that covers more than just the physical postures that you may have seen," he explained. "The path of a yogi is one of self-discovery. As a result, we may build a stronger connection with our inner selves and the divine, this will help us understand who we are and why we are here based on our karma, we may cultivate peace of mind, power, and resilience through yoga."

The idea of finding solace and healing through Ayurveda and yoga intrigued me.

As the three of us slowly continued our journey back to our own village, the path seemed familiar yet different. The village, once a place of comfort and familiarity, now held the echoes of my parents' absence. Their absence was palpable, felt in every corner and every interaction. Yet, amidst the sorrow, I carried with me a sense of resilience and a determination to honour their memory through my actions and choices.

Maadinee softly extended her arm and gently rested her hand on my forearm, pulling me out of my wandering thoughts.

"Meera," she said softly, her voice filled with empathy and concern, "are you doing, okay? I know this journey has been incredibly difficult for you."

I turned to look at her,

"I... I miss them, I find it tremendously difficult to ever imagine my life without my parents. A world without their guidance and love."

Maadinee nodded, her eyes filled with understanding. "I know, Meera. I am so sorry. But I'm proud of you for your bravery."

I smiled at her, wetting my cheeks.

"Thank you, Maadinee," I finally said, my voice filled with gratitude. "Thank you for being there for me, for helping me find strength during this challenging time."

She hugged me tightly, "You don't have to thank me, Meera. We're in this together. We'll support each other as we navigate the flow of life's journey."

We accepted an unspoken promise of friendship and constant support with those words. As we went through the village, I felt a ray of optimism in the middle of my loss, knowing that I have friends by my side who would accompany me through both the wonderful and difficult moments that lay ahead and I'd give up my life to do the same for them.

How Do I Find My Guru?

After we reached our village, Maadinee kindly agreed to stay with me in my parents' house.

Jagha was leaving but I insisted him to meet me once before parting.

We sat beneath the shade of a majestic neem tree near the village outskirts. The soft breeze gently caressed our faces. I looked into Jagha's eyes, my heart racing with anticipation, and mustered the courage to speak my truth.

"Jagha," I began, my hands sweating, "I want to talk to you about something before you leave. It's about the connection we share and the feelings that have grown within me. I think we are intended to be together in this lifetime, to travel this journey hand in hand and establish a life together."

Jagha's smile was warm and tender, "Meera," he responded, "I cannot deny the bond that has formed between us, nor the profound connection I feel. But I must seek guidance from my guru, for they hold the wisdom and insight to guide us in matters of the heart and soul. I must understand if our union aligns with the greater purpose and timing ordained by the divine."

I nodded,

"Jagha, I trust in the guidance of your guru," I replied sincerely. "I am willing to wait, to tread this path together with patience and understanding. I think our spirits will combine, and we will start on a magnificent adventure together when the time is perfect and the signals align."

Jagha reached for me, his hand gently touching mine, and a serene tranquillity washed over me. "Meera," he said quietly, "Thank you for understanding. I promise to seek clarity and guidance with utmost sincerity, for our love and union deserve nothing less. Until then, let us cherish the connection we share and nurture the bond that unites us."

As Jagha and I bid each other farewell, Maadinee's playful voice echoed in the background, breaking the bittersweet silence. "Goodbye! Don't worry, Jagha. I will be sure to keep her company while you're away!" She exclaimed joyfully.

A blush crept up my cheeks, a blend of embarrassment and surprise. I turned towards Maadinee, my eyes wide with astonishment. "Why would you say that, Maadinee? Now everyone in the village will know," I whispered.

Maadinee gazed at me with a knowing smile on her lips and a malicious sparkle in her eyes. "Oh, Meera," she replied teasingly, "you underestimate the power of village gossip. Everyone in this village already knew that there was something special brewing between you and Jagha. How could they not? His frequent visits, the time he spent with you—those spoke volumes to the keen eyes and curious minds of our villagers. They sensed the blossoming connection long before we did."

Her remarks took me by surprise. How had the villagers noticed something I was oblivious to? Their perceptive eyes had seen the subtle signs and gestures, the unspoken language that had blossomed between Jagha and me.

Blushing, I nodded in acknowledgment, my heart fluttering with a newfound self-awareness. "I suppose I have a lot to learn about our village's customs," I said, a hesitant tone in my voice.

"But let us not dwell on the gossip. Instead, let's focus on finding some delicious food to savor today."

Maadinee's smile widened, and she playfully nudged me. "Absolutely, my dear Meera," she agreed, her voice brimming with enthusiasm.

Soon, we set out to the nearby forest in search of fruits to nourish both our bodies and our spirits.

Later that day, the sun began to set, and a quietness settled over the village. I retreated to the quiet sanctuary of my room. With a heart full of anticipation, I prepared myself for an evening of meditation, hoping to connect with my Devi, Latika, in the depths of my consciousness. I sat cross-legged on a cushion. I closed my eyes and focused on my breath, allowing the outside world to fade away.

In the stillness of the room, my mind gradually quieted, and I sought to open the channels of communication with my beloved Devi. I surrendered to the vastness within, eager to receive guidance and clarity. Hours passed in deep introspection, my spirit reaching out, seeking a glimpse of divine presence. Yet, despite my earnest efforts, no visions appeared, and no ethereal whispers filled my mind.

As the night stretched on, disappointment threatened to dampen my spirits. Doubt crept in, whispering its insidious words. Had I failed to connect with Devi Latika? Was there some hidden meaning behind her silence? Uncertainty gnawed at my heart, and I yearned for a sign, a message that would illuminate the path ahead.

The following day, as the first rays of sunlight touched my eyelids, I awoke with hope.

Eagerly, I scanned my surroundings, searching for any subtle hint or whispered revelation. But the room remained silent, its emptiness echoing my unanswered questions. Frustration threatened to surface, yet deep down, a glimmer of faith persisted.

I reminded myself that the divine works in mysterious ways, and perhaps Devi Latika had chosen a different mode of communication.

Days turned into nights, and nights into weeks, as I continued my quest for divine guidance. Each day, I dedicated myself to meditation, seeking solace and connection with Devi Latika. Yet, despite my unwavering commitment, the answers I sought remained elusive, leaving me in a state of confusion and longing.

With each passing day, my restlessness grew. I found solace in confiding in my dear friend Maadinee. As we sat together under the comforting shade of the banyan tree, I poured out my frustrations and shared my dilemma with her.

Maadinee listened intently, her eyes reflecting compassion and understanding. When I finished speaking, she leaned closer and offered her perspective. "Sometimes, my father faces a similar struggle," she began. "There are moments when his prayers seem unanswered, and he, too, seeks guidance from the divine forces." She picked up a leaf and rotated it in between her fingers.

"What does he do in such situations?" I asked, hoping to find a glimmer of insight in Maadinee's words.

A mischievous smile played on Maadinee's lips as she replied, "Well, sometimes he chooses to embark on a fast. He refrains from consuming food for a day or two, immersing himself in a state of deep devotion and surrender. And more often than not, a response arrives, guiding him on his spiritual journey."

Fasting seemed like a daunting and arduous endeavor, yet the idea of seeking divine intervention through such a sacrifice held an undeniable allure.

As I voiced my thoughts, Maadinee burst into laughter, her joyous sound filling the air. "Oh, Meera, you know me too well," she chuckled. "Yes, I confess, there may be some ulterior motives in my suggestion. But fear not, dear friend, I would never let you suffer alone. I will abstain from indulging in any 'fun food' alongside you, should you choose to embark on this fasting journey."

Playfully, I raised an eyebrow, challenging her resolve. "And what if temptation proves too strong for you?" I teased.

Maadinee's eyes sparkled mischievously as she retorted, "Well, my dear, in that case, I will rely on your watchfulness to keep me in check. You have my permission to throw out any 'fun food' you may find me attempting to consume."

Her light-hearted response brought a smile to my face, reminding me of the enduring bond we shared. With a renewed sense of determination, I took a deep breath and nodded. "Tomorrow," I affirmed. "Tomorrow, I will embark on this fasting journey, trusting that Devi Latika will hear my plea and offer the guidance I seek."

The following morning, with Maadinee by my side, I embarked on my fasting journey. As the day progressed, I encountered moments of temptation, my senses heightened by the absence of food. But each time, I recalled my commitment and the potential rewards that awaited me.

Hours turned into a day and a day into night as I embraced the simplicity and introspection that fasting brought. The absence of physical nourishment became a gateway to a more profound spiritual connection as I immersed myself in prayer and meditation, seeking communion with Devi Latika.

As the first day came to an end, I felt my spirit getting lighter. But beyond that feeling, I felt a sense of calm washing over me. While I had not received any messages or visions, a quiet knowingness permeated my being. I felt a gentle reassurance that my devotion had been heard, even if the answers had not yet materialized.

The following day, I awoke with a mixture of anticipation and hunger. My stomach felt the emptiness as I lay in bed, a constant reminder of the promise I had made to myself. Today was the second day of my fast, and despite my body's need for food, I was determined to keep my promise.

I climbed out of bed and went to the familiar part of my room, where I had created a peaceful spot for meditation. I got into a comfortable position, closed my eyes, and allowed the outer world to drift away as I explored further into the depths of my own mind.

Images of Jagha danced across my mind, his smile etched into my memory. I found myself lost in a reverie, envisioning moments of togetherness that existed solely within the confines of my imagination.

In my mind's eye, I pictured Jagha and me running through a lush field, the soft grass tickling our feet as we laughed and chased one another. The wind played with our hair, carrying our joyous laughter into the open sky. The vividness of the scene brought a smile to my face, and my heart filled with a longing for such a connection to manifest in reality.

As my meditation deepened, another vision unfolded before me. I saw Jagha and me standing by the edge of a serene lake, its surface mirroring the brilliance of a full moon. The moon's gentle glow cast an ethereal light upon us as we swayed to an invisible melody, our movements synchronized. At that moment, the boundaries between us dissolved, and it felt as if our souls were united, dancing in unison.

These fantasies stirred a whirlwind of emotions within me. I yearned for a connection that transcended the boundaries of friendship, a love that could intertwine our destinies and create a shared path forward.

With a sigh, I opened my eyes, realizing that these visions were but fleeting glimpses of what could be. The realities of life, the uncertainties that lay ahead, and the need for divine guidance tempered the warmth of my daydreams. Yet, they served as a reminder of the depths of my feelings and the hope that anchored my heart.

Later that day, in the presence of Maadinee, I shared glimpses of my inner musings. With a comforting embrace, she reminded me that the path of love and connection often involved uncertainty and the need for divine intervention.

"We must trust in the divine timing, dear Meera," she whispered, her voice filled with compassion. "The universe has a way of aligning our paths when the time is right. Until then, cherish these dreams, for they are the whispers of your heart guiding you towards the love you seek."

Her words reflected rays of hope upon me.

Later that night, as I drifted into slumber, the presence of Devi Latika enveloped my dreamscape. But this time, her ethereal form exuded an air of sternness, her voice laced with a touch of frustration. Her disapproving gaze pierced through me, questioning my choices.

"Why did you stop eating, Meera?" she admonished, her voice carrying an otherworldly authority. "You must nourish your physical vessel to sustain the journey ahead. And why is Jagha consuming your thoughts? Your focus should be on finding a guru and deepening your spiritual connection. The guru awaits, but you must demonstrate your dedication. Release your attachment to Jagha and redirect your energy towards your spiritual quest."

My heart shuddered, and I felt a pull in my stomach. As I blinked away the remnants of sleep, I could still feel the weight of her message reverberating within me. The tender sensation on my cheeks served as a tangible reminder of Devi Latika's presence, an ephemeral touch that left a lasting impression.

Feeling the pangs of hunger reverberating through my stomach, I acknowledged the truth in her words. I had become so consumed with thoughts of Jagha and the possibilities of a shared future that I had lost sight of my original purpose. It was a gentle but firm wake-up call, urging me to shift my focus back to the path of spiritual seeking.

The morning sunlight filtered through the canopy of trees, casting a soft golden glow upon the village. A sense of restlessness tugged at my being, compelling me to venture into the depths of the nearby forest.

A sensation of peace rushed over me as I stepped into the beautiful woods. The rustling of leaves and the chorus of birdsong filled the air, creating a symphony of nature's harmony. I walked along the winding forest path, my senses attuned to the subtle whispers of the woodland.

Instinct guided me deeper into the forest, my footsteps were guided by an unseen force. My stomach growled harder with each passing instant. It was as if the forest itself held the answers I sought, a mystical tapestry woven with clues and nourishment for both body and soul.

Then, in the midst of the dappled sunshine flowing through the canopy, I came across a grove of fruit-bearing trees. Their branches bowed under the weight of ripe, succulent fruits as if offering themselves as a divine gift. The vibrant colors and intoxicating aroma of the fruits beckoned to me; their allure was impossible to resist.

I plucked a ripe mango and bit into its luscious flesh, satisfying my hunger.

I had an incredible feeling of thankfulness in that moment amidst the bounty of nature. The forest had fed my body, but it had also acted as a subtle reminder of the interconnection of all things. Perhaps my spiritual journey, like the forest, was a tapestry woven with intertwined threads, where the guru, Jagha, and my own self-discovery were intricately connected.

My Guru Found Me

Soon, in a couple of weeks, I established a routine of seeking refuge in the outskirts of the village. The stack of hay became my sanctuary, a humble perch where I could delve into the depths of meditation and connect with the sacred energies that enveloped our world. The canopy of coconut leaves overhead shielded me from the harsh rays of the sun, creating a serene oasis of tranquillity.

With crossed legs and a straight back, I settled onto the stack of hay, feeling its roughness against my palms. Taking a deep breath, I let the world's anxieties and diversions fade away, focused entirely on the present moment. The rustling leaves and a gentle breeze carried with them a sense of harmony as if nature itself was whispering secrets of ancient wisdom.

As my thoughts calmed, I began to explore the depths of my inner self in search of a link with the divine powers that pervaded the cosmos. With each inhale, I absorbed the life-giving energy of the earth, grounding myself in the essence of existence. With each exhale, I released any tensions or doubts, allowing them to dissolve into the ethereal realms.

Time seemed to lose its grip as I delved deeper into the realms of consciousness. My senses heightened, and I became attuned to the subtle vibrations that danced in the air. The symphony of nature's sounds—birds tweeting, insects buzzing, leaves gently rustling—merged with the rhythm of my breath, producing a harmonic song that resonated throughout my spirit.

In this sacred space, I embraced stillness, surrendering to the flow of existence. Thoughts drifted in and out like passing clouds, but I remained anchored, refusing to be swept away by their transient nature. I opened myself to the vastness of the universe, inviting the wisdom of the ages to flow through me.

As the moments of meditation grew longer, my body began to tire, and I surrendered to the urge to lie down. Gently turning onto my side, I surveyed the surroundings, my gaze lingering on the familiar figures that dotted the landscape. From this new vantage point, I observed the familiar tapestry of life that unfolded before my eyes.

The villagers, like tireless ants, moved with a sense of purpose and determination. With weathered hands, they tended to their fields, delicately nurturing the fruits of their labor. Their voices blended with the delicate rustle of leaves.

Not far from me, a group of women bustled about, their radiant smiles and welcoming gestures extending to the weary traders who sought refuge within our humble village. It was a tradition ingrained in our community, offering accessible accommodations and nourishment to those passing through.

In the midst of my observations, a shift in the atmosphere caught my attention. My gaze fixated on an elderly woman, her presence commanding and her steps purposeful, as she briskly made her way towards me. Could she be the guru I had been longing to meet? I hastily rolled off the hay, brushing away the remnants of dry grass that clung to my clothing.

She drew closer, her presence commanding respect and curiosity among the entourage that accompanied her. I instinctively straightened my posture. The villagers nearby, sensing the significance of the encounter, paused in their tasks, casting curious glances our way.

Could this be the moment I'd been looking forward to? Was this revered lady, surrounded by a group of followers, the guru I had longed to meet?

The woman's dignified presence commanded attention as she gracefully made her way toward me. Her eyes held a depth of wisdom that seemed to transcend time itself. The group accompanying her moved with a sense of reverence, their eyes filled with a mixture of curiosity and respect.

As she approached, I could sense a spiritual aura flowing from her, like a bright light that encompassed her being.

As the elderly lady arrived, her eyes met mine, and she smiled softly. It was a smile that carried with it a warmth and familiarity as if she had been expecting our encounter.

The woman's piercing gaze met mine, and with a voice that resonated with authority, she addressed me, "So, you are the one seeking to aid others through the art of medicine."

"Yes," I nodded.

"Meera," she said, her voice melodious, "I have been waiting for you. The universe has guided me to your presence, for your soul carries a deep longing for spiritual guidance."

My heart fluttered. I stood before her, feeling a mixture of awe and gratitude for this divine connection.

"Who are you?" I managed to utter, my voice filled with reverence.

She extended her hand, inviting me to rise from my makeshift bed of hay. "I am Gurumata, a seeker of truth and a guide to those seeking enlightenment," she said, her voice calm and authoritative. "The universe has conspired to bring us together, and I have been entrusted with the task of guiding you along your spiritual path."

My heart was filled with astonishment and appreciation. The universe had indeed heard my silent pleas. A surge of energy pulsed through my veins, igniting a newfound determination within me.

The villagers watched in hushed anticipation, sensing the significance of this encounter. Whispers of curiosity and speculation danced on the breeze as the news of this extraordinary meeting spread through the village like wildfire. The air buzzed with intangible energy as if the very fabric of our existence was being rewoven in this pivotal moment.

Gurumata extended her hand, gesturing for me to join her and the group that had accompanied her. I stepped forward and fell into pace beside her. As we walked together, her presence exuded a calming energy, and I felt a sense of reverence and trust growing within me.

Gurumata began to share stories of ancient wisdom and the profound experiences of seekers who had embarked on similar journeys. Her voice carried the weight of countless generations, and her words wove a tapestry of knowledge and understanding. I listened intently, my heart open and receptive to the teachings that resonated deep within me.

The more she spoke, the more clarity descended upon me like a gentle mist. The veil of uncertainty that had engulfed my thoughts for so long began to dissipate, to be replaced with a powerful feeling of purpose and direction. It was as if the ancient wisdom she shared ignited a flame within me, illuminating the path I was destined to tread.

Her expression softened slightly as she continued, her tone carrying a mix of sternness and concern, "Then tell me, why were you rolling around in that hay? The hay sustains our cows, providing us with milk, butter, ghee, and paneer. These are precious resources with numerous health benefits, and yet here you are, disrespecting our beloved animals."

I felt ashamed, and without hesitating, I apologized sincerely. However, the woman interrupted, her voice firm but not unkind, "Why are you apologizing to me? I am not the one consuming the milk from this village. Apologize to the animals and to yourself for engaging in such behavior."

Realizing the truth in her words, I gathered my resolve and expressed my regret for my actions. I informed her that the cows had been taken by the farmers to graze in the nearby woods, making it difficult to offer my apologies directly to them.

"Ah, there is a lesson to be learned here," she said after pausing, her eyes glistening with insight. "Do you know why they prefer taking the cows to the woods to feed? It is because the cows possess an innate understanding of which herbs and plants are beneficial for their well-being. When they feed themselves in the woods, they instinctively seek out the nourishment that will produce the finest milk for us. It is this wisdom that ensures the cows' optimal health and the high quality of the milk they provide."

Taking a moment to absorb her words, I acknowledged the significance of this ancient bond between the animals and their environment. The woman then extended her hand, her demeanor transforming into one of guidance and preparation, as she gently uttered, "Come, my dear Meera," she said, a hint of a smile playing on her lips. "Let us prepare you for the journey ahead."

As I walked alongside Gurumata and the group, my mind immersed in the wisdom she shared, I noticed Maadinee in the distance. Her eyes widened with interest and anxiety as she watched the drama unfold in front of her. Sensing her urgency, she quickly closed the distance between us, running towards us with a mixture of excitement and worry etched on her face.

"Maadinee," I said softly, my voice filled with a mixture of sadness and excitement, "my guru has finally found me. She has come to guide me on a sacred journey, and I have decided to accompany her."

Maadinee's eyes widened in surprise, and tears welled up in them. "But... but what about us?" she choked out, her voice laced with sorrow. "We have been inseparable since childhood, like sisters. How can you leave me?"

My heart wrenched as I saw the tears roll down her cheeks. I understood the depth of our bond and the pain she felt at the prospect of our separation. With utmost compassion, I reached out to hold her trembling hands, offering her solace amidst the turmoil.

"Maadinee, please understand," I implored, my voice filled with sincerity. "This is a path that I feel drawn to, a calling that I cannot ignore. It is a path of self-discovery and spiritual awakening. I really love you. I hope you will support me in my decision."

Maadinee's tears streamed freely, and she clutched to me, unable to let go. "I will miss you so much," she said, her voice choking with emotion. "Our laughter, our shared secrets, our dreams... They will all feel incomplete without you by my side."

Maadinee stood before us, her tear-stained face still reflecting the traces of our shared sorrow; the guru's gaze lingered upon her. I could sense a certain curiosity and intrigue in her eyes as if she was delving into the depths of Maadinee's very being. After a moment of silence, the guru spoke,

"There is something within you, Maadinee," she began, her tone filled with a profound sense of knowing. "A soul that has traversed countless lifetimes, gathering wisdom and knowledge along the way. You were destined to be a Vedic doctor, a healer of great prowess."

Maadinee's eyes widened, her tears momentarily forgotten as she absorbed the weight of the guru's words. She asked in a trembling voice, "But Guruji, how do you know that?"

With a serene smile, the guru replied, "As a guru, I have the ability to perceive the souls of my students directly. I can read your thoughts, understand your intentions, and sense the guidance of your previous teacher."

The air seemed to hum with anticipation as if the universe itself had aligned to reveal a hidden truth. I watched as a mixture of surprise, curiosity, and hope flickered across Maadinee's face.

The guru continued her voice now softer but tinged with a subtle intensity. "Though I had not planned to take on another student at this time, fate has brought us together. I offer you an opportunity, Maadinee, to embark on this sacred journey alongside us. If you are both interested, I would like to embark on a journey together—a two-year journey with me, where we will study and meet Ayurvedic doctors and priests from different parts of the world."

Maadinee stood there, her mind racing with possibilities, her heart torn between the life she knew and the untrodden path that beckoned. The weight of her decision hung in the air as if the very fabric of destiny waited with bated breath.

Maadinee glanced at me, and I returned her gaze with an affirming smile. She turned back to the guru and said, "Allow me to speak to my parents about this."

The guru nodded, her gaze filled with understanding and compassion, as Maadinee dashed off to her parents. I watched her retreating figure, feeling a mix of anticipation and curiosity about the outcome of her conversation.

After what felt like an eternity but was likely only a few minutes, Maadinee's figure emerged from the distance, her steps quick and purposeful. The radiance on her face was unmistakable, a glow that mirrored the excitement brewing within her.

With an eager smile, she approached the guru and me, her words tumbling forth in a rush of enthusiasm. "They are okay with it!" she exclaimed, her voice tinged with joy. "My parents have given their consent for me to embark on this journey with both of you. However, there is one condition—they request that I visit them once a year during our harvest festival."

The guru's voice resonated with a blend of wisdom and understanding. "Of course," she replied, her tone gentle yet firm. "It is only right to honor the wishes of your parents. Family bonds and traditions are sacred, and we must always respect and nurture them."

As I witnessed Maadinee's joy and the guru's acceptance, a wave of gratitude washed over me. The universe had orchestrated a beautiful convergence of paths, uniting us as fellow seekers on this transformative journey. I felt an increasing feeling of exhilaration and preparedness to face the unknown that lay ahead with each passing instant.

"The road ahead will not always be easy, my children," she cautioned, "there will be challenges and trials that test your determination and commitment. But remember, within each obstacle lies an opportunity for growth and self-discovery. Embrace the journey with an open heart and a curious mind."

I retired to my small cottage as the sun sank, giving a warm golden color over the town, to gather my possessions and bid farewell to the life I had known. The prospect of the lengthy travel filled me with both excitement and dread. I carefully packed my meager belongings, ensuring I had the essentials to sustain me during our travels.

Underneath the starry night sky, Gurumata gathered us together for a final evening prayer. The villagers had assembled out of admiration and curiosity. We formed a circle, our hands interlinked, as Gurumata led us in a sacred chant, invoking blessings and protection for our journey.

With each musical note, I felt a sense of belonging, as if I were a part of something bigger than myself. The energy surged through our intertwined hands, creating a palpable bond that transcended time and space. We were beginning a significant journey that would permanently change our lives.

As the chant reached its crescendo, Gurumata extended her hands, palms facing upward, and the villagers followed suit. In unison, we released our intentions and prayers into the night, offering them to the universe and trusting in its divine guidance.

With the prayers lingering in the air, Gurumata bestowed her final words of wisdom upon us. Her voice resonated with authority yet brimmed with love and compassion. She spoke of the transformative power of Ayurveda, the ancient wisdom that would unravel before our eyes. As we ventured into the realms of healing and self-discovery, she emphasized the necessity of humility, inquiry, and an open heart.

"You embark on this journey not as mere students but as vessels of light," she proclaimed, her words piercing the stillness of the night. "Remember, the true essence of Ayurveda lies not in the mere application of remedies but in the awakening of the healer within. Embrace this opportunity to connect with the divine healer that resides deep within your soul."

With the arrangements settled, we took the night to rest, knowing that the dawn would bring the commencement of our grand adventure.

That night, when I settled into my bed for the final time, the weight of the impending journey hung in the air, casting a sense of anticipation over me. Seeking solace and guidance, I closed my eyes and called upon my Devi, Latika, hoping to connect with her once more.

To my surprise, as if summoned by my thoughts, Latika appeared before me. Her ethereal presence radiated with divine energy, illuminating the room with a soft, otherworldly glow. A sense of calm enveloped me as I gazed upon her, eager to seek answers and guidance for the journey ahead.

Before I could utter a word, however, Latika's form wavered as if caught in a fleeting gust of wind. I reached out, my hand hovering in the space where she had stood just moments ago, but she vanished before my touch could make contact, leaving me with unanswered questions.

Despite the fact that Latika's visit was brief, I couldn't help but sense a spark of optimism. Perhaps her fleeting appearance was a sign, a reminder that she was watching over me and would offer guidance when the time was right. I took solace in the belief that her presence, however ephemeral, held significance and that her wisdom would reveal itself in due course.

With that certainty in my heart, I fell off to sleep, knowing the voyage ahead would be full of surprises and revelations.

The Journey Begins

As the morning sun bathed the village in its gentle warmth, I found myself drawn to my familiar spot for meditation. With a sense of purpose, I settled into a comfortable position, closing my eyes and allowing my mind to quieten.

In the depths of stillness, I focused my attention on Jagha, my childhood friend who had embarked on his journey of spiritual exploration. I yearned to connect with him, to let him know that I had set forth on the path to becoming a Vedic doctor. With each breath, I channelled my intentions, directing my thoughts toward him.

But uncertainty clouded my mind. Would my message reach him? Could he genuinely receive my thoughts through the vast expanse that separated us? Doubts tugged at the corners of my consciousness, threatening to undermine my efforts.

Yet, undeterred, I persisted. I honed my focus on Jagha, visualizing his face and the bond we shared. Like a beacon, I willed my message to traverse the distance, hoping that somehow it would reach his soul.

As I delved deeper into my meditation, a thought sparked within me. Perhaps, instead of solely directing my message toward Jagha, I could also reach out to his guru. I believed that the spiritual guide, with his heightened awareness and connection to divine energies, could better receive my intentions.

I shifted my focus to the guru. Though uncertain of his precise whereabouts, I trusted that my intentions would find their way through the cosmic realm. With my third eye awakened, I visualized beams of energy emanating from my consciousness, branching out in various directions, searching for a connection.

The sound of approaching footsteps gently pulled me back to the present moment. Opening my eyes, I saw Maadinee's mother standing before me, a warm smile gracing her lips.

Returning her smile, I greeted her with a sense of gratitude for the support she had shown throughout our journey. Sensing my unspoken words, she nodded knowingly.

Seeking reassurance, I mustered the courage to speak my heartfelt request. "Please look after my house while I'm gone," I begged, my voice tinted with vulnerability and trust.

Her response was immediate, "If you promise to take care of Maadinee, we will ensure that your home remains safe," she assured me, her words carrying the weight of a heartfelt promise.

In a tender gesture, Maadinee's mother handed me a small pouch containing three gold coins and five silver coins. Her eyes met mine, brimming with maternal concern. "Keep these with you at all times," she advised, "use them only in dire circumstances when you need them for worldly healing purposes. Remember, Mother Earth will provide for you in ways you cannot fathom."

Overwhelmed by her generosity, I accepted the pouch with reverence, understanding the significance of her offering.

Maadinee's mother talked with a mixture of grief and affection as tears welled up in her eyes.

"I know I can't stop my child's destiny, but I will miss you both so much," her voice choked with emotion. Drawing me into a heartfelt embrace, she whispered, "I accept you as my own daughter. Please take care of yourself and Maadinee. We will keep everything here in the village safe for your return. And please, do not let your sister marry without us."

We parted ways with a heavy heart, knowing that this was only a momentary stop in our lives.

I bid farewell to my dear friends, embracing them tightly, knowing that our paths would diverge for a time.

Shouldering our bags, Maadinee and I made our way to the village's main ground, where our guru and her entourage awaited us. The air buzzed with excitement and expectation, tinged with melancholy at leaving behind the familiar and entering into the unknown.

Nervous, we approached the main ground. Maadinee and I exchanged glances, a silent understanding passing between us.

Maadinee leaned in closer, her voice laced with excitement. "Meera, can you believe this is really happening? We're embarking on a new chapter, seeking knowledge and enlightenment."

A smile tugged at the corners of my lips as I responded, "I know, Maadinee. Haven't we been waiting for this moment for a long time?"

She nodded, her eyes sparkling with determination.

With renewed resolve, we stepped onto the main ground, our eyes locking onto the figure of our guru. Her presence commanded respect and awe, and she oozed knowledge and tranquility. The entourage surrounding her mirrored our own mix of emotions, their faces a tapestry of hope, curiosity, and a touch of trepidation.

As we approached, our guru's eyes met mine, a gentle smile gracing her lips. Her gaze seemed to penetrate deep into my soul, as if she could see the burning desire within me to learn and grow. A warmth spread through my being, and I felt an unspoken connection forming between us.

I turned to Maadinee, barely containing my excitement. "Can you believe it, sister? Our journey starts here. We'll learn from the guru herself, and who knows what wonders await us?"

Maadinee's eyes shimmered with anticipation as she replied, "Yes, Meera, it's incredible. We'll soak up every bit of knowledge, delve into the mysteries of the universe, and emerge as seekers of truth. I'm excited to see what happens."

The guru's voice resonated through the crowd, hushing the murmurs and drawing our attention. Her words carried a melodic quality, capturing our undivided focus. Our guru explained that our first destination would be a village located to the north, a two-day journey from our own. There, we would join a larger group of seekers, uniting our paths in a collective pursuit of wisdom and enlightenment.

Our guru's words ignited a renewed sense of purpose within me. I turned to Maadinee, a glimmer of determination in my

The Journey Begins

eyes. "Maadinee, we might face challenges on this journey, but we won't let anything deter us. We'll keep moving forward, learning, growing, and supporting one another along the way."

Maadinee squeezed my hand, her voice filled with conviction. "Absolutely, Meera. We are in this together, and we'll navigate every hurdle with unwavering resilience. Let's embrace the unknown and make this journey a transformative one."

Shouldering our bags, we stood ready to embark on this path of self-discovery and spiritual awakening.

With each step, the landscape transformed before our eyes. The bustling village receded into the distance, replaced by sprawling fields and winding paths that led us deeper into the heart of nature. The rhythm of our footsteps harmonized with the sounds of birdsong and the rustle of leaves, creating a symphony of curiosity.

As we walked alongside our guru, the weight of her wisdom hung in the air, infusing our steps with purpose and anticipation. Maadinee and I exchanged glances, silently acknowledging the privilege of being in the presence of such a revered teacher.

I mustered the courage to speak up. "Gurumata, I am grateful for this opportunity to learn from you. Your words inspire us and open doors to a world we have only glimpsed in our dreams. Can you share more about the experiences that await us on this journey?"

Our guru turned her gaze toward me, her eyes brimming with ancient knowledge. She paused as if savoring the depth of the question before responding. "Meera, dear seeker of truth, the path that lies ahead is one of profound discovery. We shall journey to villages and sacred sites where Ayurvedic doctors and priests from diverse cultures reside."

My eyes widened in excitement, ears eager to absorb every word. Maadinee leaned in closer, her curiosity mirroring my own.

"Our encounters with these practitioners will offer a glimpse into the myriad interpretations and applications of Ayurvedic wisdom," our guru continued. "From the traditional practices of the Vaidya in Kerala to the ancient rituals of the Tibetan monks, we shall witness the tapestry of healing modalities that have been passed down through generations."

I nodded, my heart filled with gratitude for the path unfolding before us.

Our guru's voice resonated with warmth and reassurance. "Dear Meera, dear Maadinee, your thirst for knowledge and your willingness to embark on this path of self-discovery will be your greatest strength. I shall be here every step of the way, offering guidance and support. Remember, true learning comes not only from the teachings of others but also from the depths of your own experiences."

Maadinee and I exchanged a glance, silently affirming our commitment to this journey of enlightenment and self-realization.

With each passing hour, the landscape unfolded like a living canvas, revealing the intricate beauty of the world.

We encountered vibrant markets teeming with spices and herbs, witnessing the exchange of ancient remedies and the richness of cultural traditions. We traversed forests alive with mystique, where ancient trees whispered secrets passed down through generations.

As night fell, casting a blanket of darkness over the landscape, our weary group sought shelter beneath the sturdy branches of a majestic oak tree. The comforting rustle of leaves whispered lullabies, lulling us into a peaceful slumber.

A mixture of tiredness and exhilaration coursed through my veins as I snuggled into my makeshift bed. The day's journey had filled my mind with swirling thoughts and questions. I yearned for a moment of clarity, an opportunity to seek guidance from our wise guru.

Gurumata, perceptive as ever, noticed the restlessness in my demeanor. She approached me with a serene smile, her presence calming the chaotic whirlwind within me. "Meera, my dear, you carry the weight of curiosity and anticipation in your eyes. Is there something on your mind that seeks expression?"

I looked into her wise, compassionate eyes, feeling a surge of gratitude for her attentive nature. "Gurumata, as we prepare to rest under this sheltering tree, I feel overwhelmed by the enormity of this journey. The path we tread is unknown and filled with challenges, yet it brims with the promise of growth and enlightenment. I wonder, how do we navigate the uncertainties that lie ahead?"

Gurumata's voice, like a gentle breeze, brushed against my troubled soul. "Meera, dear seeker, it is natural to feel apprehension in the face of the unknown. But remember, the purpose of this journey is not solely to find answers but to cultivate a deep trust in yourself and the divine wisdom that guides you."

I leaned closer, eager to absorb every word she imparted. "But, Gurumata, how do we cultivate that trust? How do we silence the doubts and fears that may arise?"

Gurumata's eyes twinkled with understanding. "Ah, Meera, the path to trust is paved with self-reflection and surrender. It requires opening your heart to the lessons that each experience brings, whether they appear as challenges or blessings. Embrace the present moment, for it is the gateway to deeper understanding."

"Thank you, Gurumata, for your guidance. Your remarks have a strong resonance with me, reminding me of the strength that resides inside each step of this path."

Gurumata placed a gentle hand on my shoulder, her touch emanating warmth and compassion. "You are about to embark on a sacred quest, a journey of self-discovery and healing, Meera." Trust in the divine guidance that has brought you here, and trust in yourself. Remember, even on the darkest of nights, the stars shine brilliantly."

Her presence engulfed me in a calm embrace. With gratitude and a newfound sense of peace, I settled beneath the sheltering arms of the oak tree, ready to surrender to the embrace of sleep, knowing that the path we had chosen was one of transformation and awakening.

We woke up on the second day of our adventure in a condition of uncertainty and terror. Our group had departed without us, leaving Maadinee and me behind. My heart started racing with my breath.

"Maadinee, wake up!" I called out. Startled, she jolted awake, her eyes widening as she surveyed our surroundings. The woods lay before us, silent and devoid of any signs of our companions.

"They left without us," Maadinee exclaimed, her voice trembling with a mix of fear and sadness. Tears welled up in her eyes, mirroring the sense of abandonment that engulfed us.

Taking a deep breath to steady myself, I reassured her, "Don't worry, Maadinee. We can catch up with them if we walk fast. We need to stay calm and focused."

We quickly grabbed our bags and began off, speeding our pace as we traversed the unknown country. The urgency in our steps mirrored the urgency within our hearts as we tried to make up for the lost time and bridge the gap that separated us from our group.

Darkness crept in, and uncertainty gnawed at the edges of our resolve. We had no knowledge of our group's whereabouts, and the fear of being left stranded weighed heavily upon us. Minutes turned into hours as we continued our determined march. The darkness seemed to stretch endlessly, testing our spirits and resolve.

Then, just as doubt threatened to overpower us, a glimmer of light pierced through the dense canopy. A clearing emerged ahead, and with it, the sight of a group of people huddled around a flickering fire.

We rushed to them, and as we arrived, we discovered a community residing within the caves, each one illuminated by the warm glow of a flickering fire. Our presence caught the attention of an elderly woman, her eyes assessing us with a knowing gaze.

"So, you must be here to meet our Vedic guru," she declared curiously. We nodded in agreement, and she indicated for us to follow.

Fatigue weighed heavy upon our weary bodies as we struggled to keep up with the sprightly old woman. She effortlessly navigated the rugged terrain, ascending the caves with an agility that belied her age. Gasping for breath, Maadinee and I pushed ourselves to match her pace, determined not to fall behind.

Finally, we reached the designated cave, and there, seated in serene contemplation, was our new guru. We approached her with reverence, seeking her blessings before settling down among the rest of the group.

With a sweeping glance, our guru surveyed the gathering, her eyes filled with a mixture of wisdom and humility. Her words carried a sense of authenticity and sincerity as she addressed us all.

"I have always made a promise to myself," she continued, her voice full of determination. "I take on only a limited number of students, ensuring that I can dedicate ample time and attention to each one. However, every year, the number of seekers grows, leaving me with a question of how I will fulfill this promise. But be assured, I am fully committed to

The Journey Begins

sharing my expertise with each and every one of you. My aim is to help you find meaning in the wisdom that unfolds before you."

Her words flowed over us, instilling faith and assurance in our chosen course. She encouraged us to embrace curiosity and assured us that our questions would be addressed in due time. But for now, she recognized our weariness from the arduous journey and advised us to take it easy, assuring us that accommodations had been arranged for everyone.

"Tomorrow morning," she continued, her gaze encompassing the room, "we will embark on our first lessons. But for now, rest and rejuvenate, for the journey ahead requires both strength and clarity of mind."

Some students instinctively raised their hands to seek immediate guidance, but our guru gently dissuaded them, recognizing the need for rest.

"Not now," she said, her voice gentle yet firm. "You have all traveled a long way, and it is important to nurture yourselves today. Trust that your questions will be heard and answered in due course. Tomorrow, we shall begin our exploration together."

With her reassurance, a wave of tranquillity settled over the cave. We surrendered ourselves to the quietude of the moment, allowing the teachings and experiences that awaited us to unfold organically. As we prepared to sleep, an atmosphere of friendship and solidarity surrounded us, suggesting the profound relationships that would be made throughout our time in this hallowed area.

And so, as the flickering flames cast dancing shadows upon the cave walls, we sought solace in the embrace of slumber, eagerly awaiting the dawn that would herald the beginning of our transformative journey into the realms of Vedic wisdom.

First Lesson – Visha Chikitsa

"Good morning, dear seekers," she greeted us the next day, her melodic voice dancing with the morning breeze. "Today marks the beginning of a new chapter on our shared path of enlightenment. Let us gather our belongings and prepare ourselves for the lessons that lie ahead."

Eagerly, we collected our bags and assembled in a circle, ready to receive the wisdom that awaited us. Gurumata took her place at the center, commanding attention and reverence.

"Before we embark on our journey today, let us take a moment to ground ourselves and connect with the sacred energies that surround us. Close your eyes and feel the earth beneath your feet as it supports you. Breathe in the fresh morning air, allowing it to invigorate your spirit."

As we followed her guidance, a sense of tranquillity settled over the group. Our breaths synchronized, creating a harmonious rhythm that united us in purpose. In this moment of stillness, I felt a profound connection not only with nature but also with my fellow seekers.

Gurumata's voice gently broke the silence,

"Now, my dear ones, open your eyes and let us set forth," Gurumata spoke, her voice infused with determination. "Today, we are going to dive deeper into the realm of Ayurvedic wisdom, investigating the healing power of herbs and the connection between mind, body, and spirit. Prepare your minds to receive the teachings and your hearts to embrace the transformation that awaits."

And then she asked, "What are you hungry for?" We all started naming dishes that we wanted to eat in excitement.

"Well, that is your first lesson; your body will tell you what you want in the situation you are based in right now; for example, we have a couple of people naming some dishes with a lot of garlic in them. Garlic is one of the main medicines to heal someone from different types of infections. Most of you have named a dish with lots of Haldi in it. Haldi is known to build a stronger body and help rebuild or balance your system."

"All different types of ingredients you eat have different healing properties. Many ingredients that we use daily in our cooking can be found easily in our country. Some other ingredients are a little bit harder. The tree we are sitting under is called the teak tree. The bark of this tree can cure a burning forehead, but if you cook it too long in water, it can also give your patient some bad experiences. Too much of this ingredient can sometimes even stop the heart. So, each and every ingredient you can find in the world has healing qualities. But in the proper amount, not too much or too little. It is important that you find balance in each and everything. Not only in making different medicine but also in your own life."

Her words illuminated the interconnectedness between our food and our well-being. It was a revelation to realize that our bodies possessed an innate wisdom guiding us toward the nourishment required for optimal health.

First Lesson – Visha Chikitsa

As Gurumata continued to enlighten us, I found myself captivated by her words.

"Meditating on the teak tree, we recognize the power of nature's abundance," I whispered to Maadinee, my voice filled with awe.

She nodded in agreement, "It's incredible how every element of the natural world holds within it the potential for healing and restoration."

Just then, Gurumata's gaze fell upon us, "Meera, Maadinee, it's heartwarming to see your enthusiasm and understanding. Indeed, nature offers us a vast array of remedies, each with its unique healing qualities. From the towering teak tree to the humble herbs that grace our kitchen gardens, the wisdom of Ayurveda lies in recognizing and harnessing these gifts."

I couldn't resist delving deeper. "Gurumata, how do we navigate the vastness of nature's offerings? How do we find balance amidst this abundance?"

"Balance is the guiding principle in Ayurveda, not only in our culinary choices but also in every aspect of our lives," Gurumata said. "It is through mindfulness and understanding that we can tap into the subtle nuances and harness the healing properties of the natural world."

I realized that Ayurveda was more than just a collection of recipes and medicines but a holistic approach to living in alignment with the rhythms of the universe.

Maadinee leaned closer, her voice filled with curiosity. "Gurumata, how do we cultivate this awareness and intuition?"

Gurumata's serene expression softened into a gentle smile. "My dear Maadinee, developing this intuition is a lifelong journey. It requires a deep connection with oneself and the natural world. Through dedicated practice, meditation, and the guidance of experienced teachers, you will gradually tune your senses to the delicate vibrations of nature. Trust your instincts, for they will guide you towards the right ingredients and their appropriate proportions. Remember, balance is not a fixed point but a dynamic state that adjusts and evolves with each unique circumstance."

The teak tree, standing tall and proud, seemed to nod in agreement as if encouraging us to embrace its teachings and weave them into the fabric of our lives.

"Ayurveda, the practice of life, is about cultivating an awareness of the elements that permeate the universe," Gurumata proclaimed, her voice infused with reverence. "It is about finding balance, not just in the creation of medicines, but in every aspect of our existence."

She paused, allowing her words to sink in, and then continued with a challenge that stirred our spirits.

"I invite you to form pairs with those who share the same dish preferences," she said, her eyes gleaming with excitement. "Embark on a quest to discover the ingredients in the surrounding woods. Many of these may be found in the wild if you have an open mind. And if you can't spot them directly, trust in the innate wisdom of your mind, body, and soul. Let them guide you to the hidden treasures nature has to offer."

We exchanged eager glances, excitement coursing through our veins.

First Lesson – Visha Chikitsa

As Maadinee, the other girl, and I ventured deeper into the woods, excitement filled the air between us. We wandered through the verdant forest, our senses heightened, attuned to the subtle signs and whispers of nature.

"What do you think we'll be making?" Maadinee asked, her eyes shining with curiosity.

"I'm not entirely sure, but I have a feeling it will be something special," I said after a little pause. "Our guru always has a way of infusing deeper meaning into even the simplest of tasks."

Kamala nodded in agreement, her enthusiasm mirroring our own. We continued our trek, scanning the foliage for the ingredients that would soon find their way into our pots.

As we ventured deeper into the woods, the excitement within our trio blossomed like the flowers surrounding us. The sunlight filtered through the canopy, casting a dappled glow on our path. Maadinee's eyes gleamed with curiosity, and Kamala's infectious laughter filled the air.

"Look, Meera! I found some fresh mint leaves," Kamalaex claimed, holding up a handful of vibrant green leaves. "These have such a refreshing scent. I can already imagine the cooling effect they will have on the body."

I smiled, admiring Kamala's find. I had watched my mother use mint when any of us suffered digestive discomfort.

Maadinee, too, was engrossed in her search. Her gaze fixated on a cluster of bright yellow turmeric roots peeking through the soil. "Haldi! Just what we need for our dishes," she exclaimed, her voice brimming with excitement.

Gurumata, who had been observing our exploration from a distance, approached us with a serene smile. "I see you have uncovered some remarkable treasures from nature's bounty. The mint and turmeric you have found are indeed invaluable ingredients in Ayurvedic healing."

Kamalabeamed at Gurumata's praise, her enthusiasm bubbling over. "Gurumata, there's so much to discover and learn. "How do we begin to understand the specific benefits of each ingredient and how to use them effectively?"

Gurumata's eyes twinkled, "My dear Kamala, the journey of understanding Ayurvedic herbs and spices is a lifelong pursuit. The key lies in immersing yourself in their teachings, seeking guidance from experienced practitioners, and observing the effects firsthand. With time and practice, you will develop an innate understanding of which ingredient to use and how it can best serve the body and mind."

Maadinee's voice resonated with curiosity. "Gurumata, as we gather these ingredients, can we also cultivate a deeper connection with nature? Can we learn to listen to its wisdom and allow it to guide us?"

"Absolutely, Maadinee. Nature is a profound teacher, whispering its secrets to those who are willing to listen. You will create a deeper connection as you interact with the elements around you, breathe in the fragrances, touch the textures, and immerse yourself in the beauty of the natural world. Nature will become your ally, offering guidance and inspiration as you walk the path of Ayurveda."

Our hearts swelled with gratitude for Gurumata's guidance and the wisdom she imparted. We continued our foraging, our bond growing stronger with each herb and spice we discovered. The woods seemed to embrace us, lending their energy and knowledge to our quest for healing.

With our hands full of nature's treasures, we made our way back to the campfire, where the aromatic scents of herbs and spices mingled in the air.

We found our guru bustling about, preparing pots and utensils with practiced ease. The tantalizing aroma of spices filled the air, awakening our senses and further igniting our anticipation.

"Well done, and welcome back my dear students," she praised. "In seeking, you have found not only the ingredients but also a deeper connection to the rhythms of nature and the wisdom that resides within."

As the rest of the group gathered, Gurumata beckoned us to wash the gathered ingredients and take our places around her. We formed a circle, multiple sets of sparkling eyes fixed on her.

"Before you embark on your culinary creations," Gurumata began, her voice gentle yet commanding, "let me share a vital lesson with you. Ghee, our golden elixir, holds immense importance in Ayurvedic cooking. It is not only a delightful addition to our dishes but also a conduit for extracting the healing properties from our base spices."

She paused, allowing her words to sink in, before continuing, "Just as ghee was Lord Krishna's favorite, it becomes our ally in the process of extracting the healing essence. However, balance is key. If we don't bring the temperature to a sufficient level, the healing properties may remain trapped within the spices. On the other hand, excessive heat can risk burning away these precious elements. It is through this delicate dance of temperatures that the magic of Ayurvedic cooking unfolds."

We listened attentively, understanding that even the smallest details held significance on our path of healing and nourishment.

"Now, my dear ones, with this knowledge in your hearts, let us begin," Gurumata declared, her eyes sparkling with anticipation. "Now, let us bring these ingredients to life, infusing our dishes with the healing power of Ayurveda. Remember, as you cook, infuse each step with mindfulness and intention, for the act of preparing food can be a sacred ritual that nourishes both the body and soul."

With her guidance fresh in our minds, we eagerly set to work, prepping our ingredients with care and attention. The vibrant colors of herbs and spices danced before us as if celebrating the alchemy that was about to take place.

As the aroma of the simmering dishes filled the air, our trio—Maadinee, Kamala, and I—found ourselves engrossed in lively conversation.

Kamala, her eyes sparkling with curiosity, turned to me and asked, "Meera, do you remember when we used to gather in your backyard, concocting simple remedies from the herbs we found? Who would have thought that our childhood exploration would lead us here, embracing the vast knowledge of Ayurveda?"

I smiled in nostalgia. "Indeed, Kamala. Those innocent experiments laid the foundation for our journey today. It's incredible how our childhood games have evolved into a profound quest for understanding the healing powers of nature."

Maadinee chimed in, her voice filled with enthusiasm. "And look at us now, creating dishes infused with ancient wisdom. I can't help but be grateful for the chance to learn and grow with both of you."

"I can hardly wait to taste our creations. I have a feeling they will not only be delicious but also a reflection of our collective energy and intention."

With laughter bubbling forth, Maadinee added, "Yes, the love and care we have infused into these dishes will surely nourish us on multiple levels."

As we continued to stir, chop, and season, our conversation ebbed and flowed like a gentle river, carrying us deeper into the realm of Ayurvedic wisdom. We shared stories of our own healing journeys, exchanged tips and techniques, and marveled at the profound impact that simple ingredients could have on our well-being.

Throughout the process, Gurumata moved among us, offering guidance and encouragement. She observed our techniques, reminding us of the balance between precision and intuition, between technique and the flow of creativity. Her presence lent an air of reverence to our endeavors, as we cooked not just for nourishment but also as a form of meditation and self-expression.

As the fragrant aromas enveloped us and the dishes took shape, we marveled at the transformation unfolding before our eyes. Each plate held not only a meal but a reflection of the love and intention we had infused into its creation.

Finally, as we gathered to share the fruits of our labor, Gurumata's smile radiated with pride and contentment. "You have embraced the art of Ayurvedic cooking with grace and skill," she praised, her words carrying the weight of wisdom. "May these dishes nourish not only your bodies but also your souls, reminding you of the profound connection between food and healing. Remember, not only the ingredients but also your intentions and energy infuse into the dishes you make."

As we sat around the flickering fire, the warmth of the flames mirrored the warmth in our hearts. Maadinee, Kamala, and I exchanged glances, our eyes reflecting a deep sense of contentment.

I gazed at Gurumata, feeling a deep sense of reverence for her guidance. "Gurumata, we are truly grateful for the teachings you have bestowed upon us. We have begun to unravel the complicated fabric of healing and self-discovery using Ayurveda. It feels both empowering and humbling."

Gurumata's smile radiated wisdom.

Kamala leaned in closer. "You know, I can't help but imagine how Ayurveda can touch the lives of our loved ones back in the village. Imagine the possibilities of healing and well-being that we can bring to them."

"Kamala, you're right." I beamed, "We have a responsibility to share this wisdom with our village, to help them discover the power of nature's healing remedies. It's a beautiful way to honor our roots and contribute to the well-being of our people."

With renewed purpose, we raised our hands in a silent vow to carry forward the teachings of Ayurveda and the spirit of unity we had cultivated in this sacred space. We knew that our journey was not just about personal growth but also about sharing the transformative power of Ayurveda with those we held dear.

As the fire crackled and our hearts overflowed with gratitude, we savored the final bites of our communal feast, the sour flavors lingering on our tongues. It was more than just a meal—it was a testament to the boundless possibilities that lay ahead, the incredible potential for healing and transformation that awaited us on our Ayurvedic odyssey.

And as we extinguished the fire, bidding farewell to the night, we carried within us the warmth, wisdom, and unity that would guide us on our path—a path illuminated by the healing power of Ayurveda and the bonds forged in the kitchen of our shared journey.

Meeting Poison Baba

That night, as I lay in my makeshift bed, the warmth of sleep wrapped around me. I yearned to connect with Devi Latika, seeking her reassurance. But despite my desperate plea, she did not appear. Frustration welled up within me, mingling with the remnants of my unspoken desires.

In my restless sleep, dreams intertwined with reality, blurring the boundaries of what was and what could be. Jagha, the object of my affection, entered my dreamscape, his presence provoking a blend of anticipation and uncertainty. It was a vivid reenactment of our last encounter, where I had confessed my feelings, only for him to express the need for his guru's approval before he could respond.

In the dream, Jagha drew nearer, his gaze intense and full of promise. Our hearts beat in unison, and just as our lips were about to meet, a trembling disruption shattered the moment. A soft voice belonging to one of the other girl students gently nudged me awake from my dream world.

Startled, I opened my eyes to the gentle rays of morning filtering through the canopy above. Reality rushed back, and I realized with a sinking feeling that I had overslept. Panic surged through me as I noticed that I was the last one to awaken from our slumber.

Feeling embarrassed, I hastily gathered my belongings and joined the others who were already engaged in their morning rituals. The girl who had awakened me offered a sympathetic smile, her eyes reflecting understanding rather than judgment.

As I hurried to catch up with the group, a whirlwind of emotions enveloped me. I pondered the significance of my dream, the unfinished conversation with Jagha lingering in my mind. Would this unexpected delay impact the trajectory of our relationship? Would I find the opportunity to revisit our discussion and discover the fate of our budding connection?

In the middle of my racing thoughts, I resolved to focus on the present moment, to immerse myself in the teachings and experiences that lay ahead. While uncertainty may cloud my path, I knew that this journey was not just about love and longing—it was about self-discovery, growth, and embracing the wisdom of Ayurveda.

As I stepped back into the group, joining them outside for our next lesson, I couldn't help but notice Maadinee sitting beside Kamala. They were engrossed in their own little world, sharing laughter and inside jokes. My heart sank a little, and a peculiar sensation tugged at my belly.

Maadinee had always been my closest friend, someone with whom I had shared countless memories and secrets. But in that moment, it seemed like an invisible thread was separating, gently pulling her away from me. It wasn't a conscious choice on her part, yet I couldn't help but feel an ache of sadness and a bit of, perhaps, jealousy.

I watched as they exchanged playful glances, their laughter filling the air. It was as if they had formed a connection that excluded me, leaving me on the borders of their newfound bond. I tried to ignore the uneasy feeling gnawing at me, pushing it to the corners of my mind, but it lingered, a constant reminder of the shifting dynamics between us.

Was I being left behind? Had I become less critical of Maadinee? Did I do something wrong? The doubts and insecurities danced around my mind, clouding my perception of our friendship.

Just as I was collecting the courage to approach Maadinee and Kamala, our guru's voice swam through the air, drawing my attention. I quickly found a spot to sit, eager to hear what she had to say.

A peculiar-looking man, dressed in vibrant green robes and adorned with intricate jewelry, stood beside our guru. He had a rounded nose and beady eyes. He had an air of mystique about him, as if secrets and ancient knowledge were etched into his very being.

With a gentle smile, our guru introduced him, "Today, my dear students, we have the honor of welcoming a special guest among us. Poison Baba." The name itself sent a shiver down my spine, conjuring images of venomous snakes and deadly potions. Intrigue mingled with caution as I looked at the mysterious figure before us.

His eyes held a depth that seemed to hold countless stories and secrets. As I observed him, a mixture of curiosity and apprehension coursed through me.

Guru continued, "Poison Baba is renowned for his expertise in herbal remedies and his vast knowledge of plants and their medicinal properties. He has dedicated his life to the study of poisons and their antidotes, unraveling the mysteries of nature's potent gifts. Today, he has graciously agreed to share some of his wisdom with us."

As Poison Baba began to speak, the entire atmosphere seemed to vibrate with excitement and curiosity.

With each word, he wove intricate tales of ancient healing practices passed down through generations. He spoke of rare plants hidden deep within the heart of the forest, possessing the power to both harm and heal. I listened, hanging onto his every word, as he described the delicate art of balance in the realm of poisons.

"It is said," Poison Baba began, "that everything in nature has its purpose. Some plants may seem dangerous or toxic, but when treated with care and respect, they can reveal their miraculous healing properties."

As the tales unfolded, Poison Baba shared anecdotes of ancient healers and their wisdom.

"The key to healing," he emphasized, "lies in understanding the essence of these substances and their effects on the human body."

In the midst of his teachings, I couldn't help but wonder about the connection between Poison Baba's knowledge and our journey in Ayurveda. Were there lessons we could learn from the darker aspects of healing? Was there a more profound significance to his presence among us? These questions whirled in my mind, seeking answers that remained vague for the time being.

"Nature, my dear students, holds within it a delicate equilibrium," Poison Baba said, his voice laced with wisdom.

"In the realm of poisons, one must tread with caution and respect. For what may cause harm in excess can also bring about profound healing when used in the right measure."

He shared stories of poisonous plants that, when skilfully prepared and administered, could cure ailments that plagued humanity for centuries. Each story was like a thread, weaving together a tapestry of knowledge that unfolded before us.

"In the grand tapestry of life, healing, and harm coexist," Poison Baba continued, "to wield the power of poisons requires not only knowledge but also reverence for the delicate balance of nature. Just as a venomous snake can hold the cure within its fangs, so too can seemingly harmful substances hold the key to transformation and healing."

His words echoed in my mind, stirring a newfound appreciation for the intricate dance of healing and harm that infused with the natural world. It was a thoughtful reminder that balance and respect were essential in our journey through Ayurveda and in our lives as a whole.

Suddenly, a hushed silence fell over as Poison Baba reached down and pulled out a small pot from his feet. As he slowly lifted the lid, gasps of both excitement and fear rippled through the students. Snuggled inside was a magnificent king cobra, its scales shimmering in the sunlight.

Poison Baba's eyes twinkled mischievously as he surveyed the group of students who sat before him. "Who among you would dare to handle the king cobra?" he challenged. The air grew heavy with apprehension as the students exchanged hesitant glances, unsure of how to respond.

Meeting Poison Baba

Among the hushed whispers, Kamala's name was uttered softly. She glanced at me nervously, her eyes wide with uncertainty. I could see the mixture of fear and curiosity in her expression. Sensing her hesitation, Maadinee encouraged her, "Go on, Kamala. This is a rare opportunity. Trust yourself."

Taking a deep breath, Kamalas summoned her courage and slowly rose from her seat. With each step towards Poison Baba, her determination grew stronger. We watched in anticipation as she approached the poisonous snake. Soon she stood before him, keeping a safe distance from the snake.

Poison Baba regarded Kamalawith with a gentle smile, his eyes filled with knowing wisdom. "Fear not, young one," he reassured her. "The cobra is a symbol of transformation and protection. In handling it, you will discover a newfound strength within yourself."

Kamalatentatively extended her trembling hand towards the serpent. The cobra, sensing her presence, remained surprisingly calm, its gaze fixed upon her. With a delicate touch, she began to stroke the sleek scales, her fear gradually giving way to a sense of awe and reverence.

As Kamala held the serpent, a tense silence hung in the air. Suddenly, the snake's demeanor shifted, its hiss piercing through the grounds. Before anyone could react, it struck, sinking its fangs into Kamala's neck. A scream escaped her lips as she dropped the snake, clutching her wounded neck in agony. Panic seized the group, with fear and concern etched on every face.

While a part of me was genuinely worried for Kamala's well-being, another part couldn't help but feel a twisted sense of satisfaction. Perhaps, in this moment of weakness, I would have my dear friend Maadinee back, entirely and only mine.

In the chaos, Poison Baba, with a calm and composed face, stepped forward. He swiftly picked up the venomous snake, returning it to its pot and securing the lid. Turning his attention to Kamala, he spoke in a reassuring tone, "Do not fear, my child. The venomous fangs of this snake were removed. You are safe."

Kamala's teary eyes widened with a mixture of relief and disbelief. She gingerly touched her neck, feeling the throbbing pain subside.

Guru approached Kamala; her voice filled with concern. "Are you alright, my dear?" Kamala nodded, still trembling from the shock. Guru gently placed a hand on her shoulder, offering comfort and reassurance. "You have faced a test of bravery, and you have emerged strong. The snake's bite, although harmless, serves as a reminder of the delicate balance between danger and protection."

The students buzzed with an assortment of relief and awe, the incident serving as a powerful lesson on the delicate nature of Ayurveda and the importance of trust in the hands of knowledgeable practitioners. Poison Baba, his gaze filled with compassion, continued, "Just as we must distinguish between poisons and medicines, we must also recognize the importance of trust in our journey toward healing. Fear can cloud our judgment, but with guidance, we can navigate the path of transformation."

As the session neared its end, our guru stepped forward and thanked Poison Baba for his enlightening words. The entire group erupted into applause.

Meeting Poison Baba

Guru then turned to Poison Baba, and their exchange caught my attention. "Your wisdom, Poison Baba, is a gift to these young minds embarking on a journey of Ayurveda. Your teachings complement our path of self-discovery and healing. We are truly honored to have you share your knowledge with us."

Poison Baba bowed gracefully, his eyes glinting with a sense of satisfaction and purpose. "Gurumata," he replied, "the ancient knowledge of poisons and remedies is intertwined with Ayurveda's essence. I am humbled to be a part of this gathering, and it warms my heart to witness these young souls seeking harmony with nature's secrets."

As the night draped the surroundings in darkness, I found myself lost in a sea of conflicting emotions. Kamala and Maadinee's friendship had become a bitter reminder of my own supposed rejection. While they shared laughter and whispered secrets, I felt like an outsider, left to navigate the depths of my own loneliness.

Restlessly, I lay on my bed, my thoughts spinning like a storm. The desire for revenge troubled my heart, fuelling my anger towards Maadinee for what I understood as a betrayal of our friendship. The weight of these emotions grew heavier with each passing moment, suffocating the fond memories we had once shared.

Just as I closed my eyes, seeking solace in the embrace of sleep, a warm presence enveloped me. I opened my inner eyes to find my Devi Latika, radiant and delicate, standing before me.

Latika's soothing voice echoed in the silence, breaking through the storm of my turbulent thoughts. "My dear

Meera, why do you let anger and revenge cloud your heart? True friendship is not about possession or control but about understanding and support. Maadinee's connection with Kamaladoes not diminish the bond you once shared. It is simply an opportunity for growth and new connections."

Her words pierced through the veil of my resentment. I realized that my anger was a barrier that separated me from the joy and companionship that awaited me if I could find it within myself to let go.

"But Devi Latika," I replied, my voice tinged with a mix of frustration and vulnerability, "it hurts to see them together as if I am no longer a part of their world. How can I find peace within myself?"

Latika's radiant presence emanated a sense of calm as if she held the wisdom of ages in her unearthly form. She gently placed a hand on my shoulder, offering her guidance. "Meera, true peace lies in understanding and acceptance. Release the attachment to what was and embrace the possibilities of what can be. Open your heart to new friendships and connections, for they hold the power to enrich your journey."

The path to reconciliation and healing lay not in revenge but in finding the strength to let go of the past and embrace the present moment.

With a newfound clarity, I looked into Latika's eyes and whispered, "Devi, show me the way to forgiveness and understanding. Help me mend the breaks within my heart and restore the bonds of friendship that once brought me joy."

Latika's smile widened, her eyes shining with compassion. "My dear Meera, forgiveness begins with compassion towards yourself and others. Let go of the pain that binds you and open your heart to the beauty that surrounds you. Trust in the transformative power of love and understanding, and you shall find the harmony you seek."

As her ethereal form gradually faded, I closed my inner eye, embracing the newfound wisdom given to me. But yet, I could not find peace.

Latika's soothing voice enveloped me, and she asked, "My dear Meera, what troubles your heart? Is it the lingering feelings for Jagha?"

I took a deep breath, feeling the weight of my unrequited affection for Jagha. "Yes, Devi Latika," I confessed, "I cannot seem to reach him during my meditations. It's as if a veil separates us, preventing our souls from connecting."

Latika's celestial presence radiated warmth and understanding. "Meera, my child, have you explored the depths of your own heart? Have you nurtured the feelings of possessiveness within you?"

I furrowed my brow, unsure of what she meant. "Possessiveness, Devi? But isn't that an undesirable trait?"

"Ah, my dear Meera, possessiveness, when understood and channeled correctly, can ignite the fire of devotion within you. It is not about controlling or possessing another person but recognizing the depth of your feelings and cultivating them within your own heart."

Curiosity mingled with hope as I listened to Latika's words. "But how do I do that, Devi? How can I grow these feelings of possessiveness in a way that restores my peace?"

Latika's ethereal form seemed to shimmer with wisdom. "Begin by turning your focus inward, Meera. Reflect upon the qualities that draw you to Jagha, the moments you shared, and the connection you felt. Embrace those emotions and let them blossom within your heart. When you nurture these feelings of possessiveness with love and understanding, they become a powerful force that can bridge the gap between your souls."

Her words rang in my heart, inspiring a new understanding. I had been so consumed by my longing for Jagha that I neglected to explore the depths of my own heart, to recognize and embrace the intensity of my emotions.

With gratitude, I nodded and spoke softly, "Thank you, Devi Latika, for your guidance. I will begin this journey of self-discovery, nurturing the feelings within me and allowing them to grow into a force that connects me with Jagha."

Latika's celestial form shimmered, her presence gradually fading. "May your path be filled with love and understanding, Meera. Trust in the power of your own heart and the connection you share with Jagha. Embrace the transformative journey that lies before you."

Soon, Latika's presence dissipated, leaving a sense of serenity in its wake. I felt a changed sense of purpose. I would cultivate the feelings within me, and that would lead me closer to Jagha's heart.

I rose from my bed and entered the stillness of the night. In the darkness that enveloped me, I settled into a comfortable position, crossing my legs and folding my hands in my lap. Taking Latika's wise guidance to heart, I closed my eyes and began my meditative state.

In the depths of my mind, I called for the precious moments spent with Jagha, allowing them to wash over me like gentle waves. His radiant smile, which could brighten even the darkest of days, etched itself into my memory. I recalled the way he gracefully moved through the woods, his steps a dance of elegance and strength. The sound of his voice echoed in my thoughts, each word blowing with a captivating melody.

With every breath, I dug deeper into the sea of memories, reliving the laughter, the conversations, and the shared experiences. But among these cherished moments, there was one memory that held a sacred place within my heart. It was the moment when our hands touched, united in a tender connection, as we scattered the ashes of my beloved parents. The touch of his warm hand against mine, a gentle comfort that I was not alone in my grief, imprinted itself upon my soul.

In the stillness of my meditation, I allowed these memories to envelop me, to become a source of strength and devotion. I allowed my feelings to flourish and deepen. With each passing moment, the bond between Jagha and me grew stronger, bridging the gap that had separated us.

I continued my meditation, feeling a sense of relief that settled upon me. I knew that this journey of self-discovery and love would not be without its challenges, but I was prepared to embrace them. Guided by the wisdom of my Devi and fuelled by the power of my own heart, I was determined to get closer to Jagha's essence.

"Jagha, are you there? Can you hear me?" My words hung in the air, a hopeful plea for connection. Silence greeted me, and a sense of uncertainty began to settle within my heart. Had my efforts been in vain? Was there no way to bridge the distance that separated us?

Just as hopelessness threatened to consume me, a soft voice, barely audible, emerged from the depths of the distance. "Meera?" The sound was faint like a whisper carried on the wind. Jagha had heard my call.

Jagha Found Me

I focused my thoughts, projecting my voice into the vast expanse of consciousness. "Yes, it's me, Jagha! Can you hear me?" The echoes of stillness surrounded me as if the universe held its breath, waiting for his response.

Seconds felt like an eternity, hanging in the balance between uncertainty and anticipation. Then, like a gentle ripple expanding across a tranquil pond, his voice carried through the spirit world. "Meera... I hear you. I've been searching for a way to reach you, too."

Relief washed over me, mingling with the joy that welled up within my being. Jagha's faint but distinct presence reassured me that I was not alone in my longing to connect.

As I continued to commune with Jagha in our separate meditative states, our connection deepened beyond the physical distance that separated us. Through thoughts and emotions, our voices tangled in a conversation that spanned over miles and transcended time.

Jagha's words reached me with clarity and warmth, carrying the weight of good news. "Meera, I have wonderful news to share," he whispered softly. "My guru has given his blessings for us to be together. He sees the love and commitment we share, and he believes that in this life, we are destined to be united in marriage."

Happiness bloomed within my heart, and a smile graced my lips. The acceptance of our union by Jagha's guru was a validation of the love that had blossomed between us. It felt like a dream come true, a confirmation that our bond was not only deep but also recognized and honored by those who guided us on our spiritual paths.

In the glow of this newfound joy, I embraced the prospect of becoming Jagha's life partner. But as the minutes ticked by, a wave of contemplation washed over me, gently nudging my thoughts in a different direction.

With a hint of hesitation, I responded, "Jagha, I am overjoyed by this news, and my love for you is resolute. I promise you this. However, I feel a calling within me, a wish to complete my studies and become a Vedic doctor. It is a path I have devoted myself to, and I believe it is crucial for me to pursue it with dedication and focus."

Silence enveloped us momentarily as if Jagha contemplated the weight of my words. Then, with a voice filled with understanding and support, he replied, "Meera, I respect and admire your dedication to your studies. Your journey to become a Vedic doctor is a noble pursuit, and I have complete faith in your abilities and your dreams. I will wait for you, my love, patiently and faithfully until the day you return to Karmana."

Relief washed over me, mingling with gratitude for Jagha's unwavering support. Our love was not bound by time or distance. We shared a deep bond that could withstand the tests of separation and the trials of individual growth.

In the depths of our meditative states, we reaffirmed our commitment to one another, promising to hold onto the love that had bloomed within our hearts. Though physically apart, our souls were intertwined, and the connection we shared would guide us through the challenges that lay ahead.

As I awakened from my deep meditative state, a sense of urgency gripped my heart. I glanced around the empty common room, realizing that I had overslept and that my fellow students had already begun their day. Panic welled up within me, propelling me into swift action.

Without wasting a moment, I hurriedly got up from my meditation spot and dashed outside, my eyes scanning the surroundings for any sign of my fellow students. My heart raced, fearing that I had missed out on essential lessons or gatherings.

As I reached the open space outside, I caught a glimpse of Maadinee, Kamala, and the other students in the distance. They were engaged in animated conversation, their laughter filling the air. Relief washed over me, knowing that I had not missed them entirely.

Taking quick strides, I approached Maadinee, the apology evident in my voice. "Maadinee! I'm so sorry I overslept. I thought I would miss everything. What happened this morning?"

Maadinee turned towards me, her eyes sparkling with amusement. "Meera, you finally decided to join us!" she exclaimed, a playful tone lacing her words. "Don't worry, you didn't miss much. We were just sharing stories and experiences from our meditative states. It was a beautiful exchange of insights and reflections."

A wave of relief washed over me as I realized that the morning gathering was more of a casual discussion rather than a crucial lesson. I let out a sigh, a mix of gratitude and light-heartedness. "Oh, thank goodness! I was so worried I missed something important. But tell me, what did everyone share?"

Maadinee's face lit up, eager to share the highlights of the morning gathering. "Well, each person had unique experiences. Kamala spoke of a profound sense of inner peace she discovered during her meditation, while another student shared a vision of interconnectedness and unity with nature. It was truly inspiring to hear how everyone's journeys unfolded and the wisdom they gained."

Listening to Maadinee's words, I felt a renewed sense of curiosity and connection with the other students. Despite my initial panic and fear, I realized that each of us had embarked on a personal journey of growth and self-discovery. We were all bonded together in this quest for spiritual enlightenment, supporting and learning from one another along the way.

As I stood there, engrossed in conversation with Maadinee, our guru suddenly emerged from the midst of the group. Her serene presence commanded attention, and a hush fell over the students.

"Today, my dear students, we embark on a journey of fasting," she announced, "Fasting is not only a physical practice but also a spiritual one. It allows us to cleanse our bodies, purify our minds, and deepen our connection with the divine."

As she spoke, she explained the various benefits of fasting, highlighting how it helps to rejuvenate the body, enhance mental clarity, and cultivate discipline and self-control.

I was aware of the profound transformative power of this ancient practice. However, as the day progressed, I could feel the effects of my sleepless night weighing heavily on me. The lack of rest made the fasting journey more challenging than I had anticipated. My body felt weak, and even the simplest tasks seemed to require immense effort.

Struggling to keep up with the daily chores, I found myself leaning on the support of my fellow students. Maadinee, sensing my fatigue, offered a gentle smile and a helping hand.

Grateful for her empathy, I mustered the strength to carry on, drawing inspiration from the teachings of our guru. I reminded myself of the importance of discipline and self-control, understanding that these challenges were part of my journey toward growth and enlightenment.

I joined the other students in carrying baskets of clothes down to the nearby river stream. We immersed ourselves in the task of washing clothes, the rhythmic scrubbing and rinsing soothing in its familiarity. Yet, with each passing moment, I felt my energy waning and my body growing weaker.

But when we returned with the wet clothes, ready to hang them on the tree branches to dry, I struggled to keep up with the others. My steps faltered, and a wave of dizziness washed over me. It was in that vulnerable state that my guru appeared, her presence both comforting and piercing.

She looked into my eyes as if peering into the depths of my soul. With a knowing smile, she asked, "Meera, why were you up all night meditating with Jagha?"

Startled by her insight, I stumbled over my words, feeling my cheeks flush. "Guruji, I... I couldn't help it," I stammered, my voice filled with guilt. "I yearned to connect with him, to share my thoughts and feelings, even in the realm of meditation."

She nodded, her expression understanding. "It is natural to feel such desires, Meera. However, it is important to remember that our spiritual journey is a path of self-discovery and growth. External attachments can sometimes slow our progress."

I lowered my gaze. "I understand, Guruji," I replied, my voice tinged with humility. "I allowed my emotions to guide my actions, losing sight of the present moment and the lessons at hand."

"Meera, true growth comes from finding balance within ourselves," she continued. "While it is important to cherish the connections we form, it is equally vital to nurture our individual paths of self-realization. Remember, your journey to becoming a Vedic doctor is your own, and it requires your complete focus and dedication."

As her words sank in, a sense of clarity washed over me. I realized the importance of staying grounded in my purpose and not allowing distractions to hinder my progress. I nodded, grateful for her guidance and understanding.

With a gentle smile, she placed her hand on my shoulder. "Do not dwell on the past, Meera. Learn from it and move forward. Embrace each moment as an opportunity for growth and self-discovery. Let go of attachments that do not serve your highest purpose. For that, you will need to cultivate the inner strength needed to persevere on your path."

As I watched her disappear into the distance, a renewed purpose rose up within me.

Gathering my strength, I resumed my tasks alongside the other students, hanging the wet clothes on the tree branches. Though weakened, I felt a changed sense of purpose and commitment to my journey. Each article of clothing I hung symbolized my willingness to let go of distractions and embrace the path of self-realization that lay before me.

As we hung the wet clothes on the tree branches, Maadinee turned to me with a concerned expression. She noticed the fatigue etched on my face and asked, "Meera, why do you look so tired? Is something bothering you?"

I hesitated for a moment, unsure of how to respond. Maadinee and I had always shared our thoughts and secrets, but this time, it felt different. Gathering my courage, I decided to confide in her.

"Maadinee, you remember the one I had feelings for?" I began, my voice filled with a mix of excitement and apprehension.

Maadinee nodded, a glimmer of curiosity in her eyes. "Of course, Meera, how could I forget Jagha?"

I nodded in response. "Yes, that's correct. Well, something extraordinary happened last night. During my meditation, I reached out to him with my inner mind, and we had a conversation. It felt so real, Maadinee."

Maadinee's eyes widened with astonishment. "You spoke to Jagha during your meditation? That's incredible, Meera! What did he say?"

A wave of mixed emotions washed over me as I recalled our exchange. "Jagha told me that his guru has accepted our marriage, and he was happy about it. At first, I felt overjoyed and ready to embrace our future together. But as time passed, doubts began to creep in."

Maadinee tilted her head in confusion. "Doubts? What kind of doubts, Meera?"

Taking a deep breath, I continued, "I realized that I still have so much to learn and accomplish on my journey to becoming a Vedic doctor. I want to complete my studies, gain knowledge, and serve others through Ayurveda. I expressed this to Jagha during our conversation, and surprisingly, he understood. He told me that he would wait for me to return to Karmana."

Maadinee's expression softened with understanding. "Meera, it's wonderful that you have such clarity about your goals and aspirations. I can see how conflicted you must feel right now. But remember, your path is yours alone, and you must follow what feels right for you."

I nodded, grateful for her support. "Thank you, Maadinee. Your understanding means the world to me. I know that our friendship will endure, regardless of the choices we make on our individual journeys."

Maadinee smiled, her warmth radiating in her eyes. "Of course, Meera. I will always be here for you, no matter what."

I continued to hang the clothes, feeling a weight lifted off my shoulders. Maadinee's words reassured me that I was making the right decision for myself. The path of becoming a Vedic doctor awaited me, and I knew I had the support and understanding of my dear friend by my side.

As the garments swayed gently in the breeze, I allowed myself to be carried away by the rhythm of the moment. The river's soothing melody, the camaraderie of my fellow students, and the guidance of my guru all converged to create a sense of harmony and purpose.

The day progressed smoothly, and soon, our conversations shifted to lighter topics. And with that, laughter filled the air once again. Together, we completed our tasks, and our shared experiences strengthened our bond.

With each passing moment, I felt a growing sense of gratitude for the clarity I had gained. I knew that my decision to focus on my studies and personal growth was the right one.

Amidst the physical discomfort and weariness, I sought solace in the wisdom shared by our guru. Her words echoed in my mind, reminding me of the purpose behind the fasting practice and the transformative potential it held. With each step, I found strength in knowing that this temporary struggle was paving the way for greater spiritual growth.

Soon, when the sun dipped below, indicating the arrival of the evening, it cast a warm glow across the courtyard. That was when our guru gathered all of us students together. We huddled in anticipation, ready to receive her guidance for the evening.

With a serene smile, she spoke, her voice carrying a sense of calm authority. "My dear students, the time to break our fasts approaches. Before we partake in our meal, I encourage each of you to go out and find food for everyone to share."

Excitement filled the air. We eagerly nodded, ready to embark on this collective mission.

As we dispersed into the surrounding areas, our eyes scanned the landscape for any signs of sustenance. Conversations buzzed among us as we shared ideas and exchanged insights on where we might find food. In this shared endeavor, we felt a deep connection with both nature and one another.

After a brief exploration, we began to return one by one, our hands filled with an array of fruits, vegetables, and herbs.

We presented the discoveries to our guru. She observed the fruits of our collective efforts with pride, her eyes shining with admiration. "Well done, my students," she commended us. "You have demonstrated not only resourcefulness but also an appreciation for the nourishment provided by our motherland."

As the sun began to set, marking the end of the fasting period, a sense of accomplishment washed over me. Despite the weakness and fatigue, I persevered and learned valuable lessons along the way. The experience deepened my appreciation for the resilience of the human spirit and the transformative power of self-discipline.

Sitting cross-legged on the ground, we formed a circle, our eyes filled with anticipation. The guru's voice rang out, guiding us through the ritual of breaking our fasts and reminding us of the sacredness of the food we were about to consume.

With each morsel, we tasted the interconnectedness of nature and our own sustenance. The flavors danced on our tongues, nurturing both body and spirit. In this simple act of sharing a meal, we experienced the profound sense of community and unity that bound us as students of the guru.

With contented smiles and full hearts, we cleared the remnants of our meal, knowing that this experience had enriched us in ways beyond mere sustenance. And as we sat together, basking in the glow of the setting sun, we felt a deep sense of fulfillment and purpose, ready to embrace the next step of our journey under the guidance of our wise and compassionate guru.

At that moment, as we gathered together, the exhaustion of the day transformed into a profound sense of fulfillment and gratitude. We shared stories of our individual journeys, expressing our struggles and triumphs and finding solace in the understanding that we were all growing together.

As we prepared for the night's rest, I reflected on the day's experiences. Despite the challenges, I realized that it was through embracing and persevering through difficult moments that we uncover our true strength and potential. With this newfound insight, I drifted off to sleep, eager to awaken to the next chapter of our educational journey.

The Art of Making a Bonsai Tree

I woke up before the sun came up. I was resolved to take my guru's advice and learn from it. Feeling a strong sense of commitment, I got myself ready for the day. I cared for my body and mind, preparing for the difficulties I knew I would face later on.

The warm rays of the early light bathed the sky with pink and orange hues as I made my way towards the courtyard.

To my surprise, I saw my guru standing beneath the large banyan tree, her serene presence commanding respect. I approached her nervously.

"Guru," I greeted her, bowing slightly, "I am ready to focus on my studies and immerse myself in the teachings of Ayurveda. I want to learn and grow to become a Vedic doctor."

She turned to me, her eyes gently gazing at me. "Meera, I am glad to see your commitment and determination. Your dedication to your studies will pave the way for a fulfilling journey. Remember, knowledge is a river that flows endlessly, and it is up to you to drink from it and quench your thirst for understanding."

I nodded, absorbing her words like a sponge, eager to absorb the wisdom she possessed. "Guru, I promise to give my best and to approach each lesson with an open mind and a willingness to learn."

She smiled a warm and reassuring gesture. "That is all I ask of you, Meera. The road to becoming a Vedic doctor is not simple, but you will succeed with determination and a strong heart. Trust in the knowledge that lies within you and let it guide you on this transformative journey."

Her comments struck a deep chord within me, instilling in me a feeling of purpose and drive. I knew that the road ahead would be challenging, but I also understood that it was through these challenges that true growth and transformation occurred.

As the sun continued to rise, casting a golden glow upon us, my guru extended her hand towards the banyan tree. "Meera, observe the strength and resilience of this tree. Its roots run deep, anchoring it firmly to the earth. Just as the tree draws nourishment from the soil, you must draw strength from your studies, rooted in a deep understanding of the principles of Ayurveda."

I followed her gaze, marveling at the majesty of the banyan tree. "Yes, Guru. I will strive to be like this tree, grounded and connected to the wisdom of Ayurveda, allowing it to nourish and shape my journey."

With a gentle nod, she placed her hand on my shoulder. "Remember, Meera, the path you have chosen requires dedication, focus, and self-discipline. It may not always be easy, but it is in difficult times that you will uncover your actual potential."

I felt ready to embrace the rigors of my studies and embark on the path of becoming a Vedic doctor.

As the students gathered in the courtyard, anticipation hung in the air. We exchanged excited whispers, wondering what the day held in store for us. The sun shone brightly overhead, casting a warm glow on our eager faces.

Our guru stood before us. Her voice was filled with enthusiasm as she cleared her throat and addressed the gathering. "Good morning, my dear students. Today, I have a special surprise for you. We will be having a friendly competition, and the prize will be revealed at the end. Are you ready?"

She glanced at each of us, her eyes wide with delight. "Today, my dear students, we will embark on a unique challenge. We are going to create a new kind of oil!"

Maadinee raised her hand, her eyes shining with curiosity. "Guru, what kind of oil are we going to make?"

The guru chuckled softly. "Ah, that is for you to discover! This task will test your knowledge of Ayurvedic herbs and their properties. You will need to combine various ingredients to create an oil that has unique healing qualities. Remember, the key is to find the perfect balance of ingredients."

The opportunity to explore the world of Ayurvedic oils ignited a sense of curiosity within each of us.

Meera spoke up, her voice eager. "Guru, where will we find the ingredients for the oil?"

The guru gestured to the lush surroundings of the courtyard. "Nature will be our guide, my dear. Look around you. The herbs and plants you need are all here, waiting to be discovered. It is your task to seek them out, to connect with the wisdom of the earth."

With renewed determination, we set off in different directions, exploring the courtyard with an attentive gaze. We examined plants, touched leaves, and inhaled fragrances, trying to discern the perfect combination for our unique oil.

As we gathered our chosen ingredients, the guru approached us, her voice gentle and encouraging. "Remember, this task is not just about creating an oil. It is about understanding the healing properties of each ingredient, their interactions, and the intentions behind their use. Let your intuition guide you."

Kamala looked at her chosen herbs, a mixture of excitement and uncertainty on her face. "Guru, what if we make a mistake? What if our oil doesn't turn out as we hoped?"

The guru smiled, "Mistakes are a part of the learning process, my dear. Embrace them, for they can lead to new discoveries. Trust in your knowledge and intuition. Even if the conclusion is not what you expected, the experience will be invaluable."

Eagerly, I wandered through the vibrant courtyard, my senses alive with curiosity. My eyes scanned the array of plants, each one holding its own secret healing properties. I reached out, my fingers gently brushing against the velvety leaves, feeling a connection to the ancient wisdom that resided within them.

As I ventured further, I noticed the other students immersed in their own exploration, their faces a mixture of excitement and determination. I approached Maadinee and Kamala, who were huddled together, engrossed in their search.

"What have you discovered so far?" I inquired, a glimmer of hope in my voice.

Maadinee turned towards me, a mischievous smile dancing on her lips. "We found this herb," she said, holding up a delicate sprig. "It has a soothing aroma and is known for its calming properties."

Kamal nodded in agreement, her eyes sparkling with excitement. "And we also stumbled upon a flower that is said to promote clarity and focus. It could be the perfect addition to our oil."

The courtyard buzzed with a sense of purpose and camaraderie as we exchanged ideas and shared the treasures we had discovered.

Our guru approached us, her presence commanding attention. "Well done, my dear students," she said, her voice filled with encouragement. "You are all on the right track. Remember, the true essence of this competition lies not in winning but in the process of discovering the healing powers of nature."

As the day progressed, I continued my exploration, allowing my intuition to guide me toward the ingredients that resonated with my intentions. I encountered a robust plant with vibrant purple flowers, known for its rejuvenating properties. Nearby, I discovered a delicate herb with a refreshing scent believed to enhance clarity and balance. These discoveries ignited a fire within me, fuelling my determination to craft a blend that would nourish and heal.

With the sun beginning its descent, casting a warm glow over the courtyard, we gathered around our guru once more. She smiled, observing our baskets filled with a diverse array of herbs, flowers, and leaves. "You have all done remarkably well," she commended us. "Now, it is time to distill your ingredients and create your unique oils."

With newfound confidence, we gathered our ingredients and began the process of creating our oils. Conversations filled the air as we shared our thoughts and insights, exchanging tips and advice. Scents of herbs and spices mingled, creating a fragrant tapestry of possibilities.

The guru moved among us, offering guidance and answering our questions. She encouraged us to experiment, to infuse our creations with our own unique intentions and desires for healing.

Excitement coursed through me as I carefully selected the tools and prepared my workspace. With focused intent, I combined the herbs and flowers, grinding and blending them with precision. As the ingredients mingled, their scents intertwined, I sensed harmony and balance being born.

Under the watchful eye of our guru, we worked diligently, channeling our passion into every drop of oil we created. The air filled with fragrant aromas, as if the courtyard itself had transformed into a sanctuary of healing.

Finally, the moment arrived when we presented our oils to the guru. She examined each one with a discerning eye, nodding in approval. "You have all shown great skill and creativity," she praised us. "These oils hold the potential to bring profound healing and balance to those who use them."

A sense of fulfillment washed over me as I held my bottle of oil, infused with the essence of my intentions and the wisdom of the plants.

Meera asked eagerly, "Guru, what will happen to the oils we made?"

The guru smiled, her voice filled with appreciation. "These oils will become a part of our collection, to be used for healing and rituals. Each one carries your intentions and the wisdom you have gathered. They will serve as a reminder of your growth and the power of Ayurveda."

We felt a sense of success and oneness as we stood there, relishing in the accomplishment of our work. The journey of creating the oils brought us closer together, deepening our understanding of Ayurveda and our connection to nature.

We realized at that point that this challenge was about more than just creating a new type of oil. It was about embracing our own creativity, exploring the healing potential within ourselves, and fostering a deep appreciation for the gifts of the earth.

Our guru carefully examined each one, her eyes shining with interest. Finally, she announced, "And the winner of the competition is Meera!"

I couldn't believe my ears. "Thank you, guru! I'm honored," I exclaimed.

The guru smiled warmly. "Congratulations, Meera. Your oil exhibits a perfect balance of ingredients and a deep understanding of Ayurvedic principles. You have demonstrated remarkable skill and creativity."

Kamala and the other students applauded, their faces beaming with happiness for me.

"But remember," the guru continued, "the true prize lies not only in winning the competition but in the knowledge and experience gained along the way."

Maadinee stepped forward, her eyes gleaming with curiosity. "Guru, what is the prize for winning?"

The guru's smile widened. "The prize, my dear students, is the art of making a bonsai tree."

Gasps of surprise filled the courtyard. Bonsai trees were renowned for their ability to embody the beauty and wisdom of nature in a compact and portable form. Ayurvedic practitioners found great value in this art, as it allowed them to bring the healing properties of trees to even the most remote areas.

Excitement rippled through us as we imagined the possibilities of creating our own miniature trees.

"But fear not," the guru reassured us, "for I will teach all of you the art of bonsai tree making. This expertise will not only improve your awareness of the natural world, but it will also help you to harness the therapeutic virtues of trees in a practical and accessible manner."

Kamala's eyes widened with wonder. "Guru, that sounds amazing! I've always been fascinated by bonsai trees."

The guru nodded, her expression filled with encouragement. "I am delighted to hear that, Kamala. We will embark on this journey together, exploring the intricacies of bonsai cultivation and the connection between nature and healing."

The art of bonsai awaited us, promising to unlock new dimensions of understanding and beauty as we continued our exploration of Ayurveda and the profound wisdom it held. We were eager to learn the art of bonsai tree making and delve deeper into our connection with nature. The guru smiled warmly at us.

"Bonsai is not just about creating miniature trees; it is a practice that embodies patience, precision, and a deep respect for nature."

The guru gestured to a collection of young saplings and a variety of tools laid out before us. "First, we must select a suitable sapling. Look for a tree that speaks to your heart and talks to you. Take your time and follow your intuition."

I scanned the assortment of saplings, searching for the one that called out to me. Eventually, my gaze settled upon a slender Ficus tree, its delicate branches reaching toward the sky.

"I have found mine," I exclaimed.

The guru nodded approvingly. "Wonderful, Meera. Now, let us begin. Carefully remove the sapling from its pot, gently untangling its roots. Treat it with the utmost care and respect, for this is a living being."

As we followed the guru's instructions, I marveled at the delicate nature of the tree's roots. It reminded me of the intricate connections within our own lives, the interplay between strength and vulnerability.

"Now, observe the natural shape of the tree," the guru continued. "With your pruning shears, trim the branches and leaves to create a harmonious balance. Remember, bonsai is about capturing the essence of a mature tree in a smaller form."

With focused determination, we carefully shaped our saplings, trimming away excess growth and encouraging the tree to embrace its unique form. The guru moved amongst us, offering guidance and encouragement.

Kamala, her eyes shining with enthusiasm, turned to the guru. "Guru, what else do we need to do?"

The guru smiled, her voice filled with wisdom. "Nurturing your bonsai tree requires patience and care. Pay attention to its watering needs, ensuring it receives just the right amount of water. Provide it with the right balance of sunlight and shade, and feed it with nutrients to promote healthy growth."

As we continued our work, the courtyard filled with the sounds of focused concentration and gentle conversation. We exchanged tips and insights, celebrating each other's progress.

Hours passed, but it felt like moments as we poured our hearts into our bonsai creations. The guru observed our dedication with pride.

"Today, you have embarked on a journey of patience, discipline, and connection with nature," the guru said. "Through the art of bonsai, you will learn to cultivate a deeper understanding of balance, both within yourselves and with the natural world. Let your bonsai tree serve as a reminder of the beauty and resilience that can be found in even the smallest of beings."

As the day drew to a close, we stepped back to admire our miniature masterpieces. The once-unassuming saplings had transformed into exquisite representations of nature's grace.

The guru's voice filled the air one final time. "Remember, my dear students, the art of bonsai is not merely about shaping trees; it is about shaping ourselves. It teaches us lessons about patience, balance, and the harmony between man and nature. Through this art, we will deepen our connection with the healing powers of the earth. As you care for your bonsai trees, let them be a mirror for your own growth and reflection. May they inspire you to nurture your own inner garden, cultivating harmony and beauty in your lives."

As the day came to a close, there was a sense of expectation in the air. The courtyard was abuzz with the energy of our studies, the gentle rustling of leaves accompanying our every move. We were on the brink of wrapping up our lessons when the tranquillity was disrupted by the sound of galloping horses approaching.

Turning our heads, we saw three men on horseback, clad in gleaming armor adorned with the emblem of King Bharata. Their arrival was unexpected, and curiosity filled our gazes as they rode towards us. With a respectful bow, one of the men approached our guru, holding a sealed scroll in his hands.

The guru accepted the scroll and began to read its contents, her expression growing increasingly solemn. The weight of the message seemed to settle upon her, and a hush fell over the courtyard. We, the students, exchanged uncertain glances, our hearts filled with anticipation and concern.

After what felt like an eternity, the guru finished reading the scroll. She turned to face us, her eyes reflecting a mix of seriousness and resolve. Clearing her throat, she addressed us with a firm yet gentle voice.

"My dear students," she began, her tone echoing with a sense of urgency, "we have been summoned by the King. He has requested our presence at the royal palace without delay."

Gasps of surprise and whispers of uncertainty rippled through the group. The gravity of the situation hung in the air, casting a shadow over our hearts. The reasons behind this summons remained a mystery.

The guru continued her words resonating with a sense of duty and responsibility. "We must heed the King's call and embark on this journey to the royal palace. It is our responsibility to serve our country and our people, and this is a chance to share our knowledge and healing skills with those in need."

Despite feeling a surge of excitement at the prospect of engaging with the world beyond our secluded studies, a tinge of apprehension and uncertainty lingered in my heart.

With a renewed sense of purpose, I returned to the guru, who was offering her guidance at this crucial moment. She assured us that our studies had prepared us well, instilling in us the skills and understanding needed to navigate the challenges ahead.

"We must remember the teachings that have been imparted upon us," she said, her voice infused with unwavering conviction. "Our path as healers extends beyond the boundaries of this courtyard. We carry within us the power to bring healing and harmony wherever we go."

As the reality of our imminent departure settled upon us, we gathered our belongings and made the necessary preparations for our journey to the royal palace. The courtyard, once filled with the essence of our studies, was now infused with an air of anticipation and readiness.

Though uncertainty lingered in the depths of our souls, we moved forward with courage, knowing that this journey would test our resolve and offer opportunities for growth. We embarked on this new chapter, united in our purpose and ready to embrace the challenges and possibilities at the royal palace.

Carpets in the Air

It had been two days since we embarked on our journey to the royal palace of King Bharata. The weariness had settled upon us, evident in the drooping shoulders and tired expressions of my fellow students. Sensing our fatigue, the guru decided to make a stop at the next village we encountered.

When we entered the village, a peculiar sight greeted our eyes. The huts stood in silence, devoid of any signs of human presence. It felt as if time had stood still in this abandoned settlement. Curiosity mingled with a sense of unease as we cautiously explored the village, our footsteps echoing through the empty streets.

The guru, ever observant, led the way, her gaze sweeping across the desolate surroundings. She paused; her eyes focused on a particular hut. "Let us rest here for a while."

We followed her lead, finding solace within the walls of the vacant hut. The air held a mysterious stillness, punctuated only by the soft rustling of leaves and distant sounds of nature. We settled ourselves on the floor, seeking respite from the journey that had taken its toll on our bodies and spirits.

The guru's voice broke the quietude. "This village holds a story, my students," she began, her eyes filled with a mixture of melancholy and intrigue. "Once vibrant with life, it now stands deserted, a witness to the receding tide and flow of existence."

The guru continued, her voice resonating with a deep understanding of the world's mysteries. "Sometimes, life takes unexpected turns. Villages, like people, can find themselves abandoned and forgotten, left to stand as remnants of the past. But within the silence lies an opportunity for reflection and meditation."

Her remarks hung in the air, prompting us to reflect on the meaning of this encounter. We thought about the lessons hidden within the stillness of the village, seeking to unravel its secrets and find meaning in our own journey.

As I closed my eyes, the village's mysterious aura enveloped me, and my weary body succumbed to the embrace of sleep.

In my dream, the village came alive with whispers of forgotten tales and faded memories. I wandered through its abandoned streets, each step unearthing fragments of its vibrant past. The village had once been a thriving community filled with laughter, shared stories, and cherished moments. Now, its empty huts stood as silent witnesses to the passage of time.

Awakening from my slumber, I found myself renewed. And our spirits were lifted by the rest and the profound connection we had forged with the village. The guru led us out of the empty huts, guiding us back onto the path that led to the royal palace.

As we bid farewell to the enigmatic village, a sense of gratitude washed over me. I realized that there are lessons to be learned and insights to be obtained, even in the most unexpected locations. Our quest seemed to be about more than just getting to the royal palace; it appeared to be about learning the depths of our own perseverance and the transformational power of the world around us.

Moving away from the deserted village, we resumed our journey with new vigor. The path seemed a little less daunting now, our spirits lifted by the rest we had received and the mysteries we had encountered. The guru led the way, her steps purposeful and sure, guiding us towards the next destination on our path to the royal palace.

As the sun cast its warm glow upon us, we ventured forth, traversing hills and valleys, our anticipation growing with each passing moment. And before long, the next village came into view, its humble dwellings standing as beacons of welcome amidst the vast landscape.

Excitement tinged with curiosity danced within me as we approached the village. The guru's words resonated in my mind, assuring us that she had dear friends awaiting our arrival. The prospect of meeting new traveling companions gave me a sense of connection and companionship.

The huts stood in a neat row, their thatched roofs blending with the surrounding landscape. The air carried a sense of enchantment, whispering of hidden wonders waiting to be discovered.

Intrigued, we approached one of the huts and peered through its open doorway. To our astonishment, we witnessed a sight that defied gravity itself. Inside, a group of youngsters and their teacher sat peacefully on floating carpets suspended in mid-air, as though in tune with the skies.

Gasps of wonder escaped our lips as we watched this extraordinary display. We turned to our guru, whose eyes sparkled with knowing wisdom. Sensing our astonishment, she spoke her voice a gentle melody that harmonized with the ethereal scene before us.

"Behold, my dear students," she began, her words carrying a hint of awe, "this is the practice of levitation, a manifestation of the extraordinary powers that can be harnessed through deep concentration and mastery of the mind."

We listened intently, our minds eager to grasp the secret behind this awe-inspiring phenomenon. The guru explained the principles of harnessing prana, the life force that permeates all living beings. Through rigorous training and disciplined meditation, these children and their teachers cultivated a heightened state of consciousness, allowing them to transcend the bounds of gravity.

"My dear students," the guru's voice resonated with calmness, "today, I want to emphasize the importance of inner stillness. In the midst of the world's turmoil and diversions, it is critical to find moments of stillness, to quiet the fluctuations of the mind, and to connect with the subtle energies that flow through the cosmos."

Her words hung in the air, their weight settling upon us, inviting us to contemplate the depths of our own potential. I listened closely, feeling a stirring inside me, a want to explore the undiscovered realms of my awareness.

"Through the practice of meditation and self-reflection," the guru went on, "we can tap into the limitless wellspring of wisdom and creativity that resides within each of us. It is a self-discovery journey, a process of connecting ourselves with the divine spirit that pervades all of reality."

I looked around at my classmates, who were looking at me with a mixture of wonder and desire in their eyes. We were all captivated by the guru's teachings, yearning to unlock the potential that lay dormant within us.

"The stillness of the mind is not a state of emptiness," the guru elucidated, her voice laced with profound understanding. "It is a doorway to heightened awareness, where we can access our intuition, clarity, and insight. In this state, we can perceive the interconnectedness of all things and tap into the divine intelligence that guides the universe."

Her words painted a vivid picture in my mind, illustrating the immense power that lies within the depths of stillness. I felt a surge of determination, vowing to embrace this practice wholeheartedly and embark on a journey of self-transformation.

"We live in a world filled with distractions and noise, but it is within our power to cultivate moments of inner stillness amidst the chaos. Through dedicated practice, we can awaken our true potential and align ourselves with the harmonious flow of life."

With a sense of reverence, we observed the levitating souls, marveling at their serenity and grace. Their existence served as a source of inspiration, lighting the way ahead of us and encouraging us to delve into the undiscovered depths of our own potential.

A sense of familiarity flooded over me as we went through the village. The air hummed with a sense of community, and the villagers went about their daily tasks with purpose and warmth. The guru's presence seemed to command respect and admiration, her reputation preceding her.

She led us through the winding streets, past vibrant market stalls and lively gatherings, until we reached a humble abode nestled among a grove of flowering trees. As she knocked on the door, she smiled, and it swung open to see a familiar face glowing with excitement.

"Gurumata!" a voice exclaimed, filled with warmth and affection. "It is a delight to see you again and to welcome your students to our humble village."

The guru embraced her friend, their laughter intertwining with the melodies of the village. And as we stood there, witnessing this reunion, a sense of belonging washed over us. We were not mere travelers passing through; we have welcomed guests, embraced by the embrace of friendship and the warmth of community.

The villagers gathered around, eager to meet the newcomers who had journeyed alongside their revered guru. We exchanged introductions and shared stories, the language of friendship bridging the gaps between our worlds.

In the hours that followed, the villagers opened their hearts and homes to us, teaching us their traditions and sharing their wisdom. We immersed ourselves in the rhythms of their daily lives, partaking in their customs and joining them in celebration.

We ventured deeper into the teachings of Ayurveda, studying the craft of herbal medicines and the complexities of healing from the guru's friends. The villagers generously shared their knowledge, passing down ancient wisdom that had been preserved through generations.

Through their guidance, we discovered the potency of nature's bounty, the healing properties hidden within the petals of flowers, the roots of plants, and the herbs that adorned their gardens.

As we bid farewell to the village, gratitude filled my heart. The kindness and hospitality bestowed upon us had left an indelible mark, reminding me of the strength that lies in community and the beauty of forging connections along our journey.

With newfound knowledge and cherished memories, we continued our expedition towards the royal palace, our steps guided by the teachings of Ayurveda and the bonds we had formed. As we ventured forth, the echoes of laughter and the whispers of friendship lingered, weaving a tapestry of resilience and togetherness that would accompany us on our path to King Bharata's grand court.

After a long and challenging journey, we finally arrived at the grand city that housed the majestic palace of King Bharata. The lively streets were packed with people from all walks of life.

The air buzzed with an undertone of excitement and expectation as we made our way through the lively metropolis. The streets were festooned with bright banners and music and laughter filled the air.

The news of our arrival seemed to have spread across the city.

The aroma of freshly baked bread and fragrant spices wafted through the alleys, enticing our senses and stirring a hunger within us. The city was a tapestry of vibrant colors and bustling activity.

My heart pounded with fear and excitement with each step.

We were about to enter the domain of the monarch, where our abilities and wisdom would be tested.

It was a significant occasion, and I couldn't help but feel a rush of pride and resolve pouring through my veins.

Just as we approached the grand palace gates, guarded by stern-looking soldiers, my breath caught in my throat. The enormity of the moment sank in, and I realized that our lives were about to intersect with the destiny of the kingdom.

The palace itself stood as a testament to opulence and grandeur. Its towering walls were adorned with intricate carvings and shimmering mosaics, reflecting the rich history and culture of the land. It was a place where power and elegance intertwined, a beacon of authority and wisdom.

Inside the palace, we were led through corridors adorned with tapestries depicting legendary battles and portraits of the noble ancestors of King Bharata. The air was thick with anticipation, the silence broken only by the soft echo of our footsteps.

We were finally led into the main hall, where the King himself awaited our arrival. King Bharata, ornated in regal attire, sat upon a magnificent throne. His presence commanded respect and awe, and we bowed before him, our hearts pounding in our chests.

The king's face bore the weight of concern, his eyes reflecting the worry he carried for his ailing son. The guru, with her serene presence, listened attentively as the king poured out his heart.

"Great guru," the king began, his voice tinged with both desperation and hope, "my infant son has been plagued by incessant crying day and night. We have tried various remedies, but nothing seems to ease his suffering. I beseech you, please, find a way to bring him relief."

The guru's gaze met the king's, a silent understanding passing between them. She nodded in acknowledgment, her voice calm yet resolute. "Your Majesty, I understand the anguish you feel as a father. I will allow my students to attempt to find a remedy for your son's ailment."

With the king's permission granted, the guru turned to us, her voice carrying a gentle yet firm command. "Students, the task before us is of utmost importance. We must delve deep into our knowledge and tap into the wisdom we have acquired. Seek within yourselves and bring forth any remedies or techniques that may alleviate the suffering of the young prince."

We knew that we held the potential to make a difference, to bring comfort to the young prince, and to bring peace to the king's heart. Each of us set out with fervor, scouring our minds for any possible solution.

Minutes turned into hours as we tirelessly experimented with different remedies and techniques. We tested herbal concoctions, conducted gentle massages, and even tried the power of song and soothing melodies. Yet, despite our best efforts, the young prince's cries persisted, his tiny frame wracked with discomfort.

The guru observed our attempts with a discerning eye, her wisdom guiding her every decision. She allowed us to explore and learn from our failures, understanding that growth often arises from challenges. Her presence provided a sense of encouragement in the trials we faced.

But as I silently observed the attempts of my fellow students to bring relief to the ailing prince, an idea sparked within me. I quickly gathered some mint leaves and ground them into a paste.

I approached the crib where the infant prince lay, his cries piercing the air. With gentle hands, I applied the mint paste to the baby's tiny tummy, hoping it would bring him some comfort. Then I closed my eyes; I let my hands hover over the child's body as if channeling the forces of nature itself.

To my astonishment, the effect was immediate. The baby's screams died away, and he was replaced by a sensation of calmness. The room fell silent, and all eyes turned to the Guru, who watched me in wonder.

"My king," the guru began, her voice soft yet resolute, "your son's affliction stemmed from an imbalance of his doshas. Through the application of Ayurvedic principles and the restoration of harmony within his body, my student, Meera, helped ease his suffering."

The king approached me, gratitude shining in his eyes. "Young lady, you have performed a miracle," he exclaimed. "Your remedy has brought solace to my precious son. You possess great talent and potential. I must offer you a position in my palace as one of my esteemed doctors."

My stomach growled. I looked around; the gold ceiling and wooden artifacts stared back at me with prestige. A great feeling of obligation, though, tugged at my heart, reminding me of my ultimate role.

With a respectful bow, I responded to the king, my voice filled with resolve. "Your Majesty, I am honored by your offer, and I deeply appreciate your kind words. However, my path lies elsewhere. I have made a commitment to my village to be a village doctor. It is there where my heart belongs and where I can have a long-term influence on my people's lives."

The king's expression softened, understanding evident in his gaze. "I admire your dedication and sense of duty. May your journey as a village doctor bring you great success and fulfillment. You have my utmost support."

As the king expressed his admiration for my remedy, a smile graced his regal face. He reached into his robe and retrieved a beautifully crafted brass lamp, its intricate design gleaming in the light.

"Meera, your skills and dedication have brought immense relief to my son and joy to my kingdom," the king said, his voice filled with gratitude. "Accept this humble gift as a token of my appreciation. May it serve as a reminder of your remarkable abilities and the impact you have made on our lives."

I accepted the brass lamp with respect, its weight a symbol of the trust and gratitude bestowed upon me. "Thank you, Your Majesty," I said, my voice full of gratitude. "I am honored to have been of service, and I will cherish this gift as a precious reminder of our encounter and the healing power of Ayurveda."

The king's gaze held a mix of admiration and understanding. "Meera, though you have chosen to follow your calling as a village doctor, know that you will always be welcomed in my palace," he said, "Should you ever seek new avenues or find yourself in need of support, do not hesitate to reach out. Your talent is extraordinary, and I believe it has the potential to touch countless lives."

I bowed respectfully, deeply moved by the king's words. "Your kindness and generosity touch my heart, Your Majesty," I expressed, my voice filled with gratitude. "I will always value your offer, and I am humbled to know that I have your support. My focus, for now, remains on serving my village and embodying the teachings of Ayurveda."

After bidding farewell to the king, there was a sense of fulfillment and gratitude that filled the air. The guru's eyes locked with mine, her gaze filled with a mixture of pride and wisdom. She approached me in a gentle whisper, yet filled with significance.

"Meera, our connection has grown stronger than I had ever imagined," the guru said, her words carrying a weight of profound realization. "It seems that the knowledge I acquired in my lifetime has begun to flow through you, guiding your path."

I looked at the guru, a blend of amazement and humility in my eyes. Her guidance and teachings had transformed me, shaping me into the healer I aspired to be. I bowed my head in respect, grateful for the knowledge she had bestowed upon me.

"Guru, I am forever indebted to your teachings and guidance," I replied, my voice filled with sincerity. "Your wisdom has illuminated my path and awakened a passion within me to serve others."

As she laid a hand on my shoulder, the guru's eyes twinkled with pride. "Meera, you have embraced the healing arts with dedication and compassion," she began. "Remember, the journey of learning never ends. Carry the flame of knowledge within you and continue to seek wisdom from every experience."

Kamala, who had been listening intently, spoke up with a smile. "Meera, you have truly become my inspiration of light and healing," she said, her voice brimming with pride. "Your talent and dedication are an inspiration to us all."

I turned towards Kamala; my heart warmed by her words. I thanked her.

And in that moment, all the enmity that I felt towards Kamala melted away.

As we exited the majestic palace, the kids flocked around me, their faces lit up with adoration and joy. Applause and cheers filled the air, celebrating the successful healing of the king's son. Amongst the joyful commotion, Maadinee's eyes sparkled with genuine happiness.

"Oh, Meera! I'm so proud of you! You truly have a gift," Maadinee exclaimed, her voice filled with excitement. She hugged me tightly, sharing in the joy of the moment. "You've amazed us all with your skills. But tell me, what will you do with the brass lamp? It's such a precious gift."

I felt its cool surface beneath my fingertips. Its intricate carvings and radiant glow were mesmerizing. I glanced at Maadinee, a mixture of gratitude and determination in my eyes.

"I will keep this lamp in my humble clinic, where I treat and heal the villagers," I explained, a soft smile forming on my lips. "Its presence will remind me of the sacred duty I have undertaken, to bring light and healing to those in need. Whenever I see its glow, I will be inspired to continue my journey as a village doctor, serving our community with compassion and dedication."

Maadinee's eyes shimmered with understanding and support. "Meera, I have no doubt that it will be a place of hope and transformation," she added confidently. "Your talent and the lamp's presence will guide you to touch countless lives and bring healing to those who seek it."

Yoga Nidra

As we returned to the comforting familiarity of our guru's ashram, exhaustion washed over me, my body yearning for rest. However, there was no time to dwell on weariness, for our guru had something important to teach us.

The guru's eyes sparkled with a blend of warmth and wisdom as she began to speak. "My dear students, you have journeyed far and wide, collecting a treasure trove of plants and herbs along the way. These natural gifts hold immense healing properties, but they must be preserved with care to retain their potency."

Curiosity danced in the air as the students exchanged glances.

"To honor the gifts bestowed upon us by Mother Nature, we must learn how to preserve these herbs properly. This will ensure their longevity and effectiveness in healing."

I listened intently, eager to learn the intricacies of herb preservation.

"The first step in preserving herbs is to harvest them at the right time," the guru explained. "Each herb has its own unique cycle and peak potency. By observing the natural rhythms and signs, we can ensure that we harvest the herbs at their optimal stage."

As the guru spoke, I found myself visualizing the lush fields and serene forests that had been our classrooms during our journey. I recalled the moments when we carefully plucked leaves, collected roots, and gathered petals, guided by the guru's wisdom.

"Once the herbs are harvested, it is crucial to handle them with utmost care," the guru continued, her voice gentle yet authoritative. "Avoid bruising or damaging the delicate parts of the plant. Treat them as if they are sacred vessels, for they hold the essence of healing within."

Her words resonated deeply within me, reminding me of the reverence we had shown toward every plant we encountered.

"The next step is drying the herbs," the guru instructed, her voice carrying a wealth of practical knowledge. "Proper drying techniques will help preserve the herbs' medicinal properties. Each herb requires a specific approach, taking into account factors such as temperature, air circulation, and duration."

As the guru shared her insights, I imagined the drying racks made of dried leaves and open-air spaces we had utilized during our journey, carefully arranging the herbs to ensure optimal drying conditions. It had been a meticulous process, but one that was essential in maintaining the herbs' vitality.

"Lastly, once the herbs are dried, they should be stored in sealed pots, ensuring that no air passes through." the guru concluded, her voice filled with conviction. "This will protect them from moisture, light, and air, preserving their potency for extended periods."

The students nodded in unison. The guru's teachings had expanded our horizons, unveiling the intricate tapestry of nature's gifts.

After receiving the guru's instructions on herb preservation, we, the students, dedicated ourselves to the task at hand. With a newfound sense of purpose, we immersed ourselves in the art of preserving the precious herbs and plants we had collected during our journey. The ashram buzzed with focused energy as we meticulously carried out each step.

As the sun rose higher in the sky, casting its warm glow upon us.

I carefully handled the herbs, paying close attention to the guru's teachings. It was a delicate process, requiring patience and precision. The air was filled with the earthy scent of dried leaves and the gentle rustling of cloth as we prepared the herbs for storage.

Kamala, standing beside me, glanced over and smiled. "Meera, do you remember when we first embarked on this journey? We were like seeds, eager to learn and grow. And now, look how far we've come!"

I nodded, a sense of accomplishment swelling within me. "Yes, Kamala, it's incredible how much we've learned and experienced. Our guru has truly guided us on a transformative path."

As we worked diligently, the guru moved among us, offering guidance and encouragement.

"Remember, my dear students," the guru said, her voice carrying a soothing melody, "the preservation of these herbs is not just a technical process. It is an act of reverence and gratitude towards nature's gifts. By carefully preserving them, we ensure their potency and harness their healing energies."

Each herb and plant held within it the essence of nature's wisdom, waiting to be unlocked and shared for the aid of all. We approached our work with a sense of devotion, honoring the interconnectedness between ourselves, the plants, and the world around us.

As the day progressed, the ashram transformed into a sanctuary of preservation. Drying racks were filled with carefully arranged herbs, labeled, and organized with precision. Aromas of drying leaves and fragrant flowers filled the air, infusing the space with their natural essences.

I glanced around, observing my fellow students engrossed in their tasks. Each of us brought our unique skills and insights to the process, contributing to the collective effort. It was a testament to the bond we had formed, a tapestry woven by shared experiences and the guidance of our guru.

Hours passed by in a gentle rhythm as we meticulously completed the preservation process. The fruits of our labor began to take shape—a treasure trove of preserved herbs, ready to be utilized in future healing endeavors. It was a tangible representation of our dedication and the wisdom we had gained.

As the sun reached its zenith, casting a warm glow upon the ashram, the guru gathered us, her students, in a circle. With anticipation in our hearts, we formed a tight circle around our beloved guru, ready to embark on another enlightening lesson. The sun's rays gently caressed our faces, infusing the air with a sense of serene energy.

"My dear students, while we wait for our herbs to dry, let us delve into the ancient wisdom of brewing a potion for longevity," she began, her voice filled with wisdom and grace.

We listened intently, our hearts open to receive the teachings that were about to unfold.

The guru spoke, her voice gentle yet commanding, "Longevity is not merely about the number of years we live but the quality of life we experience. Today, I will tell you the secrets of a potion passed down through generations—a potion thought to increase vitality and well-being."

Kamalale leaned closer to me and whispered, "Imagine the possibilities, Meera. A potion that can enhance our vitality and help us live life to the fullest!"

I nodded, equally captivated by the prospect of unlocking the elixir of longevity.

"The key to brewing this potion lies in the careful selection and combination of medicinal herbs and plants," the guru continued. "Each ingredient holds its own unique healing properties, and when harmoniously blended together, they create a potent elixir of life."

She gestured towards the vibrant array of herbs and plants that adorned the table before us. "Take a moment to observe these gifts from nature," she encouraged, her eyes gleaming with reverence. "Each leaf, each root, carries the wisdom of the earth within it. By connecting with these sacred elements, we tap into the deep well of healing that resides within ourselves."

With great care, the guru guided us through the process, explaining each step in intricate detail. She emphasized the importance of selecting the finest herbs and ingredients, for their purity and potency were crucial in harnessing their life-enhancing properties.

"This potion," the guru explained, "is a harmonious blend of nature's gifts, carefully chosen for their rejuvenating qualities."

We listened intently, absorbing the guru's words like sponges, eager to embark on this alchemical journey.

As I examined the vibrant hues and diverse textures before me, a sense of reverence washed over me—each ingredient held within it the essence of life, a gift from the earth itself. I marveled at the intricate web of interconnectedness, the profound wisdom encoded within these seemingly humble elements.

One by one, the guru instructed us on how to prepare and combine the ingredients. Her voice was a guiding melody, leading us through the delicate dance of measurement and proportion. With each action, she explained the significance of the herb, root, or flower we were handling, unveiling its unique contribution to the potion's transformative qualities.

Her voice resonated with warmth and love as she emphasized the significance of intention and mindfulness. "As you engage in the act of brewing this potion, infuse it with your deepest intentions for health, vitality, and longevity," she advised. "Allow your thoughts and energy to merge with the herbs, infusing them with your desires and aspirations. This sacred union of intention and nature's gifts will amplify the potency of the potion."

With hands-on guidance from our guru, we carefully measured and combined the herbs, their fragrances mingling harmoniously, creating a symphony of aromas. We stirred the mixture with reverence and gratitude, infusing it with our intentions and blessings.

As the brewing process unfolded, the air filled with the fragrant symphony of herbs mingling with the gentle simmering of the potion.

Finally, as the potion reached its desired consistency and aroma, the guru gestured for us to gather around. With a sense of reverence, she held a glass vial filled with the elixir in her hands, its radiant golden hue shimmering in the sunlight.

"My dear students," the guru's voice resonated with pride, "this potion represents the culmination of your dedication and the wisdom you have embraced throughout your journey. It demonstrates your connection to nature's healing abilities and your dedication to self-care."

Kamala, her eyes shining with gratitude, turned to me and whispered, "Meera, can you imagine the impact we can have on others' lives with this potion? We can spread the gift of vitality far and wide."

I nodded, a surge of purpose coursing through me. "Yes, Kamala, let us carry this knowledge with humility and compassion, using it to uplift and empower those who cross our paths."

The guru's presence enveloped us like a warm embrace as she observed our diligent efforts. "Remember, my dear students, the power lies not only in the physical act of brewing but also in the love and intention that you infuse into every step," she reminded us, her voice resonating with gentle authority. "As you sip this elixir, allow its healing energy to permeate every cell of your being, nourishing your body, mind, and spirit."

With our hearts overflowing with gratitude, we held our cups, brimming with the potion of longevity, ready to partake in this sacred ritual. The air buzzed with anticipation as we shared our intentions and blessings, collectively channeling our energy into the elixir.

As the potion touched our lips, a wave of warmth and vitality washed over us, filling us with a deep sense of rejuvenation. In that moment, we felt connected to the ancient wisdom of Ayurveda, the healing power of nature, and the transformative guidance of our guru.

With a final word of guidance and blessing, the guru entrusted each of us with a vial of the potion. We held it close to our hearts. Within its precious contents lay the potential for transformation and well-being.

As the sun started to set, casting a warm golden hue over the ashram, the guru approached us once again. Her eyes gleamed with pride and satisfaction. "My dear students, today you have embraced the art of herb preservation with diligence and care. Your efforts have borne fruit, and these preserved herbs will serve as potent allies in your future endeavors as healers."

We gathered around her, the sense of accomplishment palpable in the air. The guru continued, "But remember, preserving herbs is not just about technique. It is about cultivating an understanding and deep connection with the natural world. As you embark on your path as healers, carry this reverence and gratitude in your hearts."

As twilight enveloped the ashram, we stood together, a united group of students, guardians of nature's healing treasures. The day's labor brought us closer, deepening our bond and reinforcing our commitment to the path of Ayurveda.

With the preserved herbs safely stored and the guru's teachings imprinted in our hearts, we retired to our quarters.

Back in the common room, I retreated to my familiar corner. As I carefully unpacked my belongings, I took a moment to examine the gift I had received from King Bharata. The lamp, crafted from bronze, gleamed softly in the flickering candlelight. Its lovely design captured me, and I couldn't help but think about how happy it would have made my mother.

Running my fingers along its smooth surface, I noticed the intricate details that adorned the lamp. A handle, perfectly shaped to fit a finger, adorned one side, while a crescent-shaped opening above it provided a resting place for the thumb.

A wave of emotions poured over me as I held the lamp in my hands. Memories of my mother, her nurturing presence, and her love for beautiful objects flooded my mind. I could almost hear her voice, her words of wisdom and encouragement echoing through the chambers of my heart.

I felt a solid connection to my roots, to the community that had created me, and to the voyage that lay ahead as I gazed at the lamp.

I knew that my mother would have cherished this lamp, treasuring it as a symbol of light, guidance, and warmth. In her absence, it became a precious memento, a tangible reminder of her love and the legacy she had left behind.

Soon, we settled into our beds, fatigue tugging at our weary bodies, and the familiar presence of our guru graced the room. Her gentle voice filled the air, laden with the promise of tranquillity and rest.

"My dear students," she began, her words weaving a soothing tapestry around us, "tonight, I shall introduce you to the practice of Yoga Nidra, a powerful technique to guide you into a deep state of relaxation and restful sleep."

Curiosity sparkled in our eyes as we eagerly listened, yearning for a peaceful night's sleep after the day's exertions. The guru shared the benefits of Yoga Nidra, explaining how it can alleviate stress and promote emotional balance.

"Yoga Nidra," she continued, "is a practice of conscious sleep, where you enter a state between wakefulness and slumber. It is a journey into the depths of your subconscious mind, a sanctuary of healing and rejuvenation."

She guided us to lie comfortably on our beds, ensuring our bodies were at ease. With a soothing tone, she instructed us to close our eyes and begin deep, mindful breathing, allowing the breath to draw us into a state of deep relaxation.

"As we embark on this journey," she softly spoke, "I will lead you through a series of guided visualizations and body awareness exercises. You will explore sensations, emotions, and imagery, gently releasing any tension or worries that may linger within."

As we followed her gentle instructions, we sank into a state of blissful surrender, the cares of the day melting away. The guru skilfully guided us through a landscape of tranquillity, inviting us to envision serene natural surroundings, soothing sounds, and feelings of profound peace.

She encouraged us to witness our thoughts without judgment, acknowledging them and then letting them drift away like clouds passing across the sky. In this state of deep relaxation, our minds became still, allowing us to enter a space of pure presence and tranquillity.

Time seemed to dissolve as we traversed the ethereal realms of our consciousness, surrendering to the soothing currents of the practice. The guru's voice gently guided us back to our physical bodies, inviting us to awaken and reorient ourselves to the present moment slowly.

A sensation of calmness came over us as we opened our eyes, our bodies, and minds cocooned in a blanket of peace. The guru's smile mirrored our own, her presence radiating comfort and reassurance.

"Remember," she whispered, her voice filled with warmth, "you hold the power to find solace within, to access the depths of relaxation and rejuvenation. Embrace the practice of Yoga Nidra as a sanctuary of self-care, allowing it to nourish your body, mind, and spirit."

With a heart full of gratitude, I drifted into a peaceful slumber.

Lost in the depths of slumber, my mind immersed in darkness. I suddenly heard a man's voice calling out to me, softly whispering my name, "Meera...".

Yet, to my surprise, it wasn't Jagha's voice.

What Do You Choose

I felt a flash of frustration in the depths of my dream as the words refused to escape my lips. I desperately yearned to voice my thoughts, to express the confusion that swirled within me. The man's voice persisted, piercing through the veil of my subconscious.

"Meera, does she know about your intentions?" the voice inquired, its tone laced with curiosity and concern.

Jagha's response, barely audible, reached my ears like a fragile whisper. "No Guru, but I believe she will support my decisions. After all, her parents attained moksha. She will understand my desire to seek enlightenment as well."

Shock coursed through my veins, freezing me in place within the confines of my dream. I longed to move, to break free from the invisible restraints that held me captive, but my limbs remained unyielding.

The voice of Jagha's guru interjected, its authority resonating with wisdom. "Very well, but remember, my disciple, that the path to moksha is intertwined with the sacred bond of marriage."

"Yes, guru, we are destined to be wed as soon as she returns to Karmana."

A flicker of doubt seemed to dance within the guru's response. "Are you absolutely certain that you will not waver from this path, Jagha?"

Jagha's voice, brimming with unwavering resolve, echoed in my ears. "Of course not, guru. My heart is steadfast in its purpose."

Within the confines of my dream, emotions churned within me like a tempest, threatening to consume me. I wanted to scream, to unleash the torrent of emotions that surged within my chest. But the invisible chains rendered me powerless.

As my mind broke free from the dream's grip, I found myself drenched in sweat and gasping. The weight of the revelation lingered, casting a shadow of uncertainty over my heart. I yearned for the opportunity to confront Jagha and discover the truth that lay buried within his intentions.

With a heavy heart and a turmoil of emotions swirling within me, I fought to maintain composure in the presence of my dear friend, Maadinee. As we gathered under the soothing canopy of the banyan tree, the sweet aroma of ripe berries and succulent fruits wafted through the air, temporarily distracting me from the weight of my thoughts.

Maadinee's perceptive gaze locked onto my troubled expression, "Are you okay, Meera?"

A tight smile danced upon my lips as I replied, my voice laced with weariness, "Yes, of course. Just a little tired from our journey."

Maadinee's brows furrowed in disbelief, her eyes brimming with compassion. She reached out to gently touch my hand.

"Meera, I know something is bothering you. Please do not be shy about sharing. We're here for each other."

I swallowed the lump that had formed in my throat, grappling with the conflicting desire to confide in Maadinee and the fear of exposing the vulnerability that plagued my heart. But I couldn't deny the comfort that her presence provided, the solace from knowing I didn't have to face my inner turmoil alone.

"Maadinee, there's something I need to tell you... something I discovered in a dream." I paused, gathering the courage to lay bare the truth that had shaken the foundation of my being. "Jagha... he spoke of our future, our plans for marriage, and his pursuit of moksha. It took me by surprise, Maadinee."

Maadinee's eyes widened in disbelief, her grip on my hand tightening in support. "Meera, this is... unexpected. What are you going to do?"

I sighed, my voice trembled. "I don't know, Maadinee. I thought our connection was deep and that our journey together held a different purpose. But now... I feel lost."

Her eyes softened. She offered me some comforting words, which dispersed into the air.

The tranquillity of our breakfast was shattered as a sudden commotion erupted in the courtyard. Startled, I turned towards the entrance, where a group of men burst in, their faces etched with worry and carrying an unconscious woman in their arms.

Their urgent voices pierced the air, their words laced with desperation. "Where is Gurumata?" one of them exclaimed, his voice tinged with anxiety. "Yes, where is she? This is an emergency," another man urgently shouted, his eyes scanning the area in search of our revered guru.

Panic gripped my heart as the realization dawned upon us that our guru was nowhere to be found. A sense of unease settled over the group of students, a collective concern that mirrored the gravity of the situation before us. We frantically scanned the ashram, our eyes darting from one corner to another, hoping to catch a glimpse of our guru's reassuring presence.

But she was nowhere to be seen, leaving us with an uneasy feeling. The weight of responsibility hung heavily in the air as we exchanged worried glances, our minds racing with questions and fears. Where could she be? What had happened to the woman in need of her guidance?

As the seconds ticked by, our desperation grew. We realized we had to act quickly since time was running out. I stepped forward, "we will find her. Let us search the ashram and the surrounding areas. She may have stepped away briefly."

The men nodded in agreement, their gratitude evident in their eyes. Together, we divided into groups, combing through every nook and cranny of the ashram, calling out for our guru, hoping for a response that would ease our mounting fears. But the silence persisted, unyielding in its grip.

The minutes turned into an agonizing eternity as we scoured the grounds, leaving no stone unturned in our quest to locate Gurumata.

But the search yielded no results. Taking matters into my own hands, I moved closer to the unconscious woman who was nudged between the two men. I noticed a swollen belly, a telltale sign of a full-term pregnancy. Determined to help in any way I could, I mustered the courage to engage one of the men who seemed to be guarding her.

"Please tell me what happened," I said.

The man turned his gaze towards me, his eyes clouded with weariness and a touch of annoyance. "Who are you to ask? You're just a child," he retorted dismissively. "We came here seeking Gurumata's help. Only she possesses the power to provide the assistance we need."

His words struck a nerve. My voice rose with conviction as I firmly asserted, "I am not a child. I am a woman fully capable and in tune with the cycles of life. I bleed every moon just like any other woman."

The men exchanged surprised glances, their expressions softening as they began to see me in a different light.

"Now," I said. "Tell me what happened."

"This is my wife," the taller man explained, his voice filled with worry and exhaustion. "She suddenly fell unconscious."

Curiosity piqued, I couldn't help but ask, "Why didn't you take her to your village doctor?"

The other man sighed, his expression revealing a mixture of resignation and despair. "We don't have a village doctor," he replied. "We have been searching for remedies for someone who can ease her suffering."

A surge of compassion welled up within me as I absorbed their words. I closed my eyes briefly, seeking guidance from within, hoping that the wisdom imparted by my guru would illuminate the path ahead.

Opening my eyes, I turned to my fellow students, their faces reflecting a blend of curiosity and anticipation. Taking a deep breath, I addressed them with a newfound confidence.

"We have been blessed with knowledge and skills," I began, my voice steady and resolute. "Our guru has taught us the healing arts, and it is our duty to extend our knowledge to those in need."

"We are in a challenging situation," I acknowledged, my voice filled with empathy. "This woman is in need of our help, and though our guru is not present, we cannot turn a blind eye."

"Tell us what to do, Meera," Maadinee urged, her voice brimming with determination. "We're here to help in any way we can. All of us."

Her words echoed through the courtyard, and I could see the unwavering commitment reflected in the eyes of my fellow students.

With gratitude for their support, I began to lay out a plan. "First, let us carefully bring her inside," I suggested, gesturing toward one of the nearby huts. "We need to ensure she is in a safe and comfortable environment."

With utmost care, we laid her down on a soft mat, making her as comfortable as possible.

As the other students arranged for water and clean clothes, I turned to the two men who had brought her to us. "Do you have any ideas about what might have caused this?" I inquired, trying to learn more about her condition and how I might help her.

The taller man's brows furrowed, his expression etched with concern. "She has been experiencing severe abdominal pain," he replied, his voice tinged with worry. "It became unbearable, causing her to lose consciousness."

I nodded, absorbing the details.

With a collective sense of purpose, we began our collaborative efforts. Some students prepared warm herbal compresses to ease her discomfort, while others brewed soothing infusions to help calm her.

I couldn't help but feel a feeling of obligation and sympathy for the woman as she lay there, her face placid and peaceful. Each of us approached our task with dedication, drawing upon the knowledge imparted by our guru and the intuitive guidance within our hearts.

Hours passed as we attended to her needs, tending to her with tenderness and unwavering focus. As the evening sun began casting a golden glow across the ashram, a flicker of consciousness returned to the woman. Her eyelids wavered, and her eyes slowly opened.

The two men, her husband, and another relative watched with bated breath, their faces etched with hope and anticipation. It was a moment of profound significance, a turning point in her journey towards recovery.

With gentle words of reassurance, I approached the woman's side. "You are safe," I whispered, my voice carrying a soothing tone. "We are here to help you."

Her eyes met mine, a mix of confusion and gratitude reflecting within them. I offered her a smile, hoping to convey the warmth and compassion that enveloped the space around her. Slowly, a flicker of recognition ignited in her gaze.

The husband, unable to contain his relief any longer, stepped forward. "Thank you," he uttered, his voice choked with emotion. "You have given us hope in our darkest hour."

I nodded, feeling deeply grateful for the opportunity to make a difference in their lives.

"We are here to help," I said, my voice full of sincerity.

But just as when we felt some relief, the woman immediately began to scream, clutching her belly. Her agonizing screams reverberated through the dark night. Panic seized us all. The students swarmed around her, their voices desperation-filled as they tried to console her, but their attempts appeared fruitless in the face of her terrible anguish.

I collected the strength to approach her with a sad heart, knowing that I had to do something to help her. I placed my hands gently on her swollen belly, closing my eyes to tune into the profound stillness within.

As I connected with the depths of her womb, a wave of emotions washed over me. I could sense the distress of the unborn child, its cries echoing within the sacred space.

"There is no hope." A despairing voice echoed in my mind.

But the voice was not in my head. It was our guru who had appeared in the hut with us. She turned to the men and said, "The child is in distress. And the labor process is not

What Do You Choose

progressing as it should. This is a desperate time to make an important decision."

The men held hands, their faces furrowed with fear and anxiety. The husband, his voice trembling, looked at Gurumata and asked, "What can be done? Is there any hope for my wife?"

Gurumata's expression softened, filled with compassion as she replied, "I'm afraid that your wife's life is in danger. The only way to rescue your child is to cut it out of her womb. However, I must say that this is a dangerous treatment, and the mother might not survive the procedure."

Torn between his love for his wife and the frantic need to rescue their unborn kid, tears flowed down the man's face as he clutched his wife's unconscious body. The weight of the decision hung heavy in the air, each passing moment heightening the urgency.

Gurumata placed a gentle hand on the man's shoulder, offering solace amidst the turmoil. "I know this is a difficult decision to make, but time is of the essence. The longer we wait, the more dangerous our unborn kid will be. You must decide now."

The man's eyes searched mine, his gaze filled with anguish. I felt the weight of duty crushing down on me at the time.

I took a deep breath and took a step closer, laying my hand on the man's shaking arm. "I understand the magnitude of this decision, and I cannot pretend to fully comprehend the depth of your emotions. If it were my own child, though, I would prefer to give them their chance at life."

The man's tear-stained face reflected a mix of gratitude and agony. He turned to his wife; his voice choked with emotion. "I have to save our child. Please, do whatever is necessary."

Gurumata nodded, her eyes filled with compassion as she addressed the men. "I will gather the necessary supplies and prepare for the procedure."

As the men embraced, finding solace and support in one another, Gurumata and I swiftly organized our makeshift operating room. We gathered clean cloths, boiled water, and sterilized our meager tools to the best of our abilities.

Gurumata stood at the center of the gathering, her face a mask of focused determination. She turned to one of the students and asked, "Bring me the herbs that we dried today."

The student hurriedly fetched the carefully preserved herbs, placing them in Gurumata's outstretched hand. With utmost precision, Gurumata began to combine the herbs, carefully measuring and grinding them together, creating a potent concoction designed to induce deep sleep.

Once the mixture was prepared, Gurumata approached the unconscious woman, her eyes filled with both concern and purpose. "It is time," she whispered, her voice barely audible.

As Gurumata prepared for the delicate surgery, a sense of unease settled over the hut. Her hands moved with unwavering precision, her eyes focused on the task at hand. She carefully made an incision, guided by her vast knowledge and intuitive understanding of the human body. The repetitive sound of her motions resonated around the room as the place grew silent.

Overwhelmed by the severity of the situation, several of the pupils panicked and fled the room, seeking refuge outside the hut's walls. Yet, there were a few of us who remained steadfast in our commitment to support Gurumata and witnessed this extraordinary act of healing.

With each passing second, our emotions were filled with a mixture of hope and dread, fearful of the dangers that lay ahead.

Finally, the moment arrived. The hut was transformed into a sacred space, filled with a palpable energy of determination and love. Gurumata began the delicate procedure, guided by her years of experience and the deep well of knowledge she possessed.

As Gurumata gently eased the child out of the mother's womb, a collective breath was held. The room seemed to exhale as we heard the faint cry of the newborn, a testament to the resilience of life and the triumph over adversity. Tears welled up in our eyes, a mingling of relief and joy.

Gurumata turned to us, her eyes shining with a mixture of exhaustion and profound satisfaction. "We have done it," she said softly. "We have brought a new life into this world, a life once on the verge of death.

Tears streamed down our faces as we welcomed the arrival of the precious child, cradling them in our gentle hands. We knew at that moment that a new chapter had begun, one full of hope, healing, and the endless possibilities that life had to offer.

Gurumata turned to the men, her voice filled with both relief and gratitude. "You have made a difficult choice, one that required immense courage and selflessness. Your child is now in your arms, a sign of the love and sacrifice that brought them here."

The man's eyes shimmered with tears of joy as he embraced his newborn child, whispering words of love and gratitude. In that embrace, I witnessed the profound beauty that can emerge from the most challenging circumstances, the resilience of the human spirit, and the boundless capacity for love.

Gurumata approached the dying woman with a sense of purpose. The room became silent, each of us holding our breath. Gurumata's eyes closed as she extended her bloodstained arms towards the woman, a sacred ritual unfolding before our eyes.

As Gurumata channeled her energy, a profound stillness settled over the hut. I could feel the weight of the woman's departing soul lingering in the air as if searching for a final resting place. With each passing moment, Gurumata's presence grew more radiant, her connection to the spiritual realm palpable.

In that sacred space, the essence of the woman's soul began to separate from her physical body, and Gurumata deftly captured it, encapsulating it within an inanimate object. I watched in awe as she chose the woman's own jewelry, a bracelet adorned with a green stone tied with a black thread. It seemed to possess an inherent significance, chosen to house the essence of life on the brink of departure.

Once the ritual was complete, Gurumata gently removed the bracelet, cradling it in her hands. The woman's body lay peacefully, the physical vessel now devoid of the soul that once animated it. Gurumata turned to the husband, her eyes mellow.

"This bracelet now carries the essence of your beloved," Gurumata said softly, her voice carrying the weight of centuries of wisdom. "Though her physical form has passed, her energy lives on within this object. Keep it close to your heart, and her love and presence will always be with you and your child."

The husband, his eyes filled with gratitude and grief, extended his trembling hand to accept the bracelet. He clutched it tightly as if embracing a part of his departed wife that transcended the boundaries of time and space. A bittersweet smile graced his lips, knowing that he had been gifted a tangible connection to the one he loved.

Gurumata turned to us, her students, her gaze encompassing each of us. "Life is a delicate balance between the tangible and the intangible, the seen and the unseen," she spoke with a voice that seemed to carry ancient echoes. "In our journey as healers, we must remember that our duty extends beyond the physical realm. We hold the sacred responsibility of preserving not only the body but also the essence of the soul."

Her words resonated deep within me as I contemplated the profound impact of our actions as healers. We were not merely treating ailments or easing physical pain, but rather, we were vessels of healing, bridging the realms of the physical and the spiritual. Our purpose extended far beyond the confines of the physical body, reaching into the depths of the human experience.

As the others slowly dispersed from the hut, I felt a deep sense of responsibility settle upon my shoulders. The room silenced, with only the slight rustle of my footfall echoing through the air as I proceeded toward the woman's motionless form.

I stood there alone, my gaze fixed upon her, the lifeless body of the woman. It was then that a plan began to form in my mind. And it held the answer that I had been searching for.

The Festival of Lights

One morning, as we gathered under the shade of the banyan tree. We eagerly awaited the guidance of our beloved Gurumata. With a serene smile on her face, she appeared before us, her presence radiating warmth and wisdom.

"Good morning, my dear students. We will be celebrating Diwali, the festival of lights, in a few days. It is a time of joy, togetherness, and the celebration of inner light."

Gurumata continued to share the significance of this auspicious festival. She explained how Diwali symbolizes the victory of light over darkness, knowledge over ignorance, and the awakening of one's inner divinity.

"As we embark on this journey of self-discovery and healing, it is critical that we remember our roots, our families, and the bonds that bind us," Gurumata said. "Therefore, I have decided to offer you the choice to return home and celebrate Diwali with your loved ones."

Excitement and gratitude filled the air as we processed Gurumata's words. It was a beautiful blessing to be able to reconcile with our families, immerse ourselves in the festive celebrations, and share the knowledge and teachings we had gained with our loved ones.

Maadinee beamed with delight. "I can't wait to see my parents and celebrate Diwali together. It has been too long since we were last together."

I couldn't help but feel a sense of melancholy as I listened to my classmates discuss their expectations of going back to their homes. My own parents had passed away, and returning home for Diwali was a bittersweet reminder of their absence. Yet, I understood the importance of embracing the festival in my own way, honoring their memory and cherishing the teachings of Gurumata.

Excitement bubbled within me as I joined my fellow students in gathering our belongings. The prospect of returning home to Karmana filled my heart with joy and anticipation. Images of Jagha's warm smile and the tender moments we shared danced in my mind, adding a skip to my step.

As I folded my clothes and carefully packed them into my bag, Maadinee's infectious enthusiasm filled the room. "Can you believe it, Meera? We're finally going back to Karmana! I can't wait to see my family, the familiar streets, and, of course, to celebrate Diwali with everyone."

Her words resonated with my own excitement. "Yes, Maadinee, it's been too long since we left. I'm eager to be reunited with our village once again."

Amidst the flurry of preparations, Gurumata's serene presence filled the room. She observed us with a tender smile.

"My dear students, as you embark on this journey back home, remember the lessons and wisdom you have acquired during your time here. Carry the light within you, let it shine in every interaction, and share the love and compassion you have cultivated."

I nodded, absorbing her guidance and vowing to carry it with me as I returned to Karmana.

Gurumata's gaze shifted towards me, and she approached with gentle steps. Placing a hand on my shoulder, she spoke softly. "Meera, I see the joy in your eyes and the anticipation in your heart. But remember, Diwali is not just about external celebrations. It is an opportunity for inner illumination, a time to deepen your connection with yourself and the divine."

Her words struck a chord within me, a gentle reminder to stay grounded amidst the excitement of reuniting with Jagha. I nodded gratefully, acknowledging the importance of finding balance and maintaining my spiritual journey even in the midst of personal connections.

As the day of departure arrived, we bid farewell to the ashram and our beloved Gurumata. I carried her teachings and guidance in my heart, knowing that the true essence of Diwali lay not only in external festivities but in the deepening of our spiritual connection.

As we journeyed back to Karmana, Maadinee and I shared stories and dreams of our homecoming. The landscapes unfolded before our eyes, familiar sights reigniting a sense of belonging and nostalgia. Thoughts of Jagha's embrace and the love that awaited me brought warmth to my soul.

With weary feet and hearts filled with anticipation, Maadinee and I trudged along the dusty path that led us closer to our beloved village of Karmana. The journey had been arduous, spanning two long days of relentless walking, but the thought of reuniting with our families and the joyous celebration of Diwali kept us going.

Just when we neared the outskirts of Karmana, a wave of nostalgia washed over me. The aromas of spices and incense mixed in the air and distant noises of laughing and music reached my ears. I couldn't help but hasten my pace as excitement boiled inside me, anxious to be engulfed by the warmth of my house.

As we entered the village, the streets came alive with vibrant colors and decorations. Lamps and lanterns adorned every corner, casting a soft glow that illuminated the night. The festive atmosphere enveloped us, filling our hearts with a sense of belonging.

Maadinee and I walked hand in hand through the familiar streets of Karmana. It felt, though, as if our village welcomed us with open arms. The villagers filled with excitement and joy, greeted us with warm smiles and heartfelt embraces. It felt like we had returned to a place we truly belonged.

As we passed by the houses and shops, familiar faces emerged from the crowd. Neighbors waved and called out our names, expressing their delight at our return. The air was filled with the sound of laughter and cheerful conversations, blending harmoniously with the festive atmosphere of Diwali.

The familiarity of the surroundings brought back cherished memories of laughter and shared moments.

Maadinee's mother stood at the doorstep, her eyes welling up with tears of happiness.

"Maadinee! Meera!" she exclaimed, her voice filled with both relief and overwhelming emotions. She rushed towards us, enveloping us in a tight embrace. "Oh, my dear children, you're finally home!"

We returned her embrace, feeling the warmth and love that only a mother's hug could provide. It was a precious moment, a reunion that filled our hearts with immense gratitude.

As we stepped inside the house, the aroma of spices and freshly cooked food embraced us. The familiar sounds of clinking utensils and laughter echoed through the air.

Maadinee's mother, her eyes still moist with tears, wiped them away and smiled at us. "I've been looking forward to this day. Our home feels complete again with both of you here."

I exchanged glances with Maadinee, our bond of friendship stronger than ever. "Thank you, Aunty," I said, my voice filled with genuine appreciation. "We missed you and our dear Karmana."

Maadinee's mother chuckled softly, her eyes brimming with maternal affection. "And we missed you too, Meera. You are like a daughter to me, just as Maadinee is like a sister to you. Our home is always open to you."

We engaged in heartfelt conversations, catching up on the moments we had missed and sharing our experiences from the ashram. Maadinee's mother listened intently, her smile widening with pride as she witnessed our growth.

In the midst of the joyful chatter, Gurumata's presence seemed to fill the room. She had guided us not only in our studies but also in understanding the deeper meaning of life. Her teachings instilled a sense of purpose and compassion within us.

We gathered around a beautifully decorated table packed with a variety of wonderful delicacies as the evening proceeded. The aroma of delicacies wafted through the air, tempting our taste buds. We expressed our gratitude for the food and the abundance in our lives.

Just before we indulged in the festive feast, Maadinee's mother clasped her hands together, her eyes shining with sincerity. "Let us take a moment to offer our thanks to Gurumata, who has guided you both with such wisdom and love. May her blessings be with us always."

We joined hands in prayer, expressing our gratitude for Gurumata's presence in our lives, for the bond of friendship we shared, and for the love that enveloped us in Maadinee's home.

At that moment, as we basked in the warmth of togetherness, I realized that the true essence of Diwali resided in these moments of love, gratitude, and connection. It was a celebration of the light within each of us, illuminating our paths and spreading joy to those around us.

And in the middle of it all, I felt a profound feeling of appreciation for the path that had brought me here - to the ashram, to my beloved friend Maadinee, and to Gurumata's teachings. I knew that these events had formed me into the person I was becoming and that the light within me would continue to shine brightly everywhere I went, spreading love and compassion.

The following day, the golden rays of the sun filtered through my window, gently nudging me awake. My veins tingled with excitement as I remembered the promise of a fresh day. I quickly freshened up and shared a warm goodbye with Maadinee's mother, assuring her that I would return before nightfall.

As I made my way towards my own house, anticipation tingled in the air. I approached the veranda, and there he stood - Jagha, his presence bringing a wave of emotions crashing over me. My heart skipped a beat as I couldn't help but smile.

"How did you find out I returned?" Curiosity aroused, I inquired.

Jagha's eyes sparkled mysteriously. "Meera, when you returned to the village, I could feel it in my soul. My guru sensed your presence, and I knew deep within me that you had come back."

For a moment, I considered the extent of our relationship. It was then that a sensation of astonishment flooded over me. It was as if our souls were intertwined, sensing each other's presence even when physically apart. It was proof of the power of our bond, nurtured by love and shared experiences.

"I missed you," I confessed, my voice soft with emotion.

Jagha's smile widened, his eyes reflecting the same longing I felt. "I missed you too, Meera. It felt like a part of me was incomplete in your absence."

We stood there, enveloped in a moment of unspoken understanding before Jagha reached out and gently held my hand. The warmth of his touch sent a comforting wave through me, anchoring me to the present moment.

"Meera," Jagha began, his voice filled with sincerity, "I have something important to share with you. Something that has been weighing on my heart."

My heart skipped a beat, anticipation swirling within me. "What is it, Jagha?" I asked, my voice barely above a whisper.

He took a deep breath and fixed his sight on the ground. "I have made a decision. A decision that I believe is aligned with my path towards moksha, towards spiritual growth."

I listened intently, curiosity and apprehension intermingling within me. Jagha continued his words carefully chosen. "I have decided to dedicate my life to the path of attaining moksha, to devote myself to the pursuit of spiritual enlightenment fully."

His words hung in the air, a weighty silence settling between us. The realization of his choice washed over me, a mix of emotions swirling within my chest.

I paused for a while to collect my thoughts, wondering how to answer. The path we had envisioned together seemed to be shifting, and I needed time to understand the implications.

Jagha looked at me, his eyes searching for a glimmer of hope. "Meera, now that you're back, does this mean we can proceed with our marriage as planned?"

I took a deep breath, the words forming in my mind. "Jagha, let us take this time to reflect and rediscover ourselves during Diwali. It's a time of celebration and inner illumination. Let's see how we feel after the festivities."

Jagha nodded, understanding the importance of this transitional period. "You're right, Meera. Diwali is a time of new beginnings and introspection. We owe it to ourselves to explore our individual paths before committing to each other."

A sense of relief washed over me, knowing that Jagha respected my needs. So, for the time being, we bid each other farewell, our hearts open to the possibilities that lie ahead.

As I lay awake in bed, I found solace in the silence of the night. In the stillness, I sought the guidance of Gurumata, my revered teacher and spiritual guide. With a heart burdened by conflicting emotions, I whispered my deepest concerns into the darkness.

"Gurumata," I murmured. "I feel torn between my love for Jagha and my own path as a village doctor. How can I find clarity in this haze of conflicting desires?"

In the depths of my meditative state, I could almost feel Gurumata's calming presence. Her speech rang in my ears as if she were speaking directly to my soul. "Meera, my dear disciple," she began, her voice gentle yet resolute. "The answers you seek lie within the sanctuary of your own heart."

Her words reverberated through the chambers of my being, and I took a deep breath, allowing her wisdom to sink in. I knew that within me resided the truth I sought, a fact that would guide me toward the path aligned with my purpose.

"Listen," Gurumata continued, her voice carrying the weight of years of enlightenment. "Listen to the whispers of your heart, for they hold the key to unlocking the clarity you seek. Trust in the wisdom that resides within you, for Diwali's radiant light illuminates not only the external world but also the depths of your own soul."

I let my inhibitions go, and I absorbed Gurumata's teachings. I immediately felt a flicker of hope ignited within me. Diwali, the festival of lights, represented the triumph of light over darkness and knowledge over ignorance. It was a time for self-reflection, a moment to embrace the transformative power of inner illumination.

The air was thick with anticipation as the village prepared for Deepavali. Colorful decorations adorned the streets, and the sweet scent of delicacies filled the air. I couldn't help but feel a twinge of excitement mixed with introspection, unsure of how this celebration would shape my own journey.

As the morning sun painted the sky with hues of gold and orange, I found myself in the company of my dear friend, Maadinee. We stood at the heart of the village, gazing at the bustling activity around us.

"Meera, look at how beautiful everything is," Maadinee exclaimed, her eyes shimmering with delight. "It's as if the entire village has come alive with joy."

I nodded, my gaze shifting from the vibrant colors to the flickering flame of earthen lamps that adorned every doorstep. "Yes, Maadinee. Diwali holds a special significance for each one of us. It's a time of celebration and inner illumination."

A moment of silence passed between us as if the weight of our individual journeys hung in the air. I took a deep breath, gathering the courage to share my inner turmoil with my trusted friend.

"Maadinee," I began, my voice laced with vulnerability. "I have been grappling with conflicting emotions. Love and purpose seem to be pulling me in different directions."

Maadinee turned towards me, her eyes filled with empathy. "What is it, Meera?"

"I fear that choosing my own path may lead to heartache and the loss of a love that has been a guiding light in my life," I confessed, my voice tinged with uncertainty.

Maadinee placed a comforting hand on my shoulder, her touch grounding me in the present moment. "Meera, love is a powerful force, and it has the ability to illuminate our paths rather than dimming them. Trust that the choices you make, guided by love and inner clarity, will lead you to your true purpose."

Her words echoed within me, stirring a sense of courage and determination. I knew that within the flickering flames of the diyas, I would find the strength to embrace my journey wholeheartedly.

As the sun dipped below the horizon, bathing the village in a soft twilight, the moment of Diwali's illumination arrived. The sky came alive with a kaleidoscope of bursting fireworks, their radiant colors reflecting the hopes and dreams of each villager.

With newfound clarity, I closed my eyes and offered a silent prayer to the divine forces that guided us all. I sought the inner light that would illuminate my path and guide me toward the fulfillment of my purpose.

I found myself immersed in the joyous celebrations, spreading laughter and love among the villagers. The exchange of sweets and heartfelt greetings deepened the bonds within our community, reminding me of the interconnectedness of our lives.

I couldn't help but feel a sense of serenity settling within me in the middle of the festivities.

And just as the final fireworks lit up the night sky, I made a silent vow to honor my own journey while holding love close to my heart. The flickering sparks mirrored the flicker of hope that burned within me, igniting my path forward.

I stood amidst the bustling crowd, scanning the faces around me. My eyes searched for a familiar figure, a beacon of love in the sea of celebration. Time seemed to stretch as minutes turned into hours, and doubt started to creep into my mind.

Just as I was about to surrender to the overwhelming tide of disappointment, a voice carried on the gentle breeze, reaching the depths of my soul. "Meera." The sound of my name uttered with a hint of urgency and longing cut through the bustling ambiance, instantly capturing my attention.

I turned towards the voice, my heart leaping in anticipation. There, amidst the vibrant throng of people, stood Jagha, his eyes locked with mine. The flickering lights of the fireworks danced in his gaze, reflecting the hope and love that we shared.

The Aura of Tranquillity

"Jagha," I whispered, releasing my relief with it. I moved closer to him, our connection bridging the gap between us. "I have been searching for you."

He reached out his hand, his touch grounding me in the present moment. "Meera, I have been searching for you too. I have something I need to tell you that has been weighing heavy on my heart."

It was as if the fireworks and the surrounding festivities held their breath, eager to witness the unfolding of our story.

"I have realized that my journey towards moksha, as important as it is to me, cannot overshadow the love that we share," Jagha confessed, his voice filled with sincerity. "I want us to walk this path together, supporting each other's dreams and aspirations."

Tears welled up in my eyes, a mix of relief and happiness washing over me. "Jagha, I have been torn between my love for you and my own journey as a healer," I admitted, my voice trembling with vulnerability. "But at this moment, I understand that love and purpose need not be mutually exclusive."

His face softened with understanding, and he gently wiped away my tears. "Meera, our love has always been a guiding light in our lives. I want nothing more than to support you in your journey as a village doctor, to be by your side as we both pursue our dreams."

As the fireworks continued to illuminate the night sky, we stood there, enveloped in a shared sense of clarity and commitment. In that moment, I knew that love and purpose were intertwined, harmonizing in a dance of support and growth.

The joyous celebrations of Diwali continued around us, but our focus remained on each other. Hand in hand, we embraced the possibilities that lay ahead, united in our love and shared determination.

We took the next step in our life together, ready to tackle the difficulties and joys that were ahead. The light of the fireworks mirrored the fire that burned within our hearts, illuminating our path with the eternal flame of love.

As we joined the revelry of the festival, our laughter and smiles intermingled with the cheerful melodies and the joyous greetings exchanged among the villagers. The celebration took on a deeper meaning as we celebrated not only the triumph of light over darkness but also the triumph of love and unity.

In the midst of the festive atmosphere, Maadinee approached us, a knowing smile on her face. "I knew that the Diwali lights would guide you both towards the answers you seek," she said, her voice filled with warmth. "May your love continue to shine brightly, igniting the lives of those around you."

Jagha's words echoed in my ears, filling my heart with a mix of excitement and nervous anticipation. "Meera, we are to be married soon," he declared, his voice filled with genuine joy.

Maadinee's eyes sparkled with happiness as she heard the news. We rushed to Maadinee's house to share the announcement.

"Maa! Meera and Jagha are getting married soon!" she exclaimed, her voice bubbling with joy.

Her mother's face lit up with a joyful grin as she embraced me tightly. "Oh, my dear child, this is wonderful news!" she said, her voice full of joy. "We must inform your father immediately."

As the village pandit, Maadinee's father understood the importance of this occasion. He listened intently to his wife's enthusiastic account of our intentions to marry, nodding with a sense of approval. The news spread throughout the village, igniting a wave of anticipation and excitement among our friends and neighbors.

Preparations for the wedding ceremony began the next day. Maadinee's home buzzed with activity as relatives and friends joined hands to decorate the house and make arrangements for the joyous celebration. Vibrant flowers adorned the doorways, and the sweet aroma of incense filled the air, creating an atmosphere of warmth and festivity.

In the midst of the preparations, Jagha and I stole a moment alone. We stood in the courtyard, hands clasped, looking into each other's eyes, our hearts overflowing with love and anticipation. Words were unnecessary as our smiles conveyed the depth of our connection and the excitement of embarking on this new chapter of our lives.

"Meera, I can't wait to begin this journey with you," Jagha whispered, his voice filled with tenderness. "Together, we will face whatever comes our way. I promise to be by your side at all times."

I nodded, a mixture of emotions swelling within me. "Jagha, your love has been a guiding light in my life, and I am grateful for the bond we share," I murmured, my voice filled with sincerity. "I look forward to standing by your side, facing the challenges and joys of life together."

The air buzzed with laughter, and the sounds of music echoed through the streets. The community came together, sharing in the excitement and spreading their blessings for our union.

Maadinee couldn't help but tease me about my upcoming wedding night with Jagha. As she approached me, she had a sneaky grin on her face.

"Meera, I can't help but wonder what your wedding night with Jagha will be like," Maadinee said playfully.

I blushed and laughed, feeling a mix of excitement and nervousness. "Oh, Maadinee! You know I haven't given it much thought. But I'm hoping it will be a lovely and memorable occasion for both of us."

Maadinee giggled, clearly enjoying the teasing. "Oh, come on, Meera! You're going to be a married woman now. It's natural to have all these thoughts and feelings. Don't be shy!"

I playfully nudged her shoulder, trying to hide my embarrassment. "I guess I can't deny that. But let's focus on the present and enjoy the festivities. I'm sure everything will happen as it's meant to be."

Maadinee nodded, her smile softening. "You're right, Meera. The most important thing is that you and Jagha have a lifetime of happiness together. And tonight is just the beginning of that journey."

As the wedding day arrived, nervousness grew. I wore a red saree with a golden border, and Jagha was clad in a yellow robe. We stood before Panditji, the village pandit, ready to embark on the sacred journey of marriage. Our families and friends surrounded us, their smiles reflecting the joy that filled the air.

Panditji, with his wise demeanor and kind eyes, began the rituals, invoking the blessings of the gods and goddesses upon our union. He spoke with a gentle yet authoritative voice, guiding us through the sacred ceremony.

"Meera and Jagha, may you find everlasting happiness and prosperity in this sacred bond of marriage," Panditji began. "Today, you pledge your love and commitment to each other, promising to support and cherish one another throughout your lives."

Jagha and I exchanged glances, our eyes filled with love and excitement. We had waited for this moment, cherishing the promise of a lifelong commitment.

Panditji led us through the traditional wedding rituals. Each step is imbued with deep meaning and significance. He began by invoking the blessings of the gods and goddesses, seeking their divine grace and protection for our union. The fragrance of incense and the soft chanting of sacred mantras enveloped the temple, creating a tranquil ambiance.

Jagha then tied the mangalsutra, the sacred thread, around my neck, symbolizing our eternal bond of marriage. The gentle touch of the gold pendant against my skin brought forth a surge of emotions, anchoring us to a shared destiny.

As Panditji recited the sacred mantras, he explained the symbolic meaning behind each ritual, enlightening us about the values and principles that would guide our married life.

"Now, it is time for the phrase," Panditji announced, a smile gracing his lips. "Go around the holy fire, Agni Dev, seven times for him to witness your marriage."

Jagha and I clasped hands as we prepared to take the phrase, the circumambulation around the sacred fire. Panditji's voice resonated in the air, filling our hearts with reverence and anticipation.

"Step forward with your right foot, Meera," Panditji instructed his voice steady and filled with wisdom. "With each step, you vow to uphold the sacred bond of marriage, embracing your responsibilities and nurturing your love."

With each step we took, Panditji recited blessings and prayers, their words enveloping us with divine grace. Our loved ones watched, their eyes shimmering with tears of joy, as we embarked on this symbolic journey together.

As we completed the pheras, Panditji proclaimed, "May your love be as strong and unbreakable as these sacred vows you have taken today. May your union be blessed with harmony, understanding, and everlasting love."

Jagha and I exchanged garlands, sealing our commitment to one another.

Panditji, with a serene smile, placed his hand on our heads, bestowing his blessings upon us. "May the divine blessings guide you throughout your lives, nurturing your bond and illuminating your path," he proclaimed.

Tears of happiness streamed down my face as I looked into Jagha's eyes. The weight of the rituals and the profound meaning behind them resonated deeply within me. I felt awe and thankfulness for the sanctity of this moment.

With the completion of the wedding rituals, the air became filled with applause and joyful celebrations. Our families and friends gathered around us, showering us with blessings and best wishes for a blissful married life.

I had an incredible feeling of belonging and oneness at that time, surrounded by the love and support of our community. Jagha and I had embarked on a new chapter of our lives, bound together by the sacred bond of marriage, promising to walk hand in hand, facing life's challenges and celebrating its joys.

The rhythmic sounds of drums and the strains of traditional music filled the air as the festivities proceeded, inviting everyone to participate in the fun. We danced and laughed, our hearts brimming with love and happiness.

With the wedding rituals concluded, Panditji approached us. He spoke in a gentle voice, "Jagha, Meera, as you begin your new journey together, I advise you to visit the sacred temple of Devi Maa, which is nestled in the nearby hills. Spend the night there, seeking her divine blessings and uniting your souls as one."

Jagha and I exchanged glances, both intrigued and eager to follow Panditji's advice. We thanked him for his guidance, bid farewell to our families, and embarked on the pilgrimage to the temple. The path to the hilltop was adorned with lush greenery and the soothing sounds of nature, creating a serene atmosphere.

As we reached the temple, the aura of tranquillity enveloped us. The sweet fragrance of incense and the soft glow of oil lamps added to the sacred ambiance. We approached the main sanctum, where the idol of Devi Maa stood, radiating grace and serenity.

Jagha and I sat together, feeling the gentle warmth of the temple's divine energy. In hushed whispers, we shared our dreams, aspirations, and deepest desires, letting our hearts intertwine and strengthen the bond we had forged through marriage.

I looked at Jagha, his face illuminated by the flickering light of the lamps. "Jagha, this moment feels sacred and surreal. Let us surrender ourselves to Devi Maa's blessings and open our hearts to the journey that lies ahead."

Jagha nodded, his eyes reflecting the love and determination within. "Meera, as we unite our souls in this holy place, let us promise to support and uplift each other, to be the pillars of strength and understanding in all circumstances."

With our hands joined, we closed our eyes and offered heartfelt prayers to Devi Maa, seeking her blessings for a harmonious and fulfilling life together. In the silence of the temple, we felt a deep connection, an unspoken understanding that surpassed mere words.

I glanced at him, eager to express my thoughts and emotions, but our conversation took an unexpected turn. Our words turned into heated arguments about the concept of unification and becoming one soul, as I realized that Jagha had already made up his mind about attaining Moksha.

"Jagha, I thought we were embarking on this journey together as husband and wife. But it seems like our paths are diverging. How can we become one soul if you are set on a different path?"

Jagha's expression remained resolute, his voice calm yet firm. "Meera, I understand your concerns, but my desire to attain Moksha is deeply ingrained within me. It is my spiritual calling, and I believe it is the path that will bring me ultimate fulfillment and liberation."

His words pierced my heart, and I felt a mix of disappointment and confusion. "But Jagha, what about our love, our dreams of building a life together? Can't we find a way to align our paths while honoring our individual aspirations?"

Jagha's eyes met mine, filled with a combination of longing and determination. "Meera, I cherish our love, and it pains me to see you hurt. But my pursuit of Moksha is not a rejection of our relationship or the life we had envisioned. It is an inner calling, a journey I must embark on to seek enlightenment and spiritual growth."

He reached out, his touch gentle and tender. "Meera, I understand your heartache, and it saddens me too. Let us find solace in the love we have shared and the memories we have created. Perhaps our paths will converge again, but for now, let us honor our individual journeys and trust in the divine guidance that leads us."

I had to respect Jagha's choice and honor his spiritual path. With a heavy heart, I nodded, a mix of acceptance and sadness washing over me.

Tears streamed down my face as I bared my soul to Jagha, exposing my innermost fears and desires. "Jagha, I have always dreamed of a life intertwined with yours, a love that transcends all boundaries. But the thought of you pursuing Moksha without me fills me with a sense of loss and uncertainty. Can we find a way to unite our dreams and aspirations?"

Jagha's gaze softened, his voice trembling with emotion. "Meera, I never wanted to cause you pain or create this divide between us. My pursuit of Moksha is driven by a deep longing for spiritual awakening, but it does not diminish the love I hold for you. Let us find a way to merge our paths, to honor both our spiritual journeys and our love for one another."

In that tender moment, our souls embraced, the weight of our shared emotions merging into an embrace of warmth and understanding. Our bodies intertwined, creating a sense of unity that surpassed the boundaries of words. The touch of Jagha's hand on my back ignited a spark within me, a fire that whispered of a love so profound it could transcend any obstacle.

But in that moment, words seemed inadequate to express the depth of our emotions. We found solace and understanding in the simplicity of a warm embrace. As our bodies pressed against each other, I could feel the weight of our worries and doubts melting away.

Tears streamed down my face as I held Jagha tightly, my heart overflowing with a mix of joy and relief. I whispered, my voice quivering, "Jagha, in your arms, I feel a sense of completeness and emotional fulfillment. It's as if all my worries and fears fade away, and I am embraced by a profound sense of love and understanding."

Jagha's hold on me tightened, "Meera, this embrace transcends the need for words. In this simple act of holding each other, we find solace, comfort, and a deep connection that words fail to capture. It is a testament to the power of our love and the profound understanding we share."

As we continued to hold each other, our bodies merged as one, and a profound sense of peace washed over us. It seemed as if time had stopped, and all that was important was the love and comfort we found in each other's embrace.

In that intimate embrace, I felt a deep sense of emotional fulfillment. The worries that had plagued my mind dissipated, replaced by a profound sense of contentment. It was a reminder that sometimes, words are not necessary to convey the depth of our emotions. The simple act of holding each other spoke volumes, reassuring us that we were understood and cherished.

Together Till the End

One night, while nestled in the comfort of my home, with Jagha sleeping peacefully beside me, I found myself entering a dream state. A harsh voice resonated in my thoughts, and I recognized it as my guru's voice.

"You must not forget your purpose, Meera," the voice chastised me.

Startled, I opened my eyes within the dream and found myself standing before my guru. She gave me a serious look, her eyes full of knowledge and care.

"Forgive me, Gurumata," I murmured, feeling a mixture of guilt and confusion. "I didn't mean to stray from my path."

My guru's voice softened, and she placed a hand on my shoulder. "Remember, my dear Meera, your journey is not just about your love for Jagha. You have a higher calling as a village doctor, and your duty to serve others should never be forgotten."

My eyes welled up with tears as I nodded in agreement. "I know, Gurumata. I've been so preoccupied with my emotions and aspirations that I've lost sight of my goal. Please guide me back onto the right path."

Soon, I found myself immersed in this vivid, dark space. In this dreamland, I heard the stern voice of my guru echoing in my mind as if she were right beside me. Her remarks were tinged with anxiety and disappointment. She gazed at me with a sad yet serene expression as I approached. I had a feeling something significant was going to be disclosed.

"Meera," her voice resonated, "you have chosen the path of marriage, and with it comes a new set of responsibilities and duties. Your focus must now shift towards your role as a wife and companion to Jagha. The ashram and your studies are no longer a part of your journey."

"But Gurumata," I faltered, trying to find the perfect words, "I have so much more to learn and explore. Can't I find a balance between my married life and my quest for knowledge?"

Gurumata's gentle gaze held mine, filled with compassion and understanding. "Meera, my teachings require undivided dedication and focus. Marriage is a sacred bond that demands your attention and commitment. It is a path of its own, leading to its own lessons and growth."

I felt a pang of sadness, realizing that my dreams of becoming a Vedic doctor under Gurumata's guidance might have to be set aside. But I also understood the value and importance of honoring the commitment I had made to Jagha and the sacred journey we were embarking on together.

"I understand, Gurumata," I said, a hint of resignation in my voice. "Marriage is a new chapter in my life that I must fully embrace. Although I will miss the guidance and teachings of your ashram, I know that my path lies elsewhere now."

Gurumata nodded, a warm smile lighting up her face. "Meera, my dear, remember that true knowledge can be found in every experience and every relationship. Your journey as a village doctor and as a loving partner will offer you lessons and growth that no classroom can provide."

Startled, I sat up in bed, the words of my guru lingering in the air. I knew she had always been my guiding light, my source of wisdom, but her instructions now left me torn and conflicted. Did I make a mistake by getting married? Did my commitment to Jagha mean giving up my dreams of continuing my studies at the ashram?

I turned to Jagha, who was still sleeping soundly, unaware of the turmoil inside me. I wondered if he, too, had heard my guru's words in his own dreams. Would he understand the weight of this decision? Would he support my longing for knowledge and growth?

As the first rays of dawn gently illuminated our room, I slowly rose from the comfort of my bed, careful not to disturb Jagha. I quietly made my way to the well and refreshed myself with cool water, washing away the remnants of sleep from my face.

I walked into the kitchen on tiptoe, ready to start the day with a nutritious supper. The familiar scent of spices and warmth greeted me as I lit the hearth and began the rhythmic dance of chopping vegetables and preparing ingredients. The soothing sizzle of food in the pan filled the air, comforting and familiar.

As I stirred the pots and pans, memories of my mother's cooking came flooding back. Her gentle guidance and the aroma of her dishes had always filled our home with love and warmth. Now, it was my turn to create that same sense of comfort and nourishment for Jagha and myself.

Lost in my thoughts, I carefully crafted a meal that would satiate our hunger and bring a smile to Jagha's face.

With the dishes prepared and the table set, I called out to Jagha, gently awakening him from his peaceful slumber. His footsteps neared the kitchen, and as he entered, his eyes filled with amazement and thankfulness at what he saw.

"I couldn't resist preparing a little something for us," I said with a soft smile, motioning toward the floor filled with a delicious spread.

Jagha's eyes twinkled with appreciation as he took a seat, ready to savor the meal that awaited us.

Gurumata's words brought a sense of peace to my heart. Although my path was taking a different turn, I realized that there was still much wisdom to be gained in the world beyond the ashram.

I slowly began to accept the truth that my studies at the ashram had come to an end. It was time to embrace the new chapter of my life with Jagha and discover the profound knowledge and growth that awaited me on this path of marriage.

As I and Jagha savored each bite of our food, the morning sun streamed through the windows, casting a warm glow upon us. It was in these simple moments, surrounded by the love and nourishment of food, that I felt the true essence of our bond.

As we sat together, enjoying our meal, Jagha shared his plans for the day. He spoke excitedly about his visit to his guru, eager to delve deeper into the teachings of Moksha.

I listened closely with a grin on my face, yet a twinge of doubt pulled at my heart.

"I'm glad you're so dedicated to your spiritual path," I replied softly, trying to hide my reservations. "Take your time with your guru. I'll be here when you return."

Jagha's eyes sparkled with enthusiasm as he finished his meal. He reassured me with a gentle touch on my hand, promising to be back before nightfall. I nodded, keeping my thoughts to myself, unsure of how to express the mixture of emotions swirling within me.

As he left, my smile faded, replaced by a contemplative expression. I pondered the significance of Jagha's pursuit of Moksha and its impact on our newly formed bond. Would our paths continue to intertwine, or would his spiritual journey lead him down a different road?

Deep in thought, I cleared the space and began tidying up, the clatter of dishes echoing in the empty kitchen. I couldn't help but wonder if our paths were destined to align or diverge, like two rivers flowing in separate directions.

As I sat alone in my room, holding the brass lamp in my hands, a flood of emotions overwhelmed me. The weight of my responsibilities and the conflicting desires within my heart felt unbearable. The lamp, a symbol of my accomplishments and the encouragement I had received seemed to echo the loneliness that enveloped me.

I looked at the lamp, its polished surface reflecting the flickering candlelight. It reminded me of the wisdom my guru had imparted, urging me to choose the path of a dutiful wife.

But my heart ached, torn between my love for Jagha and the pursuit of my own dreams.

"Why does life have to be so complicated?" I asked the lamp, tears welling up in my eyes. I thought love would bring happiness, but it feels like I'm being pulled in different directions."

In the midst of my anguish, a faint whisper seemed to caress my ear, almost as if the lamp itself were responding. "Meera, the journey of life is never easy. It requires courage to make difficult choices and follow your own path. Remember, love can be both a blessing and a challenge."

With a resolute sigh, I gently placed the lamp back in its designated spot and wiped away my tears. The time had come for me to confront Jagha and share my innermost fears and aspirations. It was crucial for us to have an honest conversation about our desires and the path we envisioned for our future together.

I took a deep breath, summoning the strength within me, and whispered to the lamp one final time, "I will fight for my dreams, for our love, and for the balance that will allow us both to thrive. And if I must walk a different path, I pray that it leads us to a destination where our souls can find solace and fulfillment."

As the day progressed, I occupied myself with various duties, finding consolation in the monotony of daily existence. Time ticked away, and the sun began its descent towards the horizon. I eagerly awaited Jagha's return, longing for the comfort of his presence and the reassurance of our connection.

As dusk arrived, I found myself looking out the window for signs of his return. The sky painted hues of orange and pink, casting a warm glow over the landscape. The anticipation grew, mixed with a hint of anxiety.

Finally, as the last rays of sunlight caressed the earth, I spotted Jagha making his way back towards our home. Relief flooded over me, and I rushed to greet him at the door.

"I'm back," he whispered softly, his eyes filled with a mix of exhilaration and peace. "Today was enlightening, Meera. I learned so much."

I embraced him, holding him tightly as if trying to anchor our connection amidst the uncertainties that lay ahead. Jagha began to recount the teachings he had received from his guru that day. His voice filled with excitement and anticipation; he spoke of his readiness to embark on the path to attaining moksha.

"Meera, my guru, believes that I am prepared for this journey," Jagha shared, his eyes shining with fervor. "I've been a yogi for years, and now is the time for me to take the next steps towards liberation."

I listened attentively, a mix of emotions churning inside me. While I admired Jagha's dedication and commitment to his spiritual path, a wave of internal panic washed over me. I had anticipated this moment, but now that it had arrived, the weight of uncertainty rested on my shoulders.

Maintaining my composure, I smiled at Jagha and nodded. "I am proud of your progress, Jagha, and I support your pursuit of moksha. It is a noble path you have chosen."

Deep down, I knew that my own plans needed to be set in motion soon. The time had come for me to align my own desires and ambitions with the journey ahead. As I listened to Jagha's words, my mind raced with thoughts and considerations, weaving a web of decisions that would shape our future together.

That night, as we lay side by side, preparing to surrender to sleep's embrace, I couldn't help but gaze upon Jagha's serene face. His peaceful expression stirred a mixture of emotions within me. Deep down, I knew that I couldn't let him embark on his journey to moksha so soon.

A surge of determination coursed through my veins. I couldn't imagine a life without Jagha by my side. I wanted to be his friend, to encourage him on his spiritual path, but I also wanted us to travel through life's pleasures and trials together.

As I gazed at his sleeping form, I gently whispered, "Jagha, my love, I know your heart longs for moksha, but I believe our souls still have much to share in this earthly world. I want us to grow old together and have many children and grandchildren. And only when the God of death, Yama, deems that we're ready, and only then must we die. Please forgive me for what I am going to do."

I felt a surge of dread come over me in the serenity of the night as the moon poured its soothing shine on our surroundings. I had to be cautious with my thoughts, mindful of the fear that Jagha might somehow sense my true feelings. With these concerns weighing on my heart, I quietly slipped out of our shared abode.

Under the cover of the enveloping darkness, I found solace in the familiar surroundings of the courtyard. It was the very place where my parents had once meditated, seeking solace and guidance. Now, it was my turn to seek support from the divine.

As I settled into a comfortable position, my mind calmed, and I called upon my Devi Latika, the goddess who had been a source of strength and wisdom throughout my life. With closed eyes, I delved into a state of deep meditation, allowing my thoughts to dissolve and my heart to connect with the divine energies.

A deep transformation occurred inside me. I felt a gentle tug as my consciousness grew as if my spirit was being drawn away from the constraints of my physical body. The familiar darkness enveloped me momentarily, only to give way to an awe-inspiring sight.

In the ethereal realm that unfolded before me, I beheld the radiant presence of Devi Latika. Her magnificent figure radiated a caring, warm energy that filled the area around us with an amazing sensation of calm and tranquillity. I gazed upon her, my heart overflowing with reverence and gratitude.

Latika's voice, gentle and melodious, resonated within me. "Meera," she whispered, her voice carrying the wisdom of ages. "You have sought me with utmost devotion and sincerity. What troubles your heart, my child?"

Overwhelmed by the presence of the goddess, I struggled to find my voice. With a deep breath, I gathered my thoughts and spoke. "Devi Latika, I stand at a crossroads, torn between the love I share with Jagha and his quest for moksha."

Latika's compassionate gaze met mine as I poured out my innermost desires and concerns. She listened intently, her divine presence filling me with a sense of solace and understanding. When I finished speaking, she spoke with a soothing voice, acknowledging my pain.

"My dear child, I can sense the depth of your love for Jagha and your yearning to keep him by your side. It is a noble desire born out of the bonds of your hearts entwined. Fear not, for I have a solution that may fulfill both your dreams and your pursuit of knowledge."

She continued, her voice overflowing with conviction.

"There is a ritual, known to few, that holds the power to intertwine your destinies in a way that would allow both your journey of love and your pursuit of knowledge to flourish. It requires a sacred mantra, a profound dedication, and the unwavering commitment of both your souls. However, once embarked upon, there is no turning back."

My heart quickened with excitement and trepidation. The thought of keeping Jagha by my side while continuing my studies stirred a newfound determination within me.

"I am willing to do whatever it takes," I affirmed, my voice unwavering. "Please guide me in this ritual, Latika. I am ready to embrace the path that unites our souls."

Latika's words echoed in my mind as I pondered the weight of my decision. The realization that once embarked upon, there would be no turning back filled me with a mix of apprehension and determination. But the thought of losing Jagha, of facing the world alone, was a fear too great to bear. I knew deep down that I was ready to take this move.

With unwavering conviction, I replied to Latika, "I understand the gravity of this choice, but my love for Jagha compels me to proceed. I cannot bear the thought of losing him, of facing a world without his presence. I am committed to this path, Latika."

Latika nodded, acknowledging my resolve, and began to explain the steps of the ritual. I listened intently, engraving each instruction in my mind. As she revealed the sacred mantra, "Ohm Mha Latika namaha,"

I repeated it silently, feeling its resonance within me. I understood that this mantra would serve as a bridge, connecting our hearts in a profound way.

Her guidance continued as she directed me to prepare a fire and find an object that could contain it. The object would become the vessel to hold Jagha's soul while we forged our bond.

"When should I perform this ritual, my Devi?" I inquired, my voice filled with anticipation.

A serene smile adorned Latika's face as she replied, "Tomorrow night, under the embrace of the moonlight, when the energies align. It is during this time that the connection between realms is strongest, and your prayers are most passionately heard."

The Ritual

As the sun gently peeked through the window, I stirred from my slumber, only to find that Jagha was not beside me. Determined not to let sadness consume me, I got up and started my day.

Today was a special day, and I couldn't help but feel both excitement and nervousness.

As I worked, I was overcome with a mix of emotions—excitement, determination, and a hint of nervousness. Tonight's ritual held the key to continuing my journey with my husband, our exploration of life and love. Deep in my heart, I hoped it would bring me and Jagha even closer together, uniting us in ways we had yet to fathom.

Soon, the day passed quickly, but I couldn't wait for the night to come. Under the luminescent moonlight, I had planned to perform the ritual.

Suddenly I heard the voice of someone from the entrance of my house. Maadinee waited for me with an eager expression.

"Meera, Meera, where are you?" she called out, and I rushed to her side.

"Meera, now that you are a married woman, did you forget about me?" she teased with a playful grin.

I laughed, relieved that she had come to see me. "Of course not, Maadinee. You are my oldest and closest friend. I was simply busy cleaning the house before Jagha came back," I replied.

Maadinee's curiosity got the better of her, and she inquired, "So where is Jagha?"

I hesitated, not wanting to reveal my plans just yet. "Well, I think he went to practice yoga with his guru," I said vaguely.

But Maadinee seemed suspicious. "You seem different, Meera, more... mature," she observed, eyeing me closely.

I playfully nudged her, hoping to divert her attention. "Oh, by the way," I said, changing the subject, "I need your help with something."

Her eyes lit up with curiosity. "What is it?" she asked eagerly.

"I need some ingredients for a potion that I have to make. I find it difficult to sleep these days," I said, hoping she would believe my little white lie.

Maadinee looked concerned. "Of course, I can help. Remember the potion our guru made for that pregnant lady at the Ashram? I remember all the ingredients," she said reassuringly.

A wave of relief washed over me, knowing that Maadinee could assist me in gathering the necessary herbs. However, I couldn't share the true purpose of the potion with her or anyone else.

The Ritual

"Well, come on then. Let's go out into the wild and find them," I said with enthusiasm, eager to begin my preparations for tonight's ritual.

Together, we ventured into the serene wilderness surrounding our village. The air was filled with the sweet fragrance of wildflowers, and the gentle rustling of leaves accompanied us as we searched for the precious ingredients. Maadinee's knowledge of the herbs proved invaluable as we carefully selected each one, ensuring that we gathered the correct elements for the potion.

"Meera, look at these blooms! They're exactly what we need for the potion," Maadinee exclaimed with a sparkle in her eyes.

I marveled at her ability to recognize each herb with such precision. "You have such a gift, Maadinee. I'm grateful to have you by my side on this journey."

She grinned and playfully nudged me. "Oh, Meera, you know I wouldn't miss this adventure for the world. We're going to create something truly extraordinary."

Maadinee's expertise in identifying herbs was truly a blessing, guiding us to the right ones we needed for the potion.

"Look, Meera! This is the sacred Lavandula, perfect for calming the mind and heart," Maadinee exclaimed with enthusiasm, gently plucking a few purple flowers.

"And over here, we have chamomile," I replied, pointing to a cluster of dainty white blooms. "It has soothing properties that will surely enhance the potion's effects."

After gathering all the required herbs, we made our way back to our village, carrying our carefully collected treasures. The sun began to set, painting the sky with a myriad of colors as the day turned into twilight.

With the fading sun casting a warm glow over the horizon, Maadinee and I made our way back to my humble abode, our hands full of carefully gathered bundles of precious herbs. "Thank you for helping me, Maadinee. I don't know what I would have done without you,"

Maadinee smiled warmly. "Of course, Meera. We're in this together, just like always. Now, don't forget to follow Gurumata's instructions carefully while brewing the potion."

Nodding, I replied, "I won't forget a single step. This potion is crucial, and I want to ensure it's perfect." The responsibility weighed on me, but I knew that the outcome could make a significant difference in someone's life.

As we reached my home, I set the herbs on a clean surface, and Maadinee offered to stay and help. "It's a delicate process, Meera. Two sets of hands can be better than one."

Her offer warmed my heart. "Thank you, Maadinee. Your presence is comforting. Let's do this together."

Following Gurumata's instructions, we sorted the herbs meticulously, separating them into precise measurements. Then, I stirred the brew in a carefully calibrated pot, and Maadinee observed.

With each passing moment, the potion's fragrance filled the air, carrying the promise of healing. Maadinee and I exchanged glances, our bond unspoken but understood.

Finally, as the potion reached its final stage, I carefully poured it into earthen pots, making sure to seal them tightly. "It's done," I announced with a sense of accomplishment.

Maadinee clapped her hands in delight. "Well done, Meera! I'm proud of you."

The weight of responsibility began to ease, replaced by a sense of fulfillment. "Thank you, Maadinee. Your support made all the difference."

As the potion's aroma filled the air, Maadinee looked at me with a hint of sadness in her eyes. "Meera, it's time for me to return home," she said softly.

"Must you leave already?" I asked, trying to hide my disappointment.

Maadinee nodded, her smile tinged with melancholy. "Yes, I have responsibilities at home, and my family is waiting for me. But don't worry, we'll meet again soon."

I tried to muster a smile. "You're right, Maadinee. Family comes first. Thank you for being here with me and helping me through this time."

Her eyes sparkled with warmth and affection. "It was my pleasure, Meera."

I hugged her tightly. "Thank you, Maadinee. Safe travels back home."

As we parted ways, I couldn't help but feel a mix of emotions—joy for the bond we shared and a twinge of loneliness as I continued on my day without her by my side. But I knew that our friendship was strong enough to withstand anything. And yet, I couldn't tell her the truth about needing a sleeping potion.

As the sun dipped below the horizon, casting a warm glow upon the village, I prepared for the ritual that would unfold under the enchanting moonlight. The sky was adorned with countless stars, and I adorned my veranda with flickering lamps and candles, illuminating the darkness and creating a warm glow around our abode. The full moon had risen majestically, and its gentle radiance enveloped me, filling my heart with a sense of purpose and tranquillity.

I walked inside my humble home and reached for the brass lamp, the treasured gift from King Bharata. As I cradled it in my hands, I felt the weight of its significance, knowing that it represented not only gratitude for my service but also the guidance I sought from within. It had become a cherished symbol of my journey, a token that connected my past with the path I was now treading.

Gently, I stepped back outside, the lamp held close to my heart. At my usual meditation spot on my veranda, I set the lamp and the potion next to a single candle that cast a soft glow on my surroundings. I nestled into a comfortable lotus position and closed my eyes, allowing myself to immerse in the sacred moment.

My mind stilled, and I recalled the mantra that my beloved Devi Latika had shared with me, "Ohm Mha Latika namaha."

Its mellifluous syllables echoed in the depths of my soul as I repeated them, each utterance bringing me closer to the center of my being.

Under the luminescent moon and twinkling stars, I felt an ineffable connection with my own guru. Though she was no longer physically present, her presence was etched within my consciousness, guiding me through every step of my journey. I could almost hear her gentle voice, encouraging me to listen to my heart, to trust the wisdom within.

As I continued to chant the mantra, a sense of calm washed over me. The flickering flames of the lamps danced in harmony with the moonlight, their interplay symbolizing the dance of life. I felt a profound sense of gratitude, not just for the lamps and candles that illuminated my surroundings but for the light of wisdom that illuminated my path.

Suddenly, I sensed a subtle shift in the atmosphere, as if the very air around me held a secret. I opened my eyes to find the ethereal figure of Devi Latika before me. Her luminous presence radiated a divine aura, and I could feel her love enveloping me like a warm embrace.

"Meera," she spoke softly, her voice echoing like a celestial melody. "Your dedication to your spiritual journey warms my heart. I want to remind you that you carry the light within you. The lamp you have chosen is a symbol of the flame that burns in your soul, guiding you towards your destiny."

Tears welled up in my eyes as I gazed at Devi Latika, my heart overwhelmed. "Thank you, Devi Latika," I whispered, my voice trembling with gratitude. "Your guidance has been a beacon of hope and strength in my life. I am forever indebted to you."

Latika smiled, her radiant presence filling my heart with serenity. "The bond we share is eternal, Meera. As you continue on your path, remember that the answers you seek reside within you. Trust your intuition, and it shall guide you towards clarity."

But just as I continued deeper into my state of meditation, my mind began to quiet down, and I sensed a shift in the energy around me.

Latika's voice echoed in my mind, "Meera, it's time for me to take over, Meera."

I blinked in surprise, not fully comprehending what she meant. "Take over? What do you mean, Latika?"

Before I could fully comprehend her words, a surge of coolness enveloped me, and her spirit seemed to rush toward me, blending with my own.

Suddenly, I felt as if I was floating in an ethereal realm. My eyes fluttered open, only to be greeted by a different view. It wasn't my surroundings anymore; I was in a different place altogether. Confusion washed over me as I tried to make sense of what had just happened.

"L-Latika?" I stammered, feeling both fascinated and unsettled by the situation.

"Yes, Meera, it's me," Latika's voice echoed within me as if she was speaking from the depths of my soul. "I've merged my spirit with yours temporarily. It's a connection we share, a gift from the cosmos. You and I, bonded by destiny."

I tried to process this extraordinary turn of events. The sense of her presence within me was both exhilarating and overwhelming.

"We have a mission, Meera," Latika's voice continued, guiding me through this inexplicable experience. "There is something you must witness, something that requires my knowledge and your compassion."

With a deep breath, I nodded. "Okay, Latika. I trust you."

I opened my eyes then. It had been ages since I experienced the world through human senses, and I relished the feeling of being alive once again. I smiled, embracing this newfound existence as Meera. As I walked inside the house, the familiarity of her surroundings felt strangely comforting.

I settled myself on the veranda, eagerly awaiting Jagha's return. In this human form, I could sense emotions and desires coursing through Meera's veins. It was an exhilarating experience, one I intended to make the most of.

As I glanced around, my eyes fell upon the sleep potion Meera had brewed earlier in the day. An idea sparked in my mind, widening my smile. Without a second thought, I opened the potion's lid and conjured a few mushrooms in the palm of my hand.

With a superhuman force, I crushed the mushrooms, their essence seeping into the potion. My intentions were not to harm Jagha but to create a better experience for his soul, even if just for a while.

Minutes felt like hours as I continued to wait for Jagha's arrival, my heart pounding with anticipation. I knew I had to act swiftly once he returned before Meera's consciousness resurfaced.

Finally, the sound of footsteps approached, and Jagha appeared before me. "Meera," he called out, his eyes lighting up with love.

"Oh, Jagha," I replied, trying my best to mimic Meera's tone and gestures. "I've been waiting for you."

As we engaged in conversation, I subtly offered him the altered potion. "I brewed this sleep potion earlier. It might help you relax and rest tonight."

Jagha hesitated for a moment, then took the potion from my hands. "Thank you, Meera. Your care for me is boundless."

I suppressed a smile, knowing the potion would soon take effect. As he drank it, I observed him closely, trying to gauge the moment when its magic would unfold.

Within a short span of time, Jagha's eyelids grew heavy, and a sense of drowsiness overcame him. He leaned against the veranda, his head nodding, his body slowly surrendering to slumber.

I began the ritual by chanting ancient verses passed down through generations. The air seemed to hum with energy as the words flowed from my lips, resonating with the ancient forces that governed the universe. The fragrance of incense filled the air, and I could feel the presence of unseen spirits surrounding me, guiding and supporting my actions.

Carefully, I placed the brass lamp, the one gifted to Meera, at the center of the sacred circle I had drawn on the floor. The lamp held immense power, and its design had been perfected over centuries to serve as a vessel for capturing souls. I felt

The Ritual

Meera's heart aching at the thought of Jagha's mortal form disappearing, but this was the only way to protect him and his journey to Moksha.

As I prepared to perform the ancient ritual that would bind Jagha's essence within the lamp, my heart raced with both excitement and fear—the moment had come to merge the powerful energies of the universe and harness them for this intricate task. Taking a deep breath, I closed my eyes and focused my mind, channeling all my powers into the sacred mantra.

I went into a state where time was slowing down, everything was getting

"Ohm Unkal avi cakti muṭappaṭṭatu, Anmavin lumos Piṭipattar apmaha" the powerful Mantra got repeated through the sacred space. Each syllable vibrated with ancient energy, connecting me with the divine forces that guided this mystical ceremony. As I chanted, the air around us seemed to hum with an otherworldly energy.

I could sense Jagha's presence, his aura intertwining with mine as he surrendered himself to the process. With each chant, I could feel his soul's essence drawing closer to the lamp as if guided by an invisible force. Our connection deepened, intertwining like the intricate threads of a tapestry.

The ritual demanded complete focus, and I poured every ounce of my energy into the task. As the verses of the mantra echoed through the house, I could feel the intensity of the ancient magic surrounding us. It was as if the universe itself bore witness to this pivotal moment.

With each step of the ritual, I felt the weight of responsibility on my shoulders, as if the fate of two souls rested in my hands- both Meera and Jagha. Beads of sweat formed on my brow, but I pushed forward with unwavering focus and devotion. Every movement, every utterance, had to be precise; any misstep could lead to dire consequences.

As the ritual neared its completion, I picked up a small jar containing a mixture of sacred ash, sandalwood paste, and oil. With utmost care, I marked Jagha's forehead with a symbolic third eye, bestowing divine insight upon him. This would serve as a reminder of his spiritual quest and the path he had chosen to become the most powerful yogi.

Finally, I closed my eyes and entered a deep state of meditation. In my mind's eye, I visualized Jagha's soul rising above his physical form, free from earthly attachments and ready to embrace the journey toward enlightenment. I recited a final mantra, seeking divine blessings for his safe passage.

"Om Shanti, Shanti, Shanti," I murmured, invoking peace for Jagha's soul.

As the ritual neared its climax, a surge of energy engulfed me, as if the very essence of Jagha's being was intertwining with the lamp. The air seemed to vibrate with a power beyond comprehension. I could feel the connection between Jagha and the lamp strengthening, his presence becoming more palpable with each passing moment.

Suddenly, as the final syllables left my lips, I felt a surge of power rushing through me. Jagha's mortal form began to fade, and his essence became one with the lamp. The vessel now held his consciousness, preserving it for eternity. My heart ached with a bittersweet mixture of fulfillment and sorrow, knowing that this was the path that Meera had chosen. Jagha's essence was safely secured, and he would forever be a part of the lamp's mystical realm.

Exhausted yet fulfilled, I stepped back from the lamp, taking in the profound transformation that had taken place. I had successfully completed the binding, an ancient ritual that bridged the gap between the spiritual and the mortal realms. But as I basked in the afterglow of the ceremony, I could feel my own energy waning.

The sheer force of the energies involved threatened to consume me. My vision blurred, and the world around me spun. I fought to maintain my focus, to see the ritual through to its end, but the body refused to cooperate.

At that moment, I felt my strength slipping away, and I knew that I was losing consciousness. As my consciousness slipped away, I found solace in knowing that our destinies had intertwined, forever united through this timeless ritual. Yet, I clung to the last threads of awareness, desperate to ensure the success of the ritual. The lines between reality and ethereal realms blurred. Gradually, the world around me began to fade, and a comforting darkness enveloped me.

Latika Revenge

I stirred awake, feeling a sense of disorientation. I realized I was resting on the veranda outdoors and couldn't remember what had happened the night before. I scanned my surroundings, searching for any clues to piece together the events of what actually happened.

As I blinked, my eyes opened, confusion and disorientation washed over me. The darkness outside told me it was still nighttime, but I found myself lying on the veranda, unsure of how I got there. Panic began to creep in as I noticed Jagha was nowhere to be seen.

But I remembered that it was earlier that evening I had lit those very candles and placed them at the center of our little home. It was to be a symbol of our love, a lighthouse to guide us on our journey together. I remembered the anticipation of the night ahead had made my heart flutter.

But as the memories unfolded, I began to feel a strange sensation washing over me. My emotions were overwhelming, and I remember feeling light-headed as if I were floating away. As the memories returned, I attempted to make sense of it all. Why had I felt this way? Was it the intensity of the moment, the weight of our commitment, or something else entirely?

I longed to find Jagha, to share my feelings with him, to know that he was all right. But where could he be? Had he been worried about me?

I sat up carefully, taking a long breath and re-establishing my footing. My legs felt weak, but I was determined to find Jagha. My eyes scanned every corner as I proceeded past the veranda and into the main house, hoping to catch sight of him.

As my mind struggled to piece together the events, the flickering candlelight caught my attention, illuminating the surroundings. The soft glow of candles enveloped the veranda, casting dancing shadows on the walls. It was then that my gaze fell upon the brass lamp standing before me. The sight of it triggered a flood of memories, and suddenly, everything came rushing back. The conversations, the ritual, and the decision me and Latika had made together—it all came back to me in a vivid rush.

In the darkness, I found myself facing Devi Latika, seated gracefully in lotus position. Her ethereal presence was both haunting and captivating. With a mix of curiosity and concern, I asked her, "What did you do to Jagha?"

She looked at me with serene eyes and replied, "Nature is the ultimate judge in the Universe. It upholds the balance of Karma for everything we do. Meera, thanks to you, my Karma has finally found its equilibrium."

Confused, I protested, "Karma? I don't understand. I have never hurt you."

Latika gently smiled, her voice soft and filled with wisdom. "I need to share a story with you, Meera. Jagadeep was once my husband nearly 400 years ago. We shared a close bond, but something changed in our relationship. He became consumed with the desire to become the most powerful Yogi in the world, even more significant than God.

"We sought guidance from a revered Maharaj Swami in the Himalayas. During a ritual, he offered me up without consulting me. I had no idea what he was up to until he blindfolded me and locked me in a cage. Then he took me to an active volcano, explaining that he needed to give up all possessions, including me, as part of the ritual to become the most powerful Yogi."

In disbelief, I interrupted, "But that's terrible! How could he do something like that?"

Latika's eyes glistened with sadness, "I tried to reason with him, telling him that I wasn't his possession but his partner and equal. However, he didn't listen. He went ahead with the ritual and pushed me into the volcano."

My heart sank at the tragic tale Latika shared. I couldn't imagine the agony she must have felt all those years ago. "I'm so sorry you had to go through that," I said quietly, feeling tremendous sympathy for her pain.

"No, Meera, you don't get it," Latika said with a touch of sadness in her eyes. "I owe you an apology. I deeply regret how I used you. It took me countless lifetimes to find someone I could truly connect with, and that person turned out to be you, Meera. I believe our past issues are finally resolved now, and all the karma between us has been balanced."

I was puzzled and asked, "Karma? What does that have to do with me?"

Latika tried to explain, "You see, in a previous life, we were close friends. But back then, I made a terrible mistake and stole the love of your life, marrying him instead. And now, in this life, you ended up marrying the same person."

"Do you mean that Jagha is actually Jagadeep? The man you were married to in your past life?" I gasped, shocked by the revelation.

Latika nodded sadly, "Yes, it's true. But here's the ironic part – Jagha, or rather Jagadeep, is now the most powerful yogi, surpassing all the yogis who have ever lived on this earth. However, there's a catch. He is trapped, unable to experience the full extent of his true power freely. Instead, he's become a slave to whoever carries this lamp."

I stood there, stunned by Latika's revelations. My mind was a whirlwind of emotions and questions. How could I have been connected to Latika in such a profound way across lifetimes? And how could Jagha, whom I loved dearly, have been her husband in a past life?

Latika sensed my confusion and remorse, and she spoke softly, "I understand that this is a lot to take in, Meera. But I need you to understand that I never meant to hurt you. I was drawn to you because of our past connection, and I wanted to apologize for the pain I caused you in that previous life."

Her comments slammed into me like thunder, and I couldn't help but feel both rage and empathy for her. It was hard to believe my beloved Jagha was entangled in this web of karma.

"But why did you steal Jagha's love in that lifetime?" I asked, trying to make sense of it all.

Latika sighed, her eyes filled with remorse. "It was a different time, Meera. I was young and foolish, driven by selfish desires. I made a bad mistake that I've been regretting ever since. That's why I wanted to find you, to seek forgiveness and make amends."

I could hear the sincerity in her words, and a part of me hoped she actually regretted her actions. Yet, the thought of Jagha being a slave to the power of the lamp troubled me profoundly.

"What do you mean by Jagha being a slave of the carrier of the lamp?" I questioned.

Latika held up the brass lamp. "This lamp holds immense power, Meera. It contains the essence of a powerful yogi from ancient times. Jagha unwittingly freed that yogi's spirit, and now he is bound to the lamp's carrier, which is Jagha himself."

Confused and intrigued, I probed further, "The lamp? What's special about it?"

Latika held up an old, ornate lamp, and its golden glow filled the room. "This lamp holds a powerful secret. It's enchanted, and whoever possesses it gains control over Jagadeep. But I didn't want this type of power, and I didn't want it to be used against you or anybody else. That's why I am truly sorry for the way I've acted."

I was torn between emotions – astonishment, compassion, and confusion. Latika had been through so much, and her remorse felt genuine. Even in the middle of the weirdness of the scenario, I couldn't help but feel a connection with her.

"Is there any way to release him from this burden?" My voice trembled with passion as I inquired.

Latika nodded, her expression serious. "There is a way, but it will be difficult. The only way to free Jagha from the yogi's influence is to break the bond between the yogi's spirit and the lamp. It requires a powerful ritual that can only be performed by someone with a pure heart and deep spiritual connection. But even then, there is no guarantee that he will return back to his mortal form."

The weight of Latika's revelation crushed me, and tears streamed down my cheeks uncontrollably. "But you tricked me," I sobbed, my voice breaking with anguish. "You told me that only his soul would be trapped, not his physical body. I never wanted to harm him."

Latika's ethereal form shimmered before me, her eyes cold and unyielding. "I needed to get my revenge, Meera. For years, I've been tormented, trapped between realms, unable to find peace. With your help, I finally feel free," she said, her voice filled with a chilling determination.

Her words pierced my heart, and I couldn't comprehend the magnitude of her betrayal. "Free? But at what cost? You've trapped my husband's soul and body inside that lamp! He won't be able to attain moksha now," I cried, my grief and anger intertwining.

Latika's expression softened slightly, but the remorse in her eyes was fleeting. "It's true, Meera, and I regret the consequences of my actions, but I was desperate for release from my torment."

"How come you didn't tell me the whole truth? I would've never gone along with this plan," I pleaded, feeling a whirlwind of emotions swirling within me.

"I needed you to believe in the power of the ritual, to perform it without hesitation willingly," Latika explained, her voice tinged with sorrow. "Only then could my vengeance be fulfilled."

A flash of rage welled up inside me as she spoke, but I saw I couldn't undo the past. My focus now had to be on finding a way to release Jagha from his unintended imprisonment. I brushed my tears away and took a long breath, attempting to restore my calm.

And just like that, Latika vanished into thin air. I sat there, heartbroken and sobbing, feeling overwhelmed. It was all because of my selfishness that my husband was now stuck inside that mysterious lamp, both his soul and physical body trapped within its enchantment.

I couldn't help but feel a sense of regret devouring me as tears flowed down my face. I had been so preoccupied with my wants and needs that I had failed to contemplate the ramifications of my actions. Now, Jagha was suffering, and it was all my fault.

The morning had arrived, and I tried to dry my tears. I felt lost and broken, knowing I had to figure things out somehow. But as the day called out to me, I dragged myself back indoors, feeling drained. Collapsing onto my humble bed on the floor, I succumbed to sleep.

In my slumber, my mind continued to wrestle with the tangled emotions and the perplexing situation I found myself in. The exhaustion weighed heavily on me, and my dreams were filled with flashes of memories and uncertainties. It felt like my heart and mind were at war, leaving me restless even in my sleep.

The sun climbed higher in the sky as the morning progressed with a calm and soft drizzle, casting its warm glow through the curtains of my room. Yet, the light failed to lift the heaviness in my heart. I wished for clarity and strength, but it seemed elusive at the moment.

As minutes turned into hours, the warmth of the day gently seeped into my room, and the sounds of life outside filtered in. Birds chirped, neighbors chatted, and the world carried on without missing a beat. Yet, for me, time seemed to stand still as I grappled with the complexity of my emotions.

Eventually, as the sun reached its zenith, a sense of calm settled over me. I stirred from my slumber, my thoughts a little clearer than before. It was a brief respite, but it offered a glimmer of hope – a reminder that amidst the darkness, there were still moments of peace to be found.

I knew that I couldn't stay hidden under the veil of sleep forever. The day beckoned, and I needed to face the challenges ahead. Slowly, I rose from my bed, pushing aside the weariness that clung to me. I resolved to confront the uncertainties and search for the strength I needed to navigate this intricate web of emotions.

But then something strange happened – there it was, the old lamp, sitting right next to me! But I was sure I left it outside on the veranda. Confused, I picked it up, and to my surprise, the lamp had changed. Beautiful and intricate patterns adorned its surface, shimmering in the sunlight like magic.

I turned it around in my hands, examining the newfound designs. They seemed to tell a story of their own, like a secret language etched onto the metal. I couldn't help but be captivated by the entrancing glow emanating from the patterns.

My mind raced with questions – how did the lamp end up beside me? And where did these stunning patterns come from? Was it possible that something extraordinary had happened while I was away?

As I sat there, tears streaming down my cheeks, Latika's words echoed in my mind. My heart was heavy with regret and guilt. It was my own greed and desire for eternal togetherness that led to this unfortunate outcome.

"Jagha, I'm so sorry," I whispered, my voice trembling. "I never wanted this to happen. I never wanted to lose you."

In my desperation, I reached out to the lamp, running my fingers over its smooth surface. I could feel the warmth emanating from within. But no matter how much I wished and hoped, I couldn't break the barrier that separated us. He was there, yet so far away.

Amidst my tears, a soft voice called out, "Meera?"

As I turned to see where it was coming from, I saw a mirage of smoke swirling out of the lamp's opening. And there, in the midst of the smoke, appeared the face of Jagha, my husband.

"Jagha? Is that really you?" I asked in astonishment.

I couldn't believe what had just happened. I rushed to discuss everything that had transpired with Latika and the mysterious lamp.

"Jagha, can we talk?" I asked hesitantly.

He nodded, and I could see a hint of sadness in his eyes. "Yes, Meera. What's on your mind?"

I took a deep breath before speaking, "Latika told me about your past, about how you were her husband in a previous life. And she said something about you wanting to attain Moksha to become the most powerful yogi in the world. Is that true?"

Jagha's expression softened, and he nodded. "Yes, it's true. I wanted to attain Moksha, the ultimate liberation, to become the most powerful yogi. I believed that with such power, I could achieve great things and make a difference in the world."

I was both curious and concerned. "But why? What was driving you?"

He sighed, looking at the flowing river. "It was partly my ego, Meera. I craved recognition and admiration. I wanted to be revered and known for my exceptional abilities. But it was also about trying to make a difference in people's lives. I thought that with immense power, I could help others and bring about significant changes in the world."

I could understand his desire to do good, but I couldn't help but feel worried about the path he was treading. "Jagha, is there more to it? Why did Latika say that you are trapped and not experiencing your true power with your free will?"

He hesitated for a moment before replying, "The truth is, along the way to attain Moksha, I made some questionable choices. I became obsessed with power, and in doing so, I lost sight of my true self. I allowed myself to be bound by external influences, and now, I feel trapped by the consequences of my actions."

His vulnerability touched my heart, and I reached out to hold his hand. "Jagha, we all make mistakes, but it's never too late to find your way back to who you truly are."

I could see his eyes flicker in the haze of smoke that he was in. "Thank you, Meera. I know don't deserve your kindness, but I want to change. I want to find my true purpose beyond the pursuit of power. I want to rediscover the path to Moksha with a pure heart and a clear conscience. I got what I wanted – immense power as a yogi, but I didn't fully understand what I truly desired. Now, here I am, the most powerful yogi, yet trapped within this glowing smoke. I can't free myself from it without your help."

I was taken aback by his words. He was the most powerful yogi? It was hard to fathom. But seeing him confined to that lamp, his power rendered useless without my assistance, made me feel a strange mix of sympathy and concern.

"Do you mean to say you can't use your new powers at all?" I asked, trying to comprehend the gravity of the situation.

Jagha nodded sadly, "Yes, that's the cruel irony. Despite being the most powerful, I'm powerless when it comes to freeing myself from this entrapment. The lamp's magic binds me, and only you can help me break free."

"But why me?" I wondered aloud.

Jagha gazed into my eyes with a deep intensity, "Meera, in our past lives, there was a strong connection between us. In another lifetime, we were friends, and yet I chose to be Latika's husband. And now, I have received my karma for my actions. Perhaps, in this life, we are meant to untangle the knots of our past and find a way to set things right."

His words shot shivers down my spine. The possibility that our souls might be connected through time and space was both awe-inspiring and unnerving.

"So, do you want to experience your powers now?" I inquired, genuinely curious about the extent of his abilities.

Jagha smiled faintly, "Of course I do, but not at the cost of being a slave to this lamp's magic. True power comes from within, and right now, I'm confined to the whims of whoever holds this lamp. I want to embrace my abilities, but I wish to be free first."

I could see the longing in his eyes, a yearning for liberation and self-discovery. I couldn't turn away from his plea. It was evident that our paths had crossed for a reason, and my purpose seemed entwined with his.

Thank You

To the team who have helped me:

Nitara Talwar who help me write and edit the book

Swastika Mukherjee who help me edit the book

Sheelu Kashyap who designed the cover

Printed in Great Britain
by Amazon